Allah Akbar

The Enemy Within

Robert Grisham

Published and printed in the United States of America and Europe 2018

ISBN-13: 978-1724554482

This book is a work of fiction. Names, characters, businesses, places, events and incidents are either the products of the author's imagination or used in a fictitious manner. Any resemblance to actual persons, living or dead, or actual events is purely coincidental, although the story does include historical references.

AUTHOR'S NOTE:

The correct Muslim spelling of the book is actually Allahu Akbar but the western world appears to incorrectly understand that the cry of an Islamic Jihadist is "Allah Akbar" so I have decided to use this incorrect version as the main title of the book.

About the Author

This work of fiction is the author's debut novel.

An eye for an eye will make the whole world blind.
Mahatma Gandhi

The only thing necessary for the triumph of evil is for good men to stand by and do nothing.
Edmund Burke

Muhammed is the apostle of Allah. Those who follow Him are merciful to one another but harsh to the disbeliever.
Quran 48:29

Demoralize the enemy from within by surprise, terror, sabotage, assassination. This is the war of the future.
Adolf Hitler

It is time that we started to insist that the Muslim Council of Great Britain, and all the preachers in all the mosques, extremist or moderate, began to acculturate themselves more closely to what we think of as British values. We can't force it on them, but we should begin to demand change in a way that is both friendly and outspoken, and by way of a first gesture the entire Muslim clergy might announce, loud and clear, for the benefit of all Bradford-born chip shop boys, that there is no eternal blessedness for the suicide bombers, there are no 72 virgins, and that the whole thing is a con and a fraud upon impressionable minds. That might be a first step towards what could be called the re-Britannification of Britain.

Boris Johnson 2012

CHAPTER 1

Of course there are moderate Muslims who are not interested in destroying Western Society and imposing Sharia Law, but there were millions of Germans who were not Nazis and there were millions of Russians who were not Soviet Communists and millions of Japanese who did not want to massacre their Chinese neighbours and millions of Chinese who disagreed with Chairman Mao's policy of starvation. But they all had one thing in common, they did not do anything. They stood by and watched and the rest as they say is history. Well, we will not stand by and watch while the moderate Muslims do nothing, while our own politicians and government do nothing. England will have no page in that kind of history book.

Anonymous serving soldier of ENA.

Zarangi, Nimroz Province, Afghanistan, 1993, Iranian Afghanistan border

Jalal Johiya, his sister and his parents had travelled from his home in Helmand Province to Zarangi in Nimroz Province for his cousin's wedding. The entire Johiya family was present for what was a traditional Pashtun Afghan wedding. As the Johiya family arrived in the huge wedding tent they were met by the groom who was giving all the children attending the wedding a present. Jalal's little sister, Saadaa was given a beautiful hand crafted doll, a perfect gift for a six year old. Jalal, at fourteen was nearly a man and the groom had decided to give him a torch for his present and even had the thought to put batteries in the torch.

Jalal's mother scoffed at the decision to put batteries in the torch as she knew full well that Jalal would spend the rest of the wedding wanting to shine his new torch at anything and everything.

"Jalal, go outside and play with the torch," she said, "why don't you take your cousin Tabish with you?"

Tabish's face lit up, "yes, come on Jalal, grab some apples, I know some horses that we can find and they love apples."

"Yes, let's go and do that," Jalal said as he jumped to his feet and ran towards the tent entrance.

The two boys used the torch to walk down a small track and were no more than a hundred metres away from the wedding tent when they found the horses. Jalal held his hand over the torch to subdue its brightness so as not to scare the horses away. The two boys loved horses and horses were a prized possession in Afghanistan.

The two boys looked over towards the huge decorated tent. The wedding party was on their way out of the tent and on their way to uphold another Pashtun, Afghan tradition. The bride and groom stood in the middle of a circle and were surrounded by a dozen male guests who were holding semi-automatic rifles. As they stood in silence one of the men shouted a command and they all began to fire full magazines of bullets into the night air. The two boys held their hands over their ears as the bright flashes of gunfire stood out in the darkness of the night and did their best to try and calm down the horses who were running around the small compound in a state of utter panic.

"Come back," the two boys yelled as they ran after the horses. They were now about two hundred metres away from the wedding party. A couple of minutes later the firing stopped and silence once again descended on the wedding as the father of the bride started to give a speech to the congregation.

Jalal and Tabish knew they were being a bit disrespectful by being absent through the speech, but it was all so boring to them and anyway, horses and torches were much more fun.

Flying over Nimroz Province that night was a United States Air Force F15 fighter jet. It was making a routine patrol along the Iranian Afghanistan border. The fighter jet was making its way back to its base at Dalbandin, Pakistan, when the pilot saw flashes of gunfire coming from the ground and tracer bullets less than a mile in front of the aircraft and almost certainly getting closer.

The pilot radioed to his base that he was under attack and asked for permission to retaliate, pinpointing the exact position where the gunfire had come from.

After a few seconds his radio burst into life. "Permission granted NODAK 6."

The pilot banked the aircraft to the east and confirmed with his co-pilot that the two AIM 120s on wing station 9 and 1 were primed and ready for firing.

The two boys had caught up with one of the horses and managed to calm it down with the temptation of a succulent apple. Jalal held its leather halter as Tabish tried his best to limit its intake of the fruit.

"He's a greedy one alright," Tabish exclaimed grinning.

"What's that noise?" Jalal asked.

"What noise?"

"That whistling noise," Jalal said turning his head to the direction of the sound.

"Oh yeah I can hear it now," Tabish said.

The whistling noise grew louder and louder, then suddenly there was a massive explosion and a huge, bright ball of flame rose into the night sky as Jalal and Tabish were thrown to the floor by the force of the shockwave. A second explosion sounded just a split second later and they were momentarily stunned as a cloud of dust gradually descended on them and as they picked small splinters of wood and pieces of cement and mud from their clothes they gradually rose to their feet. Everything fell silent, it was as if someone had flicked a switch and turned off the lights. The only light that could be seen was Jalal's torch as they ran in a panic back to the wedding tent, or what was left of it. The site where the wedding had been taking place was just a dim red glow of burning fire and embers and there was a foul smelling smoke that filled the air. The two boys knew at once exactly what had happened and they searched frantically for their families among the dozens of lifeless broken bodies littering the ground.

The boys were crying and sobbing as they continued the search. There were severed heads and limbs, internal organs, bodies broken and torn apart and many of the victims were burned beyond recognition. To the two innocent boys many of the dead also appeared to be just asleep with no visible signs of injury but little did they know their internal organs had been fatally re arranged inside their bodies by the force of the blast.

Jalal shined the torch over the scene of carnage and then the beam of light landed on the bright blue and gold material. Jalal knew that this was his mother's dress and he quickly went and knelt by her side. He put the torch down as he turned his mother gently on to her back.

Tabish picked up the torch and shined the bright light into Jalal's mothers face. Jalal saw his mother's once, beautiful green eyes staring straight through him as if he did not exist.

"Mummy, talk to me mummy, please," he pleaded.

And yet he knew almost immediately that his mother would never talk to him again. He stared into the blank expressionless eyes as a trickle of blood spilled slowly from the corner of her mouth.

"No, no," he screamed. He lay his mother's head gently into the dirt as he looked around. "Dad, Saadaa, he shouted, "where are you."

As Tabish shone the torch around the bright beam settled on Jalal's father's twisted and broken body. Jalal ran over as fast as his legs would carry him, dropped to his knees and turned over his motionless body and as he did so his eyes fell on his little sisters body underneath the body of his father and the torch fell out of his hands.

As Jalal held her hand he saw flicker of movement. Saadaa began to come round and slowly opened her eyes.

"Jalal what happened, where's mother and father, and why are you crying?"

"Shush little sister," he said as he lifted her gently from the ground turning her small face away from the corpse of her father. He picked up the torch and handed it to Tabish.

"Take this Tabish, find your family, they may still be alive."

Tabish nodded in agreement and walked away.

Jalal carried her as fast as he could away from the scene of carnage. Saadaa was still clutching the beautiful doll that the groom had given her. He wiped away the tears from his eyes.

He swore to Allah that he would never cry again, Jalal's tears for his parents would be from inside his soul. As Jalal left the bomb site he heard Tabish's screams and instinctively knew that he had also found his dead family.

That night forty four Afghan men were killed, thirty six women also lay dead or dying along with sixty six of their children In addition nine babies less than six months old would never see the light of day again. They had all been murdered by United States Air Force bombs. The only survivors were two fourteen year old boys and a six year old girl.

The next day the local mosque took Jalal, Tabish and Saadaa into their cradle and gave them shelter. Weeks later a newspaper was shown to the boys by the mosque's Imam and it detailed how the USA Air Force had mistakenly bombed a wedding party and that financial compensation would be made to the victims' families.

Both Jalal and Tabish were each given envelopes by the Imam. The payment had been made through the American Embassy in Pakistan and passed through the network of mosques to reach the two boys. Each envelope contained 1000 American dollars. Later that day the Imam watched as the two boys threw the money onto the pantry fire.

As the flames gathered pace and rose into the air Jamal turned to face his cousin. "The Americans will not buy us Tabish, they cannot."

Tabish nodded, there were tears in his eyes. "We will avenge our families cousin, as sure as Allah is the most highest we will avenge them.

Jamal leaned in and placed an arm around his cousin's shoulder as he pulled him into his chest and squeezed hard. "We will cousin, we will."

CHAPTER 2

Barbara Graham Right Honourable back bench Labour MP had been anxious all day, a great big bundle of nerves. She had been summoned by Tony Hardy, the United Kingdom's Prime Minister, to attend Downing Street at 8pm, barely four hours' notice. Something was up, as sure as eggs were eggs. Tony Hardy had always been her hero. His charm and charisma aside, he had led the Labour Party back to government in a sweeping victory over the conservatives in 1997 after an absence of eighteen years which in Barbara's opinion had been far too long..

Barbara looked at her watch, it was 7.40pm and she had twenty minutes to make her appointment. She made her way out of the Houses of Parliament and walked into Parliament Square. It was raining so she decided to take a black cab taxi to Downing Street instead of walking.

The black cab taxi pulled up directly outside the formidable black gates and Barbara reached into her purse and paid the taxi driver. She exited the taxi and walked over to the side entrance. She handed over her passport and House of Commons identity card to the duty police officer and he checked the roster on a large clipboard. As he scanned the long list he confirmed Barbara Graham's appointment was for 8pm and then he motioned for her to lower her umbrella while he checked her face against the passport photo. He then took her passport and scanned it through a recognition device linked to his computer.

"Okay, Ms. Graham," he said, "your appointment is scheduled but we have to do a further security check and it will take about five minutes. All part of the procedure, we can't be too careful these days."

Barbara nodded in agreement, "That's fine, I understand," she said.

She put up her umbrella as she looked up at the ever darkening sky and waited for what seemed like an eternity. She noticed a second police officer watching her from the other side of the security gate. He was armed with a heavy looking machine gun and it made Barbara feel uneasy as every time she looked up the armed officer seemed to be staring at her. Eventually the side gate opened and she walked through the security gate check point. She'd barely taken two strides when the second armed police officer held out a hand.

"Keep to the right side of the road Ms. Graham and make your way to number ten," he barked out sternly without emotion.

A little politeness wouldn't have gone a miss she thought to herself as she walked up to 10 Downing Street for the very first time, not daring to stray from her strict instructions. The street was surprisingly dark and a little bit eerie. She thought how different it was to the huge media scrum that that she often watched on TV whenever an important announcement was made from the steps of 10 Downing Street.

A lone police officer was standing directly outside the famous black door. He looked at her without emotion and said nothing as the door opened as if by magic and she was ushered in by a man in a black suit who greeted her politely and led her through a warren of corridors and down an elegant wooden staircase. He opened a door to a large room and gestured for her to step inside. In the middle of the room was a large glass cubicle and sat at the desk poring over some documents was the British Prime Minister. After a few moments he stood up and opened the glass door that separated them.

"Please come in Barbara," he said, "it's so nice to meet up with you again."

As Barbara entered the room the PM pressed a button on the side of the desk and the glass room turned from being see-through to opaque. Barbara looked at the PM with slight concern.

"This just further ensures our privacy Barbara," he said confidently.

Inside the room was a glass table and two glass chairs. The PM pulled a chair away from the table and gestured for Barbara to sit down. The PM then sat down directly opposite her. Barbara felt slightly intimidated. She had no idea why she had been summoned by the Prime

Minister. She was not a very experienced politician and wondered if she had said something out of turn though she couldn't think what, but something told her it was almost certain that she was going to be reprimanded in some way.

Tony Hardy was good at pleasant small talk, he'd had a lifetime to perfect his art and as much as Barbara was on defensive mode, as he complained about the weather and asked about her family and what she'd be doing later that evening she couldn't help but feeling a little more relaxed and sensed that perhaps this wasn't a bad news meeting after all.

Hardy was smiling, grinning at times and he complimented her by saying he'd been following her political career with interest for some years.

And eventually he dropped the bombshell which rendered the back bench MP from Norwich absolutely speechless.

"I am considering offering you the job of Immigration Minister, Barbara," he said, as a big beaming smile drew across his face.

Momentarily stunned she began to quickly ponder the magnitude of what the Prime Minister had just said.

"What do you say?" asked the Prime Minister brashly.

Totally flustered, the words would hardly form on her lips.

"But Prime Minister do you think I have the experience... err... and the ability?"

Hardy pulled out a lever arch file from the desk drawer and placed it on the desk in front of him. He opened it.

It contained a wad of A4 papers at least four inches thick.

"We have been following your progress and your rise through the ranks for more than ten years now Barbara. On the contrary we believe you are the perfect candidate, we are not considering anybody else."

Hardy spoke for a good five minutes as Barbara sat and listened. Hardy called her loyal, and honourable and honest and she'd been screened and vetted and there were no skeletons in her closet, a perfect example of a true, card carrying Labour member, *the salt of the earth* was his final compliment. By the time he'd finished his one to one speech she was ready to take on the world, ready to do exactly as the Prime Minister requested, she was putty in his hands.

"So Barbara," he said, "what do you say, will you be my new immigration Minister?"

Without hesitation she replied. "Yes, of course, it would be a great honour, thank you very much."

"Good," said the Prime Minister, "and by the way, when we are meeting in private you can call me Tony."

The Prime Minister's eyes appeared to narrow as he opened up an official document. He looked directly at Barbara sitting across the desk from him and leaned forward.

"Listen Barbara, we have a plan that will make the Labour Party govern the United Kingdom for the foreseeable future. With your help we can make the Labour Party the dominant force in British politics."

As the formalities were completed Hardy pressed a button on the telephone. Within a second or two a voice responded.

"Yes, Prime Minister?"

"Good Evening Alfred, could you bring a bottle of my favourite champagne down and two glasses please."

"Certainly Sir, on my way."

Hardy looked at Barbara and smiled. "I think a little celebration is called for Barbara, don't you?"

The Prime Minister explained to Barbara how he thought they should relax the immigration rules to allow citizens from all over the world to settle in Britain. The PM spoke passionately about humanity and how the rich countries of the West could do more. Multi-culturism was a good thing, it should be embraced. Although a little perplexed Barbara nodded, taking everything in.

Despite the Prime Ministers vocabulary that he presented to Barbara, he actually had his own private agenda, one that could never be shared, not even with a devoted comrade person like the one sitting in front of him. Once the poor immigrants settled in the UK they would either be on benefits or in low paid employment and once they understood a little about British politics were assured Labour voters. Barbara was told that the current asylum laws needed to be revamped, they were ridiculously longwinded and bureaucratic, genuine asylum seekers should be fast tracked into the United Kingdom. Hardy wanted tens of thousands more UK citizens to flood into the country and to integrate into the British system. He may well lose the next election but his policy would guarantee Labour victory thereafter, for decades to come and even if the next government rescinded the laws it would be too late. The labour voters would already be in situ.

The United Kingdom's embassies and consulates would be advised to inform any person applying for citizenship that if they were under any threat in their home country they should apply for asylum in the United Kingdom.

"So Barbara, are you with us?" said the Prime Minister

"Yes sir, it would be an honour."

"Fantastic," Hardy said, "you'll be a great addition to the cabinet."

CHAPTER 3

Tora Bora Caves, Afghanistan December 2001

After the twin towers attack in New York, the United States of America launched their military campaign in Afghanistan to overturn the Taliban government and crush the Al Qaeda terrorist organisation that was operating without impunity from within the borders of Afghanistan. The overwhelming force of the American military campaign quickly resulted in the defeat of the Taliban and the last remnants of Al Qaeda were forced into the small enclave of the Tora Bora caves, close to the Pakistani border.

Osama Bin Laden stood before a special group of thirty men. The ceiling of the caves shook and waves of dust cascaded through the air as the American bombs landed nearby to the secret complex of caves.

"This battle is lost my brothers," he said, "the Americans are getting close and we must make good our escape. You have trained hard and learnt well in these past years. You must now leave this battle front and make your way to the infidel countries to continue this fight," he said proudly.

The cave shuddered as another bomb landed close by.

"My brothers, there are over one and a half billion Muslims in the world. If just one per cent of our Muslim brothers join this fight against the infidels we will have an army of many to fan the flames of war. Make no mistake, this is a Holy War, it is our God against their God."

Bin Laden took a deep breath as his clenched fist slammed hard against his chest.

"Remember your training," he continued, "be not martyrs, pass on your knowledge." He raised his fist into the air. "Allah Akbar."

"Allah Akbar," the men responded. "Allah Akbar, Allah Akbar, Allah Akbar."

Osama Bin Laden had anticipated that after the twin towers attack; the Americans would invade their safe haven in Afghanistan. He had been planning for years to invoke the next stage of his grand plan. His deep held belief was that Islamic countries were for Muslims and Muslims only. He saw how the liberal Muslim countries allowed the decadence of western society to infiltrate and erode true Islamic values through their permitted immigration of Muslims to western countries and then how the western culture was brought back home and spread through the Muslim's country of origin. What Osama Bin Laden really wanted was for the entire Muslim world to stay faithful to the true interpretation of the Qur'an. Muslims should live like true Muslims under strict Sharia Law.

Bin Laden bowed his head, turned to face Mecca and eased himself to his knees and started to recite from the Qur'an. The verses were etched in his soul.

"Nine, nine fifteen, fight them, Allah will punish them by your hands, sixty zero four, hatred, hatred forever until you believe in Allah alone, three eighty five, fight until there is no more disbelief, until they testify that none has the right to be worshipped but Allah," he took a deep breath, "three fifteen, we will cast terror into the hearts of the disbelievers."

Bin Laden's plan was a simple one. If he caused enough pain and suffering to the western governments and their populations, they would turn on the local Muslim population and in turn the Muslims would have no choice but to return to their Islamic homeland or join the Holy War.

Bin Laden's model of planning was based loosely on the situation in India after the Second World War, in dividing up religions as Muslims, Sikhs, Hindus and Christians fought against each other on the streets of India resulting in the biggest mass migration in history as the true Muslim population travelled to the newly formed countries of Pakistan and Bangladesh. Many Muslims were forced from their homes through extreme violence and intimidation and had no choice but to migrate. In many cases the population of many towns and villages were ethnically cleansed.

It was messy but had resulted in the pure Muslim State of Pakistan and he wanted more countries like Pakistan, he wanted them all over the world. Bin Laden had preached about pure Muslim states and every man had sworn to carry out their duty to fulfil their leader's beliefs. Bin Laden recruited specialised three man terror cells, assessed personally by himself based on IQ level, physical appearance and mannerisms and every single member had suffered the loss of a close family member at the hands of the western infidel forces. This factor alone bore a deep-seated hatred to the West and dramatically increased the odds of the terror cells carrying out atrocious acts of revenge. Each of the three man cells had been given language lessons for their chosen target countries and each of the cell had a planner, an expert bomb maker and a highly trained weapons specialist. On the last days of the American invasion of Afghanistan the ten teams made good their escape as they passed through the tribal lands of Afghanistan to the neighbouring country of Pakistan. They then dispersed and made their way to their handlers in Islamabad. Eight of the cells destinations were in Western Europe, and two had been ordered to go to Australia and Canada.

Jalal Johiya, Tabish Othmane and Pasha Talpur made up one of the three man cells and had safely escaped the Tora Bora caves. They met their handler in Islamabad where they obtained fake Pakistani passports, finance and operations details. They were to head for the United Kingdom, given a list of the weaponry that would be sent there just as soon as they had set up a business ready to take delivery. They were advised that an existing Al Qaeda network already existed in the UK. They were to memorise contact details, nothing would be written down. The three man terror cell spent several further weeks training and briefing before they left Islamabad and made their way down south to Karachi. At Karachi they boarded a freighter to the port of Durres in Albania. The Albanian customs officers at the port gave nothing more than a momentary glance of their passports as they were waved through passport control and entered the country.

The three men bought airline tickets for the flight from Tirana to London, UK. They landed at Heathrow airport and immediately claimed asylum at passport control. They were provided with a government appointed interpreter who assisted the men in filling out the asylum application forms. The government interpreter advised them to state that they were under threat due to their political beliefs in Pakistan. Once the forms were lodged with the Heathrow UK border agency the three men were then free to enter the UK. The only condition of entry was that they had to attend specifically arranged appointments at Hounslow immigration office with the appointed interpreter. The interpreter would assist them with applications for emergency accommodation due to their vulnerable asylum status.

By nightfall the three men had been lodged in a comfortable hotel. Within three weeks the men had been interviewed by a very overworked asylum visa department and were told that they were likely to be granted permission for indefinite stay in the UK. It was just a matter of time, it was as easy as that.

Talpur and Othmane followed their orders and moved north to Bradford, while Johiya resided in Stevenage. The men followed Bin Laden's orders and went into sleeper mode. They would simply act like Englishmen and not display their Islamic lifestyle or beliefs in public. It was critical that they were completely nondescript, that they blended in with western society and therefore not give any reason to cause suspicion of any kind.

Within a year of arriving on UK soil Talpur and Othmane had used the finance provided by Al Qaeda to set up a car and exhaust business on the outskirts of Bradford. Johiya went to work for a local accountant in Stevenage.

Once Othmane and Talpur's car exhaust business was fully established and legal, Johiya made a long distance call to his handling officer in Islamabad. The cell handler congratulated them and asked them how life in England was treating them. Neither of the men had any complaints. After the call had ended the cell handler made another call to a man in Karachi.

CHAPTER **4**

ANF Engineering Works – Karachi, January 2003

The tentacles of the Al Qaeda network had spread throughout Pakistani society. Many moderate Muslims turned a blind eye to the activities of the terrorist network and although many Muslims were not prepared to fight they were obliged to participate in the struggle against the non-believers of the western world.

The ANF engineering works and its owner, Faisal Sadique, were part of the Al Qaeda network. Faisal Sadique's role was to smuggle arms into various countries using his engineering works as a cover. The difference between the Al Qaeda terror operation and other previous Islamic terror groups was the financial backing achieved through Osama Bin Laden's contacts in the highly conservative Saudi Arabian society. This financial backing allowed the Al Qaeda network to fund and perfect the planning for all their terror activities.

One of Al Qaeda's prized possessions was a Clear Image 100 D model x-ray scanner. They had done their research and had managed to buy it on the international black market, the exact same specification x-ray scanner currently used by UK container port customs. Possession of the exact same x-ray scanner would allow Faisal to see exactly what the UK customs officer would see if they chose to search the hidden deadly cargo.

Faisal went to work. He had to hide twenty Kalashnikovs, ten thousand rounds of ammunition, 20 kg of Semtex, timing detonators, a large bore mortar, and two stinger handheld ground to air, heat seeking missile launchers. He had been told that the cover story for the cargo would be lorry exhausts. This was perfect, as the sheer size of lorry exhausts would easily hide the list of weaponry that needed to be sent to the UK. The catalytic converters contained in the lorry exhausts were particularly beneficial as they contained palladium. Palladium was a heavy metal that blocked out x-rays. The catalytic converters were ideal for hiding the Semtex and the timing detonators.

Faisal did some research and discovered which specific exhaust was best suited to hide each specific weapon. The commercial lorry exhausts were then ordered from different manufacturers and as they arrived from all over the world they were dismantled and prepared to secrete their deadly cargo. It was vital that the weapons did not attract any unwanted attention. The only concern for Faisal was the added weight of the weaponry. It was one aspect of the smuggling operation that caused him some difficulty as he had to reduce the weight of the exhausts to match the specific weight of the hidden weapons.

The Semtex had to be handled with great care and was hidden deep inside one of the catalytic converters. Faisal put the exhaust through the x-ray scanner several times so that they were 100% positive it would not be revealed if subjected to an inspection by the UK customs. All the weapons were equally well hidden and in some cases the steel tubing on the exhausts had to be double skinned to thwart faint signs of the weapons as they passed through Faisal's own x-ray scanner.

After a month of tireless work, the final exhaust was passed through the x-ray scanner with no signs of detection. Faisal had completed his work, he was overjoyed. The lorry exhausts were then loaded into a container and sealed with the ANF Engineering Works' cargo seal. Faisal knelt beside the container and said a silent prayer.

"Allah Akbar," he said as he gently touched the outside of the container.

The next day Faisal watched as a lorry came to collect the container and take it on its short journey to Karachi docks from where it would be loaded onto a ship for its long passage to the UK.

Felixstowe Customs Clearance, April 2003

Customs officer Jamie Green looked at the thousands of containers stacked up in the huge customs clearance area. Docket 8732 came to his attention as it originated from Pakistan. There was no hard intelligence that this container had anything illicit or illegal inside but due to the general consensus that as much as fifty per cent of the heroin smuggled into the UK came from Pakistan, the container had to be inspected and subjected to a series of checks.

Container 8732 was pulled out and moved to the inspection area. There were at least a hundred other containers marked for drug sniffer dogs and x-rays. The docket said the cargo was lorry exhausts destined for an exhaust fitting centre in Bradford.

Officer Green put both the export company and the import company into the risk register. Neither importer nor exporter flagged up as a risk. Customs protocol still stated that all imports from Pakistan had to be checked by a drug sniffer dog and their cargo subjected to random x-ray. Officer Green walked over to the inspection area and broke the seal on the container. The 40ft container was packed with commercial lorry exhausts. Max the sniffer dog was trained for drug detection and not for the chemicals used in military ordnance.

Officer Green began to pull out random exhausts from the cargo. Max began to run over each of the selected exhausts, and he watched as the sniffer dog ran around, tail wagging as normal. He waited and watched the dog who was trained to bark and howl if he smelled the slightest trace of heroin. The officer waited patiently, the dog was clearly bored and after three circuits of the packages trotted over and sat by his handler's side.

Officer Green patted Max on the head and tossed him one of his favourite biscuits. The next stage of the customs inspection was to run several of the randomly selected exhausts through the Clear Image 100D x-ray machine; the very same type of x-ray machine used by Faisal in Karachi. Officer Green watched as the large lorry exhausts he selected, passed through the machine. Nothing untoward showed up on the scanner and Green replaced the exhausts back in the container. He placed a tick in the box on his form, he had followed the correct protocol and this container was good to go. He stamped the release docket and the container was resealed and moved to the collection point. An Eddie Stobart lorry collected the container and started the long journey from Felixstowe to the city of Bradford.

Talpur and Othmane had been patiently waiting for the container. They had received an email once it had been cleared by customs and a further email that tracked the delivery along the route. Estimated time of arrival had been noon that day and the lorry arrived just fifteen minutes after its ETA. Talpur nodded politely at the truck driver and signed for the container and he and Othmane unloaded the exhausts and placed them in a large exhaust rack. The rack had a sign that stated *obsolete exhausts* and a cover note said they were not to be thrown away for scrap. The sign was written in English and Pakistani Urdu.

Talpur smiled as he turned to Othmane, "we are ready brother, we have been waiting for this a long time and

God willing we are prepared to kill the infidels in the name of Allah."

Othmane smiled as a shiver ran the length of his spine.

"Allah Akbar," he said, "I am ready, brother."

CHAPTER 5

Manchester, 2004

John Dodds had been partying hard since his last earner. He had been smoking crack and playing video games on his PlayStation for the last thirty-six hours. His kill rate on Tour of Duty went through the roof when he took a hit of his crack pipe. He liked to think he was a little different to other crack heads in that he preferred to be alone when he went on a drug binge. He could concentrate on his video games and more importantly he didn't have to share the crack with anyone else.

He looked at his stash of crack cocaine with a little rise of panic as he realised that he would have to go out again for another little earner. He jumped up from his sofa and pulled back the curtains slightly and took a quick glimpse outside. The bright sunlight shone right into his crack widened eyes. He looked at his watch. It was 10.30am but it could have been midnight, as he had no idea of time when he was partying hard. As luck would have it, 10.30am was a good time to go out for an earner. It was a warm, sunny day and from experience he knew that many householders would take the opportunity to go out shopping when the weather was hot and what was more, many of these householders made the mistake of leaving windows open. *Stupid bastards*, he thought to himself as he stretched his body with a long audible groan as a smile ran from his face.

He looked out of the window again, he wanted to continue partying and he couldn't face the thought of climbing the walls on a crack comedown during the daytime so he had no option, he needed to get enough crack to last him till the sun went down and the quickest and easiest way to raise some money was to rob some unsuspecting householder while they stocked up on their groceries at the local Tesco.

He found his sunglasses and a pair of gloves and then put on a hoodie, his official works uniform. He was an experienced house burglar and he was ready to go. He had four rocks of crack left and decided to smoke one before he jumped in his car and prepared to start his search for a suitable target.

Dodds had been driving around for an hour or so and had already stopped twice to have a smoke of his crack pipe. He had one rock of crack left and he was starting to panic. Doing crack in his car was risky but it gave him the boost he needed to continue with his search. At last he finally found what he was looking for… a nice corner house with an alleyway running down the back of the garden. He could see an open downstairs' window and despite the fact that he was high on crack he prided himself in believing he could still think just like a burglar should think. He parked his car about fifty yards from the front of the house and quickly made his way to the front door. He rang the doorbell and then rapped firmly on the front door knocker. He looked up at the window and walked back slowly to his car. He waited patiently for some minutes watching the house to see if there was any sign that someone was at home.

"Nothing, this one will do" muttered Dodds to himself. He would normally watch the occupants of a house go out so he could be sure the house was empty but he didn't have the time to do that today as he was down to his last rock of crack. That was all that mattered. They hadn't answered the door and that was good enough for him.

He put the last rock in his pipe and quickly lit up the drug, inhaling deeply, drawing the smoke into his lungs. He held the smoke in for as long as he could, making sure he got the maximum hit from the drug. The crack cocaine did its job very quickly and the powerful drug soon hit the spot... he was bloody well flying! He jumped out of his car and walked quietly down the side road and then down the alley that ran down the back of the house.

He scaled the back fence and as he dropped down into the garden he quickly walked up to the back of the house. He found a dustbin by the back door and stood on it to reach the open window. The crack gave him the energy to pull himself up and through the window.

Being a skinny crackhead had its advantages, as he easily squeezed through the window and tumbled head first into the kitchen, smashing a neatly stacked pile of plates which had been sitting on the draining board.

"Fuck, bastards and shit," he cursed to himself, "silence is golden," he whispered as he brushed himself down from the fall and listened carefully. Nothing, not a sound. He made his way to the upstairs of the house to begin his search for money and valuable items of jewellery that could be easily offloaded in any one of numerous public houses he usually frequented. Even his crack dealer was prepared to take a little gold or a diamond or two now and again. He walked along an expensively carpeted hallway and entered the first bedroom. How neat and tidy it looked he thought to himself, in comparison to his own bedroom that is. He would soon change that. He looked at the furnishings, the ornaments and the picture frames and grinned. It was an old codgers house, he should have known by the smell and he'd grinned because he knew that the old folks didn't believe in credit cards and banks, no, they believed in good old fashioned cash and hoarded family jewellery and watches like they were going out of fashion. Somehow he sensed that today was his lucky day. He took a step forward and began to ransack the room turning over the drawers in a stand-alone corner unit. He struck lucky in the third drawer down as he lifted a wad of cash tied up with an elastic band. In a jewellery box by a bedside cabinet he found gold rings, at least a half dozen necklaces, earrings and an old fashioned heavily weighted pocket watch. He turned it over and grinned as he noticed the small stamp signifying that it was genuine gold. His pickings in bedroom two and three were poor, he had hit the jackpot in bedroom one with enough loot to keep him in crack for a month. It was time to go.

As he walked down the hallway he stopped dead in his tracks. A noise. What was it?

"Shit," he muttered to himself, "a door, someone coming up the stairs."

Panic started to well up inside him as he realised that the owner was home and he or she was blocking his only means of escape. He rushed back into the bedroom and ran towards the window and looked out. It was too high to jump out, a broken ankle or leg at the very least. He couldn't risk it. And as his breathing got harder and the sweat began to build on his brow he remembered his initial assessment of the owners, just as soon as he'd entered the first bedroom. He smiled. An old man or an old woman, what possible resistance could they give him? He crept back along the corridor and as he turned the corner and looked down the stairs he saw her. Eighty five, eighty six, perhaps even older and very frail, so frail she was taking an age to climb the stairs. He didn't want to hurt her, he had no intention of hurting her but as he sprinted down the stairs the silly old bitch just froze and because she froze she blocked his route of escape. He had no option but to move her and held out the palm of his hand and the momentum of his movement took control as the bottom part of his hand caught the corner of her left eyebrow and as he connected with her face there was a sickening crack and a scream. The velocity of his movement and gravity took over as the old lady lifted into the air and turned a full summersault as she landed in an unconscious heap at the bottom of the stairs. Dodds bolted down the stairs three at a time and vaulted over the prone body.

Every Thursday morning Joe Henderson took his elderly mother shopping and today was no exception. He pulled his car into his mother's driveway and came to a stop. Joe followed the normal routine and went to the boot of the car to get his mother's shopping while his mother opened the front door of the house and went into the house to put the kettle on. It was almost a tradition, a cup of tea with old Mum before returning back home to his family. Moments later Joe heard his mother screaming from the house. A split second later a man appeared, running through the front door and headed down the driveway clearly making for the street in a mad, blind panic. Instantly Joe put two and two together. The man was wearing a hoodie and sunglasses and clutching a carrier bag. Joe ducked down behind the car, the man clearly hadn't seen him and as he ran past the car, he stood and with all the strength he could muster propelled his fist into the side of the man's head. He went down like a sack of potatoes and Joe leapt on his back with both feet. He turned him over and hit him a few more times then dragged the man back to the front door of his mother's house. He recoiled in horror as he saw his mother lying in a heap at the bottom of the stairs. He could see bone protruding from his mother's leg and blood seeping from a wound to her head.

Dodds was regaining consciousness, the first thing he saw was another clenched fist smashing into his face and then again and again and then blackness. The next time he regained consciousness was when he was sitting in the back of a police car. Waves of depression and anxiety swept through his mind as the last effects of the crack cocaine left his body.

Instead of smoking crack and playing video games, he spent a crack cocaine comedown in a police cell. He was battered and bruised and the police doctor would not give him any medication for his pain until the crack cocaine had left his system. Dodds was climbing the walls.

He was charged with aggravated burglary and GBH with intent. The Magistrate denied bail and he was remanded in custody at HMP Strangeways. As soon as he landed on the remand wing he bought a small wrap of heroin on tick. He quickly swapped his crack cocaine addiction for a heroin addiction.

Six months later John Dodds found himself at Manchester Crown court awaiting sentence. He was by now a fully-fledged heroin addict. He knew he was going to be sentenced to a long term in prison, and then some, so before he went up for his sentencing he smoked a full wrap of heroin to ease the pain.

"Stand up," said the judge.

Dodds stood slowly and looked around the court room. Everything seemed hazy and surreal as the heroin did its job of dulling the mental pain. He recognized the old woman sitting in the court alongside a burly, thick set man. He remembered the man from a picture in the local newspaper. The local newspaper decided to do a 'have a go hero story' with Dodds as the evil crack burglar and the rugby playing son as the hero. The newspaper seemed to take great delight that the burglar had needed seventeen stitches to facial wounds, had a broken nose, a broken jaw, two cracked ribs and had lost three teeth.

The fella should have been a boxer not a poxy rugby player, he thought as he stared at the man across the courtroom.

How unlucky had he been that the son was a professional rugby player who just so happened to take his mum shopping that day.

His mind went into a spin as the judge rambled on about how evil he was and that crack cocaine was a blight on our society. The words fifteen years did however bring him back into the real world.

"Fifteen years? You're taking the piss," he slurred in his heroin induced stupor.

"Take him down," ordered the judge.

As Dodds was led down the stairs the last thing he saw was a broad grin on the face of the rugby playing son.

"Bastard, cunt, motherfucker," he muttered to himself.

"I'll get you one day, wait and see," he screamed at the Judge as he was manhandled down to the court cells.

"Make a note of that comment Mr. Ford," the judge said, "and make sure it goes on his file." The clerk of the court nodded politely to the Judge.

It was not the first time the Judge had heard idle threats but noting that on file would make it more difficult for Dodds to progress easily through the prison system and finish the last years of his sentence in an open category prison.

He sat in the court cells trying to come to terms with his sentence. His longest previous sentence had been three years and he was out on a tag after one year. Fifteen years, fifteen bloody years, thought Dodds. His solicitor had told him that he could be out after seven and a half years. *For fuck's sake,* he thought, *I'll be thirty four when I get out.* He needed another hit of heroin quickly as he reached in his pocket for another wrap but before he could roll it up and smoke it the court cell door opened and two prison officers appeared.

"Dodds," shouted one of the prison officers.

"Yeah, that's me," he replied.

"You're being transferred to HMP Full Sutton," said the officer.

His heart skipped a beat and his head fell into his hands. He knew enough about the prison system to know that HMP Full Sutton was a maximum security, category A prison, built to hold the worst of the worst… England's most violent criminals and terrorists.

"Why am I going there?" he groaned.

"Length of sentence, danger to the public, aggravated burglary and GBH with intent on a eighty five year old woman, you worthless piece of shit. Plus you just threatened a judge."

The other officer stepped forward. "Come on Dodds, we gotta go now."

As he was led to the waiting prison van the officer made one more passing remark.

"It's a bit noncey doing an old woman Dodds, you'd better watch your back at Full Sutton."

The prison officer was right, he knew that and the words echoed round his mind as he began to think what the other prisoners would do if they discovered he had put an old woman in hospital for the best part of a month.

CHAPTER **6**

London 2004

Chelsea's football hooligan firm was busy smashing up Watford town centre. They had just lost two - nil to Watford and they wanted to take a firm revenge on the shops, cars and anything else that they could smash up as they made their way from the football ground to Watford underground tube station. They were a thousand strong and after wrecking Watford they were intent on heading back into central London looking for another soft target to finish the day off. The Chelsea firm got on at Watford station and then got off at Northwick Park. Only their top boys knew where they were heading next. They walked to South Kenton tube station on the Bakerloo line and entered the underground complex. They failed to notice one amongst them drop away, not a Chelsea fan at all, far from it.

Young Billy Smith was fifteen years old and a member of the notorious West Ham ICF youth firm known as the Under Fives. He was also a trusted lieutenant of

Taylor. He had ordered young Billy to go to the Watford Chelsea game and carry out undercover surveillance on the Chelsea firm. It was not without risks as anyone in the Chelsea firm could have recognised young Billy. But it was unlikely because the problem with the Chelsea firm was that it was so big they didn't know who was who in their ranks. This chink in their armour made it easy for young Billy to tag along with them and then slip off the back of the firm without anyone noticing. Young Billy made a call on the mobile phone Taylor had given him.

"It's South Kenton on the Bakerloo Line, it's an above ground station so I'll be able to see when they actually get on the train," Billy said.

"You done well young Billy, you're moving up the ranks. Make sure you keep them in sight but be careful eh." Taylor said and then pressed end on his phone.

Taylor turned to the other senior members of the firm gathered around him.

"Okay lads, listen in. Those Chelsea mugs are getting on at South Kenton, that's the Bakerloo line," he looked at his underground map, "Maida Vale," he announced, "that's where we are going to hit the cunts."

There were a few nods and grunts, some murmurs of approval as the tension in the air built. The ICF had been waiting in the bars and cafes around Baker Street. They had been mingling with the general public as best they could so as not to pick up a police escort. They were acting as nondescript as possible. It was all set up nicely, very little police attention as West Ham United's football team were playing in Sunderland, up in the north east of England that afternoon. The police would naturally assume that the top ICF boys were heading that way but there would be little trouble in Sunderland that day as the ICF had other carefully laid out plans in the capital. Within minutes the ICF top boys sent text messages to their own individual firms and each firm then made their way down to the Baker Street underground station and onto the westbound platform.

Taylor made another call to Billy before he too made his way underground where his mobile would not work.

"Where they at, Billy?" he asked.

"Half their firm are on the platform, they're still making their way through the station. Some of 'em are still hanging around outside. There's a lot of 'em Mick," Billy said.

"Yeah, a lot of fuckin' mugs. Don't worry about how many there are Billy, they won't know what's fuckin' hit them."

Taylor was the last man on the platform and saw all the regular faces who were spread out and casually mingled in with normal underground tube travellers. The ICF were well disciplined, under orders to be smartly dressed and polite to everyone until the action started. The large group of smartly dressed young men then boarded the Bakerloo line train in small groups of two and three. Precisely nine minutes later the ICF disembarked at Maida Vale tube station and again mingled in with the general hustle and bustle outside the London tube station.

Taylor sprang into action on the phone and spoke with three members of the Under Fives outside the station. The Under Fives only ever took orders from Taylor and not from any of the other ICF leaders. They only had respect for Taylor.

"Okay, you know what to do," said Taylor

"Yeah Mick, we won't let you down."

Taylor watched as the three Under Fives put on their hoodies, pulled up their scarfs and made their way back down onto the platform.

Maida Vale Underground Station Platform

Two of the boys made their way to the very end of the station where the front of the train would come to a halt. The other under five member went to the front end of the platform where the train would first come into view.

The plan was a simple one. As the trains pulled into the station the first Under Five member at the front end of the platform would check to see whether Chelsea's firm were on the train. Once he knew they were on the train he would signal to the two youths at the other end of the platform. The boy waited patiently, ready and willing to carry out his duty. The first two trains that pulled into the platform drew a negative, but as the third train pulled into the station and he peered into the windows he knew it was the one they had been waiting for.

It was still slowing down but he could see the train was packed full of men. It wasn't too hard to work out that this was the Chelsea firm. He quickly waved down the platform to his two mates.

The driver of the train was about thirty metres from the end of the platform as he engaged his brake a little more anticipating bringing the train to a halt just before the tunnel entrance. As he was about twenty metres from his stop point he saw two youths with hoodies run towards his train. He let out a gasp as they both threw something at the window. All of a sudden his front window was completely blacked out as he realised that they had obviously thrown balloons filled up with some sort of paint that had exploded on impact. The two youths, their task complete made their escape as they ran back up the platform and jumped the barrier ignoring the shouts and protests of the ticket inspector. The first youth acted a little more casual as he made his way leisurely out of the station and gave the thumbs up signal to Taylor.

Once Taylor saw the sign he put on his ear phones and banged on Adagio for Strings by Tiesto and set it for auto play. This was how Taylor got the Mad bit added to his name. Taylor's closest ICF mates all looked at each other with a nudge, nudge, wink, wink, when Taylor put on his earphones and banged on some fucking crazy trance track. Most football hooligans had a vice that got them ready for a big off, be it a line of

Charlie, a dab of speed or a can of special brew, but Taylor had found his own unique hit to prepare for a big off.

Everyone knew that Taylor didn't need anything to fight and he was as fearsome as the next man but this music sent Taylor into a higher level of psychotic violence that always seemed to give him the edge when it kicked off proper with a big firm. Taking on Chelsea's firm on a match day in London was a big ask when West Ham's actual team were playing up north in Sunderland. It meant that the ICF could not rely on any help from normal run of the mill West Ham fans who always swelled their numbers when the ICF kicked off on a match day.

The entire ICF firm were all waiting for Taylor to give the signal. He stood watching the entrance to the tube station, eyes wide open, just staring; staring and not blinking; just staring and staring as if he was in a trance.

Richie Freeman was in the lead carriage when he saw the two youths running down the platform. Freeman was pissed off. Chelsea had just lost to poxy Watford. Still it had been a decent end to the day smashing up their town centre. Freeman became even more pissed off when the Tannoy spluttered into life and made an announcement.

"This train will be delayed for some time due to an act of vandalism. All passengers can either embark from the train or wait until we make a further announcement."

Freeman made an instant decision. "Fuck this for a laugh we're in Maida Vale let's get out of here and find a boozer."

The word spread down the tube train and the Chelsea firm got off the train and made their way through the tunnels and escalators that took the passengers up to the surface.

Most of the top hooligan firms had their gamest fighters at the front and at the back of the firm because this was where they were most likely to be attacked. Chelsea were blasé that day as they knew both Millwall and West Ham were playing away and had no other hooligan firms to fear in London that evening. The Chelsea boys began to congregate outside Maida Vale station, waiting for the rest of the firm who were still underground. The Chelsea firm's best and gamest fighters were now spread out. In football hooligan terms that was a bad mistake to make.

Freeman stood outside the station with two hundred Chelsea firm members who were standing around, waiting for the rest of the firm to come out of the station. Freeman would normally always have his top boys in close vicinity but that day he saw a lot of the wannabes mixed in with his trusted top boys.

Taylor was twenty-five metres away and he could see Freeman standing in the centre of his firm. Freeman stood out from the crowd. He was a huge black man and that in itself was unusual as most of Chelsea's firm was white and racist. From previous offs, Taylor knew that Freeman would not run, he was as game as you like.

Taylor's alter ego entered his persona and Mad Micky surfaced. The only difference was a strange sheen that passed over his eyes. Taylor's closest ICF lieutenants watched Taylor's eyes and when they saw Mad Micky appear they knew it was time.

Taylor raised a clench fist in the air. "Now, now, come on West Ham, let's fuckin have it," he screamed, his crazy blue eyes gleaming with madness. One of his ICF firm blew a whistle, the signal for all of the West Ham ICF firms to join up and come together en masse to attack the enemy.

The chant started up from all directions.

"ICF, ICF," and as youths and grown men seemed to appear from everywhere running towards the Chelsea Firm, Freeman's blood turned to ice as he realised he'd been stitched up and completely outflanked.

"Stand firm," he shouted, but even as he tried to rally his troops, he could see the fear the ICF chant had struck in the faces of those closest to him and all of a sudden the ICF were on them like a pack of wild dogs as they steamed straight into the rank and file of the Chelsea firm. Some Chelsea boys were standing firm trying to repel the attack but most of them had cut and run, fleeing desperately into the tube station trying to escape the attack.

In the ensuing chaos Freeman saw Taylor coming straight for him, leading his Canning Town firm. It was a perfectly executed and well planned attack as his top lieutenants from the Canning Town firm headed straight for Chelsea's top boys.

Now there were no more than twenty of Freeman's men who had stood firm and refused to run together with a few wannabes who were trying to make a name for themselves.

Taylor was at the front of his Canning Town firm. He had one target in mind and that was taking out Freeman. In the madness that followed, Freeman proved why he was Chelsea's top boy. Not only was he fighting but all the time he was screaming out orders and words of encouragement to stand and fight.

In the cauldron of the mass football brawl Taylor headed straight for Freeman. As Taylor ran towards Freeman he could see that he was holding a telescopic truncheon in his right hand. It was a good weapon for a football brawl. Freeman flicked out the truncheon to its full length.

"Come on West Ham boy, I'm going to teach you a lesson, you're going down you fucking cunt," he shouted.

The words were wasted as Mad Micky only had Tiesto's Adagio for Strings banging into his brain.

Taylor was handy, about six foot tall and weighed eleven stone. Taylor could fight but in football hooligan terms it was about how game you were and what weapon you used. Freeman was an intimidating sight. At least six foot eight tall and carrying eighteen stones. As Taylor came for him Freeman took a big swing with his telescopic truncheon but Taylor was ready for him with his favourite weapon. As Taylor took a swift step to the side, the truncheon clipped his shoulder blade. It was mistimed, bad judgement and it would cost him dearly as Taylor pointed and sprayed a small plastic bottle directly into Freeman's face.

Freeman felt the noxious liquid in his eyes and immediately fell to the ground screaming in agony as the fumes from the household concoction of domestic products burned into the eyes of the Chelsea top boy.

In all the confusion of the mass brawl taking place around him Taylor calmly flipped the lid back on the bottle and pulled out a small Stanley knife. He pulled Freeman's hands away from his face and sliced a large cut down Freeman's left cheek right to the bone. He pulled a card from his back pocket and slipped it inside Freeman's jacket. The card read

'Congratulations, you have just met the ICF.'

Freeman was done as he lay screaming on the ground but the ICF were far from happy and there was still much work to be done. It was a classic ambush by West Ham's Inter City Firm. The rout of Chelsea did not end with Freeman's demise but continued into Maida Vale Tube station and deep into the complex of tunnels that led to the underground platforms. The entire Chelsea firm was cornered; they were getting well and truly battered by the highly organised ICF even though they outnumbered them by at least three to one. Weight of numbers were not a factor in the close confines of the tunnels and the beating of the Chelsea firm continued as they retreated en masse back to the platform. In a bid to seek sanctuary some of the Chelsea firm boarded the train which was still stranded at the platform. They were now well and truly trapped and the ICF attack continued, with those attempting to fight beaten to the ground and then kicked, punched and in some cases sliced up with razor sharp Stanley blades.

The onslaught continued and in their desperation to escape some of the Chelsea firm smashed through the windows of the stricken underground train and ran across the track. It was a poorly thought out escape plan as they were met by more ICF fighters who had been waiting on the other side of the platform and at least a dozen of the Chelsea Firm ran into the actual tube tunnels to escape.

Taylor looked at his watch and gave a signal. A shrill whistle sounded out and the ICF stopped their attack immediately. It had been exactly six minutes since the attack had started and within the next few minutes the station would be overrun by police. They made good their escape from the station and melted away into the London evening.

That day the Chelsea hooligan firm got well and truly butchered. The Maida Vale ambush would go down in football hooligan folklore and reinforced West Ham's reputation of being the top hooligan firm not only in London but in the whole of England.

Taylor rendezvoused as pre planned, with a few of his trusted lieutenants in a quiet pub in Newham. They discussed the day's events and congratulated each other. Taylor allowed himself just one pint. He needed to return to his family, he wasn't the sort to spend too much time in pubs.

As Taylor arrived home he opened the front door and his son Danny was waiting for him. He dived from the stairs into his arms.

"Hello, Dad."

"Hello, son," he replied as he planted a big kiss on his cheek and ruffled his hair.

"Did we win today?"

"Today was a draw, but never mind son, West Ham always win somewhere," he beamed.

A voice sounded from the kitchen. It was his wife.

"Mick, can you come into the kitchen."

She sounded serious.

As he walked into the kitchen Sandra stood by the sink, her face was like thunder.

"What?" Taylor said.

"Well I hope you're proud of yourself," she snapped.

"What are you talking about?"

She placed her hands on her hip. "So you weren't involved in the incident at Maida Vale tube station?"

"I don't know what you're talking about," he lied.

"It was on the radio that there had been a serious incident of football violence at Maida Vale tube station between West Ham and Chelsea fans, two stabbings, numerous faces slashed and even some poor bastard nearly blinded with some sort of ammonia."

Taylor shrugged his shoulders.

Danny clung to his leg. "Will you play a computer game with me Daddy?"

He eased his young son's arms from his leg, "sure I will little man, just you go into the lounge and I'll be through in a while."

The boy let out a sigh and wandered through the open doorway.

"When will you ever grow up Mick? And you just so happen to have been out all day, that's a strange coincidence isn't it?"

"I've been in the pub all day."

"Liar," she said, "you've been out fighting with your mates like a fucking teenager. Why don't you take Danny out for the day like a proper Dad?" she screamed, "what sort of an example are you to your son especially with what he's going through?"

The abuse and accusations went on for some minutes. Taylor tried to put up a decent sort of defence but it was all too futile, there was something different about Sandra this time, she appeared so much more determined than she usually was.

"Give it a rest will you Sandra."

On she went, the police had CCTV, arrests were imminent.

Eventually he'd had enough.

"Ah bollocks to all this, I'm going out down the pub," he said, flinging his arms up in despair.

"No you're not, you're not going to the pub we need to have serious discussion about Danny," she shouted.

"What, another fucking lecture?"

She didn't answer him and all at once he knew. In that uncomfortable half minute of silence Taylor knew that something was seriously wrong and he could see tears welling up in his wife's eyes.

Sandra stood up and closed the kitchen door.

"What is it Sandra, tell me?"

Sandra sat down at the kitchen table as two identical tears rolled the length of her cheek.

"It's Danny isn't it?" he asked.

She nodded. "I've had the results back, Danny is ill, very ill, it's not good news."

Her words stopped Taylor in his tracks.

"What's wrong with him?" he asked nervously, "he's just a little worn out that's all, anaemic the doc said. Tell me that's all it is?"

Sandra shook her head as the flood gates opened. "I wish it was just anaemia."

Taylor shook his head, "not anaemia?"

"No."

"Then what?"

"You should have been with me at the Doctors Mick."

He lost the strength in his legs, he thought they were about to buckle underneath him and he pulled out a chair and sat down.

"Tell me Sandra, tell me now darling."

She nodded slowly as she wiped at the tear that had roiled the full length of her face. "Danny's got leukaemia," she wailed as her head dropped onto the kitchen table.

Taylor was momentarily frozen in time. He hadn't heard that, surely he hadn't heard that?

He leaned in towards her and held her in his arms as she sobbed uncontrollably. He wanted to speak, wanted to find the right words to tell her everything would be fine but he couldn't. He couldn't find any words to comfort her as tears welled up in his eyes and he looked over her shoulder and saw his son standing in the doorway wondering what all the fuss was about.

CHAPTER 7

Sandra was taking her early morning bath. She was worrying about Danny's hospital appointment with the cancer specialist and was due the results from his last round of his treatment. It was a very important day for the family. She was annoyed that she couldn't make the appointment but despite Danny's illness blighting the family the one good thing that had come out of Danny's diagnosis was that Taylor had now changed for the better. He was spending more time with Danny, he was a better father and a better husband. Taylor had even stopped going to football on a Saturday and instead took Danny bowling and did other things that he enjoyed or at least could manage during his treatment. *It wasn't right, it shouldn't be happening, God shouldn't be putting little children through this sort of thing, the chemotherapy was draining the life from him.* And yet the doctor was positive, he kept throwing statistics at her that survival rates were good and even if the current treatment didn't work, there were other alternatives like bone marrow replacement, stem cell therapy, immunotherapy and radiation.

If anything Taylor had become too soft with Danny and sometimes let him run riot. This usually meant Sandra telling off her son when he needed reining back in. More often than not Danny would go running to Taylor complaining that mum was telling him off for no good reason and of course Taylor would always take his side. Taylor had changed, there was no doubt about that, he had changed during the past eight months of treatment, he was absolutely devoted to his son but could sometimes forget about some aspects of family life.

Sandra was scared about today, there was no other word to describe it and because of work commitments it was impossible to get the time off and accompany her two boys on the journey. She looked at her watch. There was no sound, why weren't they getting ready? She jumped out of the bath and shouted downstairs.

"You're going to be late boys, I want Danny to keep to his routine, he should be dressed by now, it will be a bloody nightmare getting him up for school tomorrow."

Taylor eased himself from the kitchen table, poured the last dregs of his coffee down the sink. "Come on little man, you heard your Mum, I'm going to get in trouble if we are late so up the apple and pears and put on your school uniform. Remember, today you're seeing Doctor Barnes and you're not having any treatment so you'll be off to school after we get out of the hospital."

Danny frowned, "dad can't we go to the park after, just for a little bit, please dad?"

Taylor lowered his voice, put a finger across his lips, "course we can, just for a little bit but keep it a secret yeah?"

"Yeah just our little secret," he laughed.

By the time Sandra Taylor left the house she only had time for a quick kiss for her seven year old son.

"Bye Danny, I love you very much, try to be brave at the hospital and be good for your daddy."

She reached across the table and picked up her handbag.

"Love you too, Mum," he replied.

Sandra turned to Taylor. "See you later Taylor, make sure you're not late okay. Call me as soon as you get his results,"

Sandra gave a quick wave goodbye and walked out down the path cursing under her breath that her boss should have been a little more understanding and allowed her the morning off. Taylor shut the front door and went back into the kitchen. Danny looked up from the table as he spooned the last remnants of Rice Crispies into his mouth. He chewed for a second or two.

"When are West Ham going to win the FA cup, Dad?" he asked.

"Next year, son," said Taylor confidently.

"You said that last year, Dad."

"Now don't start on West Ham Danny," Taylor said. He knew what was coming next.

"West Ham never win anything because there…" he dragged out the word… "rubbish."

Taylor clenched his fist and grinned, "right little man, you're in trouble now. You'd better watch out 'coz I'm coming to get you," he laughed. Right on cue Danny leapt from his seat and Taylor started to chase him around the table. The fun lasted just a couple of minutes and Taylor looked at his watch. Time was getting on a bit.

"We'd better get going Dan, or I'll get your mum giving me the ear 'ole if I'm late for your hospital appointment. Finish your toast and get your teeth cleaned for me."

"Okay Dad," Danny said. He laughed, reached for the last piece of toast and ran upstairs.

Taylor checked the London Underground map again, even though he knew it like the back of his hand. He had to take a couple of trains to get Danny to his hospital appointment. He had to get a Metropolitan line train from his home in Bethnal Green, then change at Liverpool Street for a Circle Line train to St James's Park.

Kings Cross Underground Tube Station

The capital had four other unwelcome visitors that day. One of those visitors was Shehzad Tanweer. He was a member of a home-grown cell of terrorists who had travelled to the capital that day to bring their version of Islamic fundamentalism to the citizens of London.

Tanweer had boarded train 204 at Kings Cross Station carrying a backpack, the contents of which did not contain everyday items but a highly volatile homemade bomb. He had completed two previous dummy runs and knew that the trains leaving on the Circle Line from Kings Cross had been sparsely populated with passengers. Tanweer positioned himself in the centre of carriage three and waited patiently for a seat to become available.

Tanweer's biggest concern was the lurching backwards and forwards of the train and the possibility of another passenger accidentally hitting his backpack and exploding the highly sensitive bomb. The bomb could be easily damaged with the resulting scenario of the bomb going off at the wrong time, leaving very few victims, or a worst case scenario that the bomb could be easily damaged and fail to work at all.

The train pulled into the Barbican Tube Station. A few seated passengers stood up to leave the train and Tanweer quickly sat in an empty seat. He placed the backpack on his lap and waited for the carriage to fill up with people. He was getting close, the next stop was Moorgate.

At Moorgate the train increased its passenger load and then left for Liverpool Street. As the train pulled into Liverpool Street Station Tanweer saw that the platform was packed with people. He smiled a smug grin of satisfaction. The time was nigh, *Allah would be waiting for him in Jannah, Allah would take care of everything.* He opened up the zip on the backpack and let out a deep sigh and noticed that his hands were shaking uncontrollably. A bead of sweat ran down his brow and down the length of his nose. He put one hand around the detonating cord and began to pray silently to himself. He knew in his head that the last moments of his life beckoned and he wondered why he felt so afraid.

The Metropolitan Line train had pulled into Liverpool Street underground station and they made their way through the mass of tunnels to the Circle Line platform. Taylor didn't need to look at any of the signs as he knew Liverpool Street Station like the back of his hand. Eventually Taylor and Danny were through the last tunnel and walked onto the Circle Line platform. The platform was packed with people and Taylor held Danny's hand tightly while they waited patiently for the next train.

Taylor was looking at his watch wondering whether he would be late for the hospital appointment when at last, the Circle Line train appeared at the end of the tunnel and came to a halt in the station.

The doors of the train opened and a few dozen passengers got off and squeezed past the mass of passengers waiting to get on. Taylor and Danny were just about to get onto carriage two when they realised the carriage was completely full, they were jammed in like sardines.

"Dad, this one quick," Danny shouted as he pulled on his father's hand trying to get onto the train.

Taylor felt uneasy, it was a ridiculous tight squeeze and wouldn't be comfortable, he worried that Danny might get crushed.

"C'mon dad."

Taylor checked his watch. "Shit," he whispered to himself, "no option, have to get on otherwise we'll be late."

"Dad... hurry."

"Okay quick son, before the doors shut."

They were the last passengers to get onto carriage three. The carriage had just about enough space to stand. Taylor held the railings with one hand and Danny's hand with the other.

Simon Hass was thinking how lucky he was to grab a seat eight minutes earlier when he boarded the Circle Line train at London Kings Cross. He watched the man with a young boy hesitating as they decided whether or not to jump onto the packed train. The little boy looked sick, not well at all but eventually the little boy stepped onto the train holding his father's hand. To this day Simon Hass never actually understood why he gave up his seat but on that particular day he chose to offer his seat to the frail looking boy.

"Would you like my seat little fellow, I'm getting off at the next stop?" he said as he stood up and beckoned the little boy forward.

Danny Taylor looked up at his dad and his dad nodded to Danny that it was okay to take the seat. Danny Taylor squeezed past several people and swapped places with the stranger. Danny sat next to an Asian man who looked very hot and sweaty.

Nice gesture, Taylor thought to himself, *not many like him around these days.*

He called out to his son, "stay there Danny we have about ten stops to go,"

Danny looked a little anxious as Taylor moved a few feet away from his seat but soon relaxed when he could see that his father was looking at him through the glass partition near the exit doors. Danny was just a few yards from his dad with two people between them on the packed train. A buzzer sounded, and the doors automatically closed. Train 204 lurched forward and began its journey to the next stop, Aldgate East. It was 8.47 a.m. on Thursday 7th July 2005.

Tanweer said another prayer and silently chanted in his head, *Allah Akbar, Allah Akbar, Allah Akbar.*

The plan was to detonate the bomb between stations to cause maximum damage and increase the effect of the blast wave in the close confines of the tunnel. Train 204 was just one hundred metres down the tunnel when Tanweer made his decision. The time was right, everything was perfect, so many infidels. He rose slowly to his feet and took a tight grip on the detonating cord.

Several people noticed the young Asian man rise to his feet. Some noticed the demonic, almost vacant look on his face and the sharp determined look in his eyes.

"Allah Akbar," he screamed at the top of his voice as he pulled hard on the detonating cord inside the rucksack.

Danny Taylor gazed up at him and wondered to himself why he couldn't understand the words the man said.

Those were the last words that many passengers in train 204 ever heard. The man appeared to explode and disintegrate in a blinding white and red flash and a blast wave containing six inch nails and nuts and bolts ran through the train at 8000 metres per second. In the immediate vicinity of the explosion at least a dozen people were quite literally ripped apart. Body parts, broken bones, personal effects of the unfortunate victims, glass and steel were added to the initial blast wave and it continued through the train. The blast wave tore into Danny's young body rupturing every one of his internal organs and several nails and bolts and other shrapnel smashed into his skull shredding his brain into a thousand pieces. Danny Taylor died instantly.

In that first millisecond of the bomb blast Taylor felt a blinding flash of heat and the explosion catapulted Taylor and several passengers through the train window and out into the tunnel. They were the lucky ones. The blast wave continued to roll through the train, taking its deadly toll on human flesh and bodies turning the carriages into a mangled mass of death and sheer carnage. Several minutes passed before Taylor regained consciousness.

He was aware of the acrid smoke that filled his lungs as he coughed and spluttered for air. There was a sweetly sick smell in the air, *what was it* he thought to himself, it smelled like half cooked chicken and then the horror dawned on him as he realised what had happened and that the smell could only be that of burning flesh. Taylor looked up at the carriage of the train, several fires were burning and he could hear terrible screams echoing around the tunnel. He was concussed and confused but he could only think of one thing.

"Danny, he screamed, "where are you?"

Taylor pulled himself groggily to his feet and held onto the side of the train for balance. The only light in the tunnel was from the glow from the fires as he realised where he was, in a narrow space between the train and the tunnel wall.

"Danny," he mumbled to himself, "I need to find Danny."

Taylor tried to pull himself up into one of the smashed train windows but was beaten back by the heat from the burning fires coming from the carriage.

"Danny, Danny," he screamed.

There was no way that Taylor could climb back into the train. He looked along the tunnel and saw flashes of light coming from the back of the train. He searched his pockets; luckily and found his mobile phone. He turned on the built-in torch and miraculously it worked. It gave him just enough light to see where he was going. He stumbled and tripped over something and pointed the torch to the ground. It was the body of a young woman, stripped of clothing, half her head was missing along with an arm

"Holy fuck, he said, "Holy fucking shit."

He continued to make his way along the narrow space between the train and the tunnel wall as he stepped over even more bodies, limbs and what looked like huge chunks of meat, discarded bags and suitcases. Bodies were hanging from the shattered windows as he noticed flashlights coming from the back of the train. Was help on its way?

He looked up at two figures moving towards him. As they got closer he recognised the uniforms of the London underground staff. They were rushing towards him.

"Are you okay Sir?" one of them shouted.

"Yes," Taylor said, "I'm looking for my son, help me please, I need to find my son, I've lost my son, his name's Danny has anyone seen him?"

"I'm sure he's okay," the man said, we've been taking the survivors back to Liverpool Street station, there are paramedics and doctors and nurses, I'm sure you'll find your son there.

The man stepped forward with a cloth. "Hold this cloth on your face, you've got a nasty cut to the side of your face."

"I don't care about my face, I need to find Danny."

The other underground worker put a blanket around him, "C'mon mate, we need to get you into the station, I'll help you find your son."

"Danny, Danny," he shouted as he was led along by the man, his words echoing along the tunnel walls.

As he began to make his way back to the station he saw powerful beams of light shining through the tunnel as the first of London's emergency services arrived on the scene. There were blue flashing lights and he could hear the screams and moans of the injured and dying.

Taylor and his helper eventually arrived at the main concourse at Liverpool Street station. The scene was utter mayhem, the concourse milling with scores of injured passengers, he noticed several bodies lying on the ground, with their faces covered with white sheets.

"It was a crash," said one voice.

"No it was definitely a bomb," said another.

Taylor scanned the platform

 "I'll take over now," said a medic to the man who had helped him from the tunnel.

"Good luck," he said then he disappeared into the crowd.

The medic quickly attended to his wounds not wanting him to know the extent of the cuts that would permanently disfigure his face. As the adrenalin wore off, the waves of pain started to flow through his body but they were secondary to the mental anguish of his missing son. He looked out across the station concourse and saw a row of wounded men and women propped up against the station wall. Could Danny be there, he thought to himself. He pushed the medic aside and walked towards the group. One of the wounded men looked familiar and as their eyes met he realised it was the man who had swapped places with his son. The man lay on a stretcher.

Taylor limped over to him, "you mate, you gave up your seat for my son. Have you seen him?"

"I'm so sorry, so very sorry," he said.

"What do you mean sorry?" he said, aware that his stomach had begun to cramp up and a feeling of nausea was sweeping over him. "I don't want a sorry, I want to know if you've seen my son."

The man nodded. Almost in a whisper he spoke. "Yes, I saw your son."

"Great," he said as he tried to fix a smile on his face, "then where is he?"

The man took a deep breath, Taylor hung on his words and something deep inside told him to cover his ears for the words the stranger was about to speak would be with him in nightmares until his dying day.

"I'm sorry… your son sat next to the suicide bomber."

No Taylor wanted to scream, *don't tell me that.*

A tear rolled down the stranger's cheek. "He didn't stand a chance."

Sandra Taylor's entire office were watching the day's events unfold on the rapidly updated news flashes. It seemed that every report gave a different account but by 10.30 a.m. it was more or less a given that the explosions were most likely to be a series of terrorist attacks on the London underground network. There were also reports of an accident on a London bus that was now also said to be a bomb. Once again Sandra pressed the redial button on her mobile phone. No answer. Straight to voicemail. She had no idea if Danny or Taylor were safe. The only grain of comfort was that everybody's mobile telephone had stopped working and the news channels were reporting that the whole telecom network had crashed due to the fifteen million people in the London Metropolitan area using their mobile phones in the space of thirty minutes.

Sandra looked around her office and she saw the deep lines of anxiety etched on the faces of her colleagues. No one in her office knew for sure that their loved ones were safe and it seemed every person in the office had a friend or a member of their immediate family who were quite likely to have been in the near vicinity of the areas that had been targeted. Sandra would have been that bit more relaxed if Danny had left for school that morning. It would have been just a short walk to school, no need for any form of public transport whatsoever. She started to think what route Taylor and Danny would have taken to get to St. Mary's hospital. With ten million people living in London she hoped the odds were well in her favour and that her family were safe. The TV news reports were stating perhaps a dozen victims, no more. Her boys would be fine, she was sure of it.

CHAPTER 8

HMP Full Sutton

Dodds was lying on his bed watching TV. He was thinking back to when he first landed on the induction wing at Full Sutton. He ended up sharing a cell with some stupid 'Paki' from Burnley' who had just been given a life sentence for a so called 'honour killing.'

What the fuck was the point of that? he thought to himself. Dodds could never see the point in committing any crime unless there was an earner in it and an honour killing was about as stupid as it got. He'd read in a newspaper about an honour killing where a mother had burned her own daughter alive. According to the details of the incident, 18-year-old Zeenat Rafiq was burnt alive by her mother Parveen Bibi in Lahore's Factory Area. Zeenat had eloped with a man named Hassan Khan and later married him. Zeenat's family was infuriated over her actions but they pretended to forgive her and asked her to come back to her home so that she could be given a proper wedding reception. The girl fell for the trap and returned to her home just a week after her marriage. When she came back, her mother, helped by her son and son-in-law, threw kerosene on her and set her on fire. It simply defied logic, how could a mother do that to her own daughter?

He hadn't particularly liked the Pakistani's and the Muslims and couldn't quite relate to their beliefs and their strange customs and their faith, but being banged up with Imran Bakar ending up being a proper stroke of luck. When Dodds landed in HMP Full Sutton's induction wing he had no money to buy any heroin and started to go into cold turkey. His attitude to Bakar quickly changed when he gave Dodds a free wrap of heroin. He knew there was no such thing as a free ride in prison but Bakar asked for nothing in return and stated he was taught to help others in need.

On that first day Dodds noticed how all the other Muslims on the induction wing gave Bakar the utmost respect. Bakar seemed to be a bit of a face and it was obvious that Dodds needed to befriend Bakar before he hit the main wings at Full Sutton. Over the next two weeks of induction he slowly but surely wormed his way into Bakar's friendship. Dodds had to put up with Bakar's continuous preaching about the way of Islam and the regular praying sessions but for Dodds the most important thing was to make Bakar like him so he was prepared to put up with it. It was a means to an end.

Dodds didn't give a fuck about religion, fucking invisible men in the sky, it was all complete nonsense, an invention of man to control the people, nothing more than that. Anyone who immersed themselves in religion, dedicated their lives to it was brainwashed and deluded. *The Sun* newspaper always said it was the vicars and priests who nonced up the little choir boys. Islam or Christianity, it was just the same. An American Evangelical preacher, a Jew who prayed for Armageddon or a nutcase in charge of a cult, they were there to control, nothing more, nothing less. Even so, the more Dodds integrated with Bakar it was clear that he was truly devoted to his religion, and despite his general dis-interest in religion, Dodds did begin to take an interest in what Bakar was talking about. On the day before Dodds went onto the main wing at Full Sutton, Bakar invited Dodds to attend Friday prayers.

"But I'm not a Muslim," he stated honestly, "It wouldn't be right, I mean I don't even believe in Islam or Allah, or any god?

Bakar smiled. "I think in time you may look upon Islam differently but in the mean time I think you need us. We know why you're here, we know about the old woman you put in hospital. Your soul is dirty, you need redemption, you need to be cleansed."

He waived a hand in the air. "Pah! I'm my own man, I need nothing, I don't know what you're talking about."

Bakar let out a quiet sigh. "It will be dangerous for you to go on the main wing Dodds, you know that."

"I can take care of myself, I'm no mug."

Bakar laughed out loud, "you couldn't take care of yourself with the rugby player though could you?"

He was lost for words as Bakar continued.

"If you come to Muslim Friday Prayers I can arrange for the Imam to have you moved to E wing. I can protect you there and help you with your drug problem," he added.

It was exactly what Dodds had been hoping for because it made good sense for him to tag along with Bakar.

Bakar smiled. He had seen this sort of reaction many times and it was all about patience. Siding with the Muslims would offer Dodds a certain protection along with a good source of prison heroin. Bakar had a hidden agenda. Very few Muslims indulged in drug taking but there was plenty available on their Wing. It was the perfect tool to corrupt and manipulate those prisoners with a drug addiction, the first stage in the process of radicalisation. They were there to be exploited and used. It was why Allah had put them there.

Dodds continued to play the game and resisted just long enough so that Bakar wouldn't give up trying to persuade him altogether.

"Okay, I'll go with you on Friday."

"And you'll listen to what the Imam has to say?"

"Of course."

Bakar rose to his feet. "A wise decision Dodds, perhaps we can still save you after all."

As the prisoners walked into the prayer room, Bakar introduced him to each and every person who attended the prayer meeting. The majority of the Muslims were either black or of Indian and Pakistani race, but surprisingly there were a few white faces amongst the prayer group which puzzled him. Despite some contemptuous looks, the fact that Bakar had introduced him seemed to put the rest of the prayer group at ease. They even seemed to show Dodds a little respect. It was then that he realised that Bakar was not only very highly respected but feared too, and in prison, respect was only ever gained by fear.

Bakar had even introduced him to the Imam and he found the hour long service strangely comforting and peaceful.

As he left the Imam made a point of stopping him.

The Imam hugged him warmly. "I look forward to seeing you next Friday Mr Dodds and I'll make arrangements for you to be moved to the Islamic wing," he whispered.

Dodds nodded, he couldn't help but break out into a smug grin as he walked away.

"Muslim fuckin' mugs," he whispered quietly to himself as he looked at the copy of the Qur'an the Imam had handed him as a gift. As he walked away he wondered why someone as important as the Imam had genuinely shown him so much respect.

He attended the next Friday's prayer meeting and each and every prayer meeting thereafter. After four weeks he started to read the Qur'an. He learned to recite certain verses from the book.

Dodds had been attending prayers and reading the Qur'an for nearly two months. He sat on his bunk most days for several hours absorbed in the text of the Islamic book. The cell door opened and Bakar walked in.

"Brother," he said.

"How are you?"

"Good, just finishing off my studies."

Bakar smiled, "you are a good student and I have a little present for you."

Bakar placed the wrap of heroin on his bed.

"No thanks," Dodds said.

"You have another supplier." Baker asked suspiciously.

"No, of course not"

"Then what is going on?"

"This book, the Qur'an, I have read it twice already, studied it in great detail.

"Really, twice?"

"Yes Bakar, I do not feel the need for drugs anymore. My new drug is the Qur'an."

A month later Dodds was invited to read a passage of the Qur'an at Muslim Prayers. Bakar looked on. His skin was clear, his eyes bright, a different man from the junkie Bakar remembered some months previously. The Muslims in HMP Full Sutton not only accepted Dodds as one of their own but began to look up to Dodds as a confidant and a bit of a right hand man of Bakar. Dodds, for the first time in his life actually felt that he 'belonged.'

That acceptance became enshrined when Dodds, with the agreement of the Imam, was offered 'shahada,' the declaration of believing in the oneness of God.

He knew the words off by heart, he had been determined to show everyone present that he was more than serious about immersing himself in Islam.

"I bear witness that there is no god but Allah, and I bear witness that Muhammad is the Messenger of Allah," he recited to the Imam.

The Imam looked on him with a display of genuine pride.

"Now you have accepted Shahada and you are a true believer, you must now take a new name," said the Imam.

"Yes Imam."

"I declare you to be named as Muhammed Khan."

"Thank you Imam, thank you from the bottom of my heart, I agree to be named as Muhammed Khan."

The following week he attended his first Friday prayer meeting as Muhammed Khan and Bakar and the Imam introduced him to the rest of the group as Muhammed Khan. He received a small round of applause from his fellow Muslims. For the first time in his life he felt accepted within a true family, he was truly among brothers, he was a believer.

Wherever he walked in prison he felt a certain level of protection and despite the snide looks and sniggers of the non-believers as he walked along the prison corridors he held his head up with pride.

It was an official Category A dispersal policy that no one group should dominate any particular prison wing and apart from the IRA prisoners back in the eighties and early nineties this rule stood. However, by 2004 all of England's four maximum security prisons had their own unofficial Muslim wing. At Full Sutton, E wing was designated as the Muslim wing. And so Muhammed Khan and Imran Bakar found themselves on E wing when the London bombings took place.

Imran Bakar was reading the Qur'an when his door flap opened up and an excited prisoner known as Ali was talking rapidly and incoherently through the small inspection space. Bakar rose slowly from his bunk and walked to his cell door

"What is it Ali? talk slowly and calmly," he said.

"Allamah, Allamah, I have great news," said Ali.

"Okay, speak of this news, Ali."

"It's on the news in the TV room."

"What is on the news, Ali?" Bakar replied, growing increasingly frustrated.

"Bomb attacks in London, the TV speaks of bombings in London."

Bakar removed his glasses. "Bombs in London?" he enquired.

"Yes," Ali said," they are the bombs of our brothers, they have slaughtered the infidels."

Bakar reached for his Qur'an as he looked skywards and whispered a quiet prayer. Ali looked on, hardly daring to breath as he waited for Bakar to finish."

Bakar leaned towards the door. "You have brought me wondrous news Ali, I thank you from the bottom of my heart, you can go now and please close my hatch."

Bakar switched on his TV and watched the events unfold on the BBC.

Further down the Wing Khan heard a tap on his door and Ali's face appeared at his door flap.

"Go to the news, go to the news channel Khan, it has started, Allah Akbar," he said as he rushed away to the next cell to spread the word.

Khan switched on his prison cell TV and tuned into the BBC news channel and watched as the aftermath of the London bombings were being played live on TV. He thought back to the preaching's of both the Imam and Bakar, who stated that there would be a day of reckoning for the UK's oppressive treatment of all Muslim brothers throughout the world. That day had apparently arrived.

Ali continued to pass the message around and within thirty minutes E wing was buzzing as the news channels simultaneously relayed the story of the London bombings to the Muslim prisoners on E wing. The channels all seemed to suggest that it was an Al Qaeda suicide style attack in retaliation for the UK wars in Afghanistan and Iraq.

Prison Officer James and Senior officer Smith were sitting in E wing's high security bubble reading the prisoners' newspapers that were delivered every morning. Televisions were not allowed in the security bubble so they had no idea that the bombings had taken place. All of a sudden the whole of E wing erupted in a crescendo of banging as the prisoners on E wing kicked their doors in celebration of the news that the bombings had been confirmed as an Islamic Al Qaeda linked attack.

"What the fuck is that?" Smith said.

"Fuck knows, sir, I've no idea what's going on," he replied.

Smith covered his ears with his hands. "What a fucking racket, I want it stopped pronto."

The noise continued unabated and could be heard throughout the whole prison.

Smith could hear the words, "Allah Akbar" being screamed from some of the cells.

"Go and see Bakar," Smith yelled, "he's the only cunt who can stop this."

"Yes sir," he said as he jumped to his feet and ran towards the door and ran out into the corridor. He was a little out of breath as he reached Bakar's cell door. James opened Bakar's door flap and saw that Bakar was lying quietly on his bunk reading, seemingly oblivious to the crescendo of noise that filled the wing. Smith reached for his keys, unlocked Bakar's door and stepped inside.

"What the fuck is going on Bakar, can you sort this out?" he screamed in a bid to be heard above the din.

"What makes you think I can influence my Muslim friends to appease you?" Bakar said calmly.

"Look Bakar, if this racket don't stop, E wing will lose its association time tonight, I'll personally strip you of all privileges."

Bakar smiled at the grossly overweight prison officer. *A pathetic little specimen of nothingness.* James knew that he was speaking to the top dog on E wing and he knew that he had the powers that no Prison Officer could yield. Generally when there was a problem between the officers and the Muslim prisoners Bakar was always called upon to calm things down.

Bakar eased himself off his bunk and with great sarcasm said, "Your word is my command Sir, anything to keep the peace, Sir."

Smith frowned, "stop belittling me Bakar, just get it fucking sorted, there's a good lad."

"So officer Sir, what exactly do you want me to do?"

"I want you to stop this banging on the doors or I'll be taking a few of your buddies down the block," he said.

Bakar swung his legs over the side of his bunk and let out a deep sigh. "Permission to leave my cell Sir, permission to talk with my Muslim brothers."

"Stop taking the piss Bakar," the officer said, "just quieten things down."

Bakar walked out onto the landing and even he was surprised how loud the banging seemed to be on the open space of the wing. He also noticed that Officer James was not alone and he had four other officers supporting him just in case Bakar decided to cause any trouble.

The officers watched as Bakar went from cell to cell and with his fingers to his lips motioned the other prisoners to quieten down. Within a matter of minutes E wing was eerily silent. Bakar walked towards the four prison officers slowly. As he drew alongside them he bowed his head.

"Your wish is my command gentlemen," he smiled, "the Muslim brothers are at peace now."

Bakar returned to his cell and quietly closed the door. He reached for his prayer mat and placed it carefully on the cell floor. He knelt. Bakar began to pray.

CHAPTER 9

Taylor sat patiently in the A & E department of Whitechapel hospital. His face was heavily bandaged and the morphine based pain killers dulled most of his physical pain. His mental pain however was very real indeed. Despite the hushed voices Taylor could hear medical staff discussing what do with his face. He could just about pick up most of the conversation but the words meant nothing to him.

"I'm not qualified nor do I have the skills to do that man's face, let alone the rest of his injuries." an attractive looking nurse whispered to a junior doctor.

"Well, the alternative is to let him bleed to death," he replied.

"He needs a plastic surgeon," the nurse said.

"I'm well aware of that nurse but we only have one plastic surgeon on duty and this man is way down the pecking order I'm afraid, he may look bad to you but I have at least three patients with half their damn faces missing. Look, you are the best person on this ward. None of us asked for this nurse, none of us, just do the best you can."

Nurse Johnson was left feeling way out of her depth as the doctor walked away to discuss the next bomb victim with another overworked member of staff.

Taylor watched as the attractive nurse walked in the cubicle, picked up his medical chart and read the notes. She studied the hand written addition at the bottom of the page and took a sharp intake of breath.

Proceed cautiously, Mr Taylor's son is believed to have been killed in the Aldgate underground bombing.

The notes stated that the ambulance staff had noted very deep lacerations to the right side of the man's face as well as a deep neck wound that they had patched up quickly. There was evidence of head trauma and concussion. Next of kin was his wife, Sandra Taylor, she is believed to be safe, Mr Taylor said she was at work.

"Hello Michael, my name is Sarah, I'm going to be looking after you for the time being."

Taylor didn't respond. He was numb with shock, could hardly hear and what happened to him from now on simply wasn't important. Why had he let little Danny sit next to that man?

"You have a wife Michael, is it okay to call you Michael? I believe she's on her way here now."

Taylor nodded.

"This may hurt a bit but I need to remove some pieces from your face, we don't want any infection."

He nodded.

The nurse sat on a chair with wheels and moved in closely with a pair of tweezers. She placed a cardboard bowl into Taylor's hands.

"Hold this for me please Micheal."

He nodded just once.

The nurse proceeded to remove bits of glass and tiny shards of metal that had been embedded in Taylor's face. It was only pure luck that he had not been blinded. She removed a quarter inch splinter of glass and a fragment of six inch nail just millimetres from the corner of his right eye.

"All good," she said, "it's going well but some of the shrapnel is too deeply set, I'm afraid you are going to need surgery to remove them."

Nurse Johnson went about her job in silence. She had the experience to know that when a patient had lost a very close loved one it was generally best not to force a conversation. She had dealt with many patients in road traffic accidents where family members had been killed.

The nurse attended to him for the best part of an hour. She lifted the final shard of glass from Taylor's eyebrow and announced that it was all over.

"You'll be pleased about that won't you?"

Taylor shrugged his shoulders, "thank you, I hope I haven't taken too much of your time."

Not at all Michael, that's what we are here for. Now, if you'll excuse me I'll need to speak to the junior doctor."

She found the doctor in another cubicle on the next ward.

"Man, he's a tough one," she said, "I removed a hell of a lot of shrapnel from his face and I swear he didn't flinch once."

"Really?" the Doctor questioned, "that's a first, they normally scream the house down."

"He really needs an MRI scan to find out exactly where the rest of the shards are and there are half a dozen pieces at least that need taken out, they are too deep for me."

The doctor let out a sigh. "Look, Nurse Johnson, we have a major incident on our hands, we are the closest hospital to the two of the bombings and as I said before, this man is at the back of the queue, especially as far as MRI scans go."

"But there's at least three or four pieces that are in too deep Doctor, I can't just sew his face up and leave them there."

"Then get them out," the doctor replied, "you've just said he's a tough bastard. If not he's got at least a two day wait for surgery."

Nurse Johnson was furious, this was not what she had signed up for and it was exactly these sort of incidents that exposed the vulnerability of the NHS. She left the cubicle and made her way hastily towards her patient's room. She was not qualified to do this, it was a specialist surgeon's job, the poor bastard would be in agony.

She pulled back the cubicle curtain and looked at Taylor. She explained how the hospital was stretched to the limit, how there wouldn't be a slot in the operating theatre for at least two days.

"It won't be pleasant, she said, "in fact it will hurt like hell."

"Just get on with it, I'm sure you'll do your best," he said.

Nurse Johnson spent another forty-five minutes removing seven deep set foreign objects from Taylor's face. His sweatshirt and the towel which had covered his lap looked like something from an abattoir. She eventually sewed up Taylor's face in silence. Not once had he complained, not once had he cried out in pain, not once had he even flinched. She gave him yet another pain killing injection and warned him that he would be in some discomfort for the next few hours. She spent another twenty minutes applying bandages and led him towards a wheelchair.

As he spotted the wheelchair eventually he spoke. "I don't need that, I can walk."

"No you can't, you've had a head injury, you could collapse at any moment."

Before the nurse could say another word Taylor had walked out of the door.

The nurse ran after him. "Michael please, do as I say, get into the wheelchair, I need to get you onto a ward quickly and safely."

Taylor turned to face her. "A ward?" he questioned, "I aint going on no ward, I'm going home."

Nurse Thompson had had enough. "Now look here," she said, her voice raised just a decibel or two. "you listen to me because I've had one hell of a day and the last thing I need is someone like you thinking that you know better than me. Do you want to tell me where you were medically trained and if I rate the place then you can walk out of here with my full blessing."

Taylor hesitated for a second and unless he was mistaken he was beginning to feel a little dizzy. He looked over at the wheelchair.

"Get in," the nurse said forcefully.

Taylor nodded and shuffled towards the chair.

There were no beds available in any of the wards. From his position in the A & E department's corridor, Taylor watched the chaos that the bombings had brought to the hospital. Since the IRA ceasefire back in the mid-nineties the UK hospitals had massively cut back on training for bomb blast injuries. The reality was that none of the emergency workers or the hospital staff had any real experience of how to deal with these types of injuries. He heard the nurses and doctors whispering about what to do with this or that patient. Despite the noise and mayhem around him he eventually drifted off to sleep. It was a very disturbed sleep and he dreamt that little Danny was holding his hand as they walked to the park. Taylor slowly opened his eyes and saw that it was actually his wife, holding his hand.

He tried to speak, the words wouldn't come, his lips and his mouth were dry and at last his face was beginning to burn and sting as the anaesthetic wore off.

"Don't speak Mick," Sandra whispered, "it's okay, I know."

"Danny..." he whispered.

"I know."

"It's my fault," he said.

"No," Sandra cried as she burst into tears."

"My fault…the seat.. the man."

Taylor discharged himself from the hospital twenty four hours later against the advice of the doctors and nurses and despite the protests of his wife. He'd sent Sandra home, said he would take a taxi back, there was one final thing he needed to do.

He was still shaky on his feet, his face and body ached, his limbs were stiff as boards and an express train thundered through his head. He shuffled along the corridor holding onto the wall for support and took the lift down to the basement. As the doors opened he quickly looked up at the hospital direction sign and turned to his left. It was eerily quiet, unlike any other part of the hospital. He followed the corridor for fifty metres and then turned to his right. He saw the lone hospital worker sitting at his desk staring blankly into a computer screen. As Taylor approached him he looked up.

"Yes Sir, can I help?"

"Yes," Taylor cleared his throat. "My name is Michael Taylor and I've come to identify the body of my son."

Three months later

Sandra opened the front door. "Hi Mum, thanks for coming round," Sandra said.

"How are you, darling?"

Immediately tears welled up in Sandra's eyes. It was always the same, something as innocuous as *how are you* brought everything flooding back.

As she broke down her mother took her arm and led her through to the kitchen, "I'll put the kettle on."

Sandra sat nursing her cup of tea. The routine was the same, the conversation a repeat of the previous visit and the one before that and the one before that.

"If only I'd taken Danny to hospital… he would still be alive."

"You don't know that."

"I do Mum, I do and he had beaten leukaemia, he had beaten that awful disease just to lose his life for nothing," she sobbed.

Jean took a deep breath and for the first time in years raised her voice at her daughter.

"I know how hard it is but you have got to snap out of this Sandra. Danny's gone, it's hard, it's hard for all of us but you still have Mick and you need to try and save your marriage. It wasn't Mick's fault, it was the bastard suicide bomber who blew himself up. It was his fault Sandra not Mick's," she said sternly.

Sandra lifted the tea cup to her mouth, said nothing.

"It's tearing him apart, Sandra, you can't blame him for Danny's death just because he was late for that hospital appointment."

"Typical of you to defend Mick in a situation like this," Sandra scowled at her mother.

"I am not defending him, I'm just saying that it wasn't his fault."

"He left Danny, he let him go and sit beside that bastard so he must take some of the blame."

Jean stared at her daughter. She had black rings around her eyes, she wasn't sleeping and cried almost permanently. It had been three months since the London bombings and her daughter seemed to be getting worse, she was heading downwards in a spiral of depression and no amount of help or counselling or doctors or drugs could change her direction.

"Where's Mick now?" Jean asked.

"How should I know? Probably in the garden shed smoking dope," she replied sarcastically.

Jean stood up. "He's doing what he has to in order to cope. Don't knock him if he takes an odd smoke now and again, at least he's trying to do something which is more than I can say for you."

Jean walked towards the back door. "I'm going to see the poor lad. Do you want me to tell him anything, should I make you both a nice bit of lunch and you can sit down together, just the two of you?"

Sandra looked back into her tea cup and shook her head.

Jean walked down the garden path towards the shed and tapped on the wooden door. As the door opened he sighed with relief. *Thank God it wasn't Sandra,* he thought, *the last thing he needed was another argument.*

"How are you son?"

"Bearing up," he replied.

He saw Jean's eyes waiver as she looked at the deep red scars on his face. They both felt a touch of embarrassment and Jean quickly asked about Taylor's injured leg.

"The leg is improving fast and the doctors said it should function fine but I will have a slight limp forever and a day."

Jean shrugged her shoulders, "shit happens."

"That's what I said."

Taylor knew that many of his friends and family simply avoided him due to the uncomfortable way they felt about his son's death. Jean was one of only a few people that Taylor saw on a regular basis.

There was a moment's silence before Jean spoke again.

"I'm really sorry Mick. I don't know why Sandra is like this, she has no right to blame you for what happened to Danny."

"I love her Jean but since Danny's death it's like a black cloud has descended over this house. She needs to see another doctor or do something. I'm really worried."

"We're all worried about her," Jean sighed.

"Have a word with her, you're the only person she'll listen to," he said, "because she sure as hell won't listen to me."

"I'll pop back to the house now, it's getting a bit cold... I think autumn is well and truly here now," she said in an attempt to lighten the mood.

"Take care Jean."

He was too absorbed in his thoughts to even acknowledge her attempt at small talk.

Jean walked over to Taylor and gave him a hug. "You too darling."

As she hugged him she noticed a mass of newspapers on an old table just behind him. As his mother in law left he picked one up. Each and every one of them had been checked and double checked and every single headline or sub headline relating to anything to do with Muslim terrorism had been ringed with a thick red marker pen. It seemed that the whole of the UK was on alert for some new Muslim outrage. Taylor was absorbed in his task, which was to document everything to do with this new campaign of violence. He was caught up in the fear and paranoia that was sweeping the nation since the 7/7 London bombings which had claimed the life of his son, scarred him for life and had taken his marriage past the point of no return.

Sandra's mum had sat with her for another two hours after she had been to Taylor's shed. She somehow sensed that her daughter was acting just a little differently than she usually did and seeing an occasional smile cross her daughter's lips for the first time in three months had been more than a welcome change. As Jean had left, Sandra had even hugged her and gave her a kiss on the cheek. It was cause for optimism, perhaps even celebration and although she wanted to run down to Taylor's shed and tell him a snippet of good news she thought it best to leave it for another day. As Jean almost skipped down the garden path she felt for sure that her daughter had turned a corner, she seemed at peace with the world.

"About bloody time," she muttered to herself as she closed the garden gate and turned around.

Sandra stood at the open door. "See you Mum."

"See you tomorrow darling," she waived.

Sandra closed the door and returned to the kitchen. She opened the cupboard and reached inside for the whisky. Jesus how she hated that shit, *how could anyone drink that?* She poured the whisky into a pint glass and started to drink. It took her a good twenty minutes to finish the glass and as she staggered to her feet she walked through the door and headed towards the stairs. In the en suite bathroom she opened the medicine cabinet and reached inside for the bottle which she carried towards her bed.

Later that evening Taylor went back indoors and called out for his wife. There was no response. He went upstairs and found his wife lying quietly in their bed. She was propped up against the headboard holding one of Danny's favourite teddy bears. He knew instantly that his wife had taken her own life. He calmly called an ambulance and when they arrived they did their best to resuscitate her but all to no avail. In a way he was relieved. It had been what she wanted, at least she was at peace. Not him. He wouldn't be going down that road because he had made a pledge to himself, Danny and now Sandra. Sandra had taken a lethal cocktail of prescription drugs and had slowly slipped into unconsciousness and then death. She was happy now, she was with Danny once again and Sandra Taylor became another casualty of the radical Islamic bombers. He was alone now and that's the way he wanted it. He asked his friends and family for space and privacy and for the most part they respected that. They became worried that Taylor might want to take his own life too, after all what did he have to live for? But Taylor had plans and within weeks of Sandra's funeral he put the house up for sale. He accepted the first offer he got even though the Estate Agent advised he should hold out for more. The sale went through in six weeks, the following week he had enlisted to join the paratroopers.

CHAPTER **10**

Infantry Training Centre Catterick, 2006

Taylor had unpacked his kit in the barracks when his corporal announced that Sergeant Thorpe wanted to see him. Taylor closed his locker door, locked it and walked the short distance to the sergeant's office. He knocked on the door and was motioned inside.

"Shut the door Taylor," Sergeant Thorpe said.

Taylor's file was on the sergeant's desk.

"I've been reading this and to be honest I'm more than a little concerned."

"Why is that Sergeant?"

"I understand that you applied to join the paratroopers soon after the death of your son and your wife. Is that correct Taylor?"

"Yes sir," he replied.

"I'm going to be straight with you Taylor, the powers that be think you are only here on some sort of revenge mission against the Muslims and that worries me. Is there any truth in that Taylor?"

"No sir," he said, "I'm here to serve my Queen and country, to make a new life for myself and to leave behind unpleasant memories, no more than that."

Thorpe leaned forward on his desk, removed his spectacles and placed them on the desk. "Very noble sentiment Taylor, and I hope you are being straight with me because we only have time for team players here. We watch each other's backs here and there's no place for any fucking loose cannons. You might think that you're a bit different because of your situation but be sure that there is no special treatment for anyone here. Understand?"

"Yes sir."

Sergeant Thorpe spoke for fifteen minutes while Taylor stood to attention and listened. He laid down the law, told him that the Para's were not prepared to carry anyone or be an outlet for any sort of revenge. They were disciplined, professional, the toughest unit in the world and any bad eggs would be found out and sent packing.

"Understand Taylor?"

"Yes Sarge, one hundred percent understood Sarge."

"Okay Taylor, we'll leave it at that, go and finish what you were doing."

As Taylor left the room the sergeant picked up the phone.

"Captain Rogers, do you have five minutes?"

Sergeant Thorpe sat in the Captains office. Despite Taylor's apparent genuine reasoning he still had major concerns regarding his mental state and was not one to burden his other soldiers and officers or place them at risk.

"He's an interesting one," the captain said, do you think he'll make it through, do we want him to make it through? He clearly has issues?"

"Do we want him in the British army, is that what you're really saying, sir?"

"Look Thorpe, those above don't want some psycho, ex soccer thug, soldier running amok in Afghanistan. He's hell bent on revenge, that's as clear as day but of course we can't prove it. Plenty recruits drop out. Do you understand me?"

"Yes sir, I believe so. I'll keep an eye on him, I'm sure we can break him, after all it won't be the first time."

Thorpe stood, saluted the officer and left the office.

It was not the first time that orders had unofficially been passed down to reject a recruit. But orders were orders and Thorpe was sure that a little extra pressing on Taylor would ease him out. Enough recruits dropped out in normal circumstances let alone with a push from the instructors. Taylor had lost his son and his wife and been severely wounded, yet he had the look of someone who would not easily buckle. Maybe he would need a little bit more than a small push. Only time will tell, he thought to himself.

Thorpe had seen many injuries in his time, although usually from combat or army related. Taylor had already been hurt bad, Thorpe could see that. He had also seen the look in Taylor's eyes many times before. It usually came from witnessing the deaths of friends killed in combat. Most soldiers either gave in to their injuries or became bitter and sought revenge. It wasn't too hard to realise which of those emotions was driving Taylor.

Taylor made his way to his barracks to finish unpacking his kit. A man walked towards him extending his hand.

"Hi, I'm Sofian Ahmed, it's my first day here, I've been assigned to this billet."

Taylor looked up, the man waited for a handshake. It never came.

"This dorm is full mate, Taylor said as he lowered his head in the direction of his kit bag, "find somewhere else."

Ahmed stood. He was embarrassed but not altogether surprised. He was warned about certain elements in the British Forces and he had been especially warned about Taylor. He knew about his history, the tragic circumstances that had brought him into the parachute regiment at such a late age.

"No worries mate," Ahmed replied as he turned around and walked towards the door. "I'll find another room."

"You do that mate."

Taylor let out a sigh as Ahmed left the room. Two minutes later another man breezed in.

"Well fuck me, if it aint Mad Micky Taylor," a voice said in a northern accent.

Taylor looked up to see a face that he couldn't immediately recognise but the fact that he had called him 'Mad Micky' meant that this fella could only have known him from his past football hooligan life.

"You probably don't know who the fuck I am but I was once with the Leeds Service Crew and we kicked off a few times with your lot over the years. You were well known up our end," the man said.

Taylor didn't say anything. He stared back at him.

"Sorry," he said, my name is Dave King, I heard about your family, sorry to hear 'bout that," he added awkwardly

"Thanks, mate but life goes on eh?"

Dave King held out his arm and the two men shook hands.

King pointed to the empty bed. "Is that free?"

"It's got your name on it mate, park your kit."

"Cheers."

"But do me a favour yeah?"

"Sure."

"Can you keep the Mad Micky bit out of the barracks."

"Yeah mate, no worries," he said.

"The top brass don't need any more excuses to fucking send me home."

The two men bonded almost immediately as they took up the challenge of the paratroopers' basic training. And basic training to become a paratrooper was no picnic. For Taylor it was that much harder as he had the added attention from Sergeant Thorpe. But it did not weaken his resolve and if anything it made Taylor stronger in his ambition to become a paratrooper. For the first time in many months Taylor's despair over his family's deaths were laid to the back of his mind as he strove to prove that he had what it takes. He nearly didn't get past the medical, that was touch and go because as a result of the bomb injuries his right leg was slightly shorter than the left and although it was barely noticeable, Taylor carried a slight limp. The medic had picked up on it and said that he might struggle in the Battle Fitness Test, a basic requirement before training even commenced. Taylor had told him to bring it on and had posted the fourth fastest time among sixty seven men hoping to make the grade. 'Not bad for an old bastard,' the PT Instructor had said.

Six weeks later red squad sat nervously in the gymnasium waiting for Sergeant Thorpe to call the next two names for the latest round of the milling contest. The squad had made a semi-circle with a raised platform completing the small arena. On that platform sat Sergeant Thorpe and Doctor Barnes. All milling contests had to have a medic present in cases of emergencies.

"Baker, Lennox, you're next," said Thorpe, "gum shields, head guards and gloves, now." Moments later Thorpe checked the two recruits gear and motioned them into the centre of the circle. The rest of the squad sat in anticipation as Thorpe squared up the two opponents.

"Right you've seen your mates who went before you so you know the score. Sixty seconds, no slacking. Remember this is the real test, okay?"

"Sir," grunted Baker and Lennox.

"Hands up. Go," Thorpe shouted.

Baker and Lennox were game on. They battered each other for the full sixty seconds not giving an inch to each other. One could argue that Baker got the better of Lennox but milling was not about winning it was about proving you had real guts for a fight and would not hide when the fight was going against you.

"Time," Thorpe yelled.

Both Baker and Lennox stopped swinging punches and gave each other a hug as they staggered back to the bench. Both men received a patter of applause and nods of acknowledgement from their colleagues.

Captain Rogers had been watching the events from the gym window and decided it was time to make his entrance.

"Attention," Sergeant Thorpe ordered as he saw Captain Rogers make his entrance into the gym. The squad quickly jumped to their feet and saluted him.

"As you were men," the Captain said.

He sat on the platform and looked at the list and the mini reports on the milling test.

"So, we have four recruits left," he said with a voice just loud enough for the squad to hear.

"Yes we do Sir," Sergeant Thorpe replied.

Captain Rogers and Sergeant Thorpe knew full well who was left as they had decided who would be fighting who on the previous evening. Army regulations stated that all milling contests had to be based upon each individual's particular height and weight. This allowed some form of fairness although it was really left to the discretion of the sergeant to choose who fought who. This so called discretion was about to play its hand.

"Okay Sergeant Thorpe, carry on," Captain said.

"Ahmed and let me see…Taylor, you're up next," Thorpe shouted.

The recruits sitting on the benches all looked at Sergeant Thorpe as if he had done something wrong, but no one said a word to challenge his decision.

Ahmed was at least three stone heavier than Taylor. He was a big man, with a muscular build and a three inch height advantage over his opponent. He was also the only Muslim in the group of recruits and pitting him against Taylor was causing quite a stir amongst the other recruits. They all knew what had happened to Taylor's family at the hands of Muslim extremists. It was a ridiculous mismatch for many reasons.

Sergeant Thorpe checked the gum shields and headgear of both milling opponents.

"Okay, square up. Right Taylor, Ahmed, you both know the rules, no dodging, ducking or any other tricks, head shots only."

"Yes Sarge,"

"Yes Sarge,"

The two opponents inched a little closer to each other.

"Just get it on," he ordered.

In a milling contest the opponents were not allowed to dodge or weave about, they were ordered to stand toe to toe and batter each other. There was no other way to describe it. Taylor squared up to Ahmed and although he could sense his physical disadvantage against his opponent it was not something unknown to Taylor. He had had many situations at football where he had to fight bigger men in the random melee of a mass hooligan football fight.

Ahmed looked down at Taylor and decided he would win this easily. He was fully aware of all the gossip in the barracks in regard to Taylor's family in the London bombings but Ahmed did not get involved in all the gossip. He had heard enough gossip from his own Muslim community when word went round that he was going to join the paratroopers. Ahmed believed he was British first and that his religion came in a close second. Fighting Taylor was just another hurdle that he had to overcome.

But Ahmed also knew the rules on milling and knew that any participants in a milling contest should be of similar height and weight.

"Sergeant Thorpe," said Ahmed.

"Yes,"

"Is this fair? I'm much bigger than Taylor and I've boxed for nearly ten years."

"Fair, what the fuck is fair? Listen Ahmed, this is the Paras not a fucking kindergarten. We can't choose the size of our enemy when we are pitched against them on the battlefield, do as you are ordered," he shouted, he looked over to another man who sat by the ring. "Doctor Barnes is in attendance, he can stop the contest any time he wants."

Taylor stood quietly, eager for the contest to start, the adrenaline was building.

"Okay, are you ready?" said Sergeant Thorpe.

"Yes sir."

"Sir."

"Remember, it's for sixty seconds and if you go down I stop the clock. Start milling," he shouted.

A whistle sounded and both Ahmed and Taylor immediately started throwing measured punches. Taylor's speed counted and his punches were connecting with Ahmed's head, which threw Ahmed of balance a little. Ahmed's punches weren't landing and at that precise moment any thoughts of fairness left Ahmed as he felt the strength of Taylor's punches pushing him backwards. He needed to step up or his smaller opponent would get the better of him. Ahmed took a deep breath, stepped forward and began punching, his natural ability in the ring coming into play and eventually he landed a powerful strike on the side of Taylor's head, just below his temple. The weight advantage and technique immediately became apparent as the blow knocked Taylor to the floor.

"Up, up," the sergeant shouted.

Taylor grabbed at the rope and leapt to his feet to re-join the fight and immediately landed a few of his own punches that pushed Ahmed back. But once again as Ahmed threw a flurry of well-timed punches and connected with another powerful thump to the side of Taylor's jaw which again knocked him to the floor.

Sergeant Thorpe stopped the clock.

"Get the fuck up Taylor, what are you, a fucking pussy?" he screamed.

Taylor's head was spinning from the heavy punch and he could hear Sergeant Thorpe screaming at him along with the rest of the squad. Taylor rose to his feet once more and squared up to the bigger man.

"Fight," the Sergeant screamed.

As Taylor climbed gingerly to his feet Ahmed jumped in and landed half a dozen quick powerful blows to Taylor's head and on the final punch there was a sickening crack as Taylor's nose popped like a party balloon and a collective groan could be heard among the recruits. Taylor staggered against the ropes but refused to go down. Ahmed took another step towards him as the blood streamed from his broken nose.

"That's it, Taylor's had enough," the Doctor shouted.

"No, he's okay," Thorpe said, "he's still on his feet."

"He's not okay, look at his face." The Doctor turned to his left, "Captain Rogers I must ask you to intervene and stop this immediately."

Taylor had recovered his senses; he put his gloves to his face and turned towards the Captain. "Permission to continue Sir."

All eyes in the room turned to Captain Rogers.

"You're sure you want to continue Taylor?" he said.

"Yes Sir."

The Captain smiled at the doctor, "There you go Doctor Barnes, you've heard it from the horse's mouth, the man wants to fight."

"This is ridiculous, I will report this to Colonel Sanderson if this is not stopped now. You have broken every rule in the book."

"I'll thank you not to threaten me Doctor Barnes, this is my battalion and my men and one of my men is happy to continue so the decision is not yours or mine. Taylor has taken the decision." He looked back towards the ring. "Fight on," he ordered.

It was Sergeant Thorpe's turn to intervene as he got to his feet. "Actually Sir," he turned to the Captain, they've been fighting for fifty eight seconds so we can call it a day now."

Captain Rogers looked at his watch and then back at Taylor. "Box on," he announced.

The exchange between Doctor Barnes, Sergeant Thorpe and Captain Rogers gave Taylor time to completely clear his head. It was plainly obvious that he was being targeted when he was ordered to mill with Ahmed. As far as Taylor was concerned both Sergeant Thorpe and Captain Rogers wanted Taylor to take a good beating and walk away from the Paras and as the doctor had said, they had broken every rule in the book. Taylor took a deep breath, it was time to break a few rules himself. If the powers that be could break the rules then so could he, especially as he was on the receiving end of a beating. Taylor was a good fighter and knew that he could win and had already spotted a weakness in Ahmed's armoury.

"Okay, ready yourselves, square up now," Sergeant Thorpe said.

Ahmed and Taylor faced each other. In the previous onslaught Taylor had noticed that Ahmed raised his head just a split second before he threw a punch. With that little weakness Taylor had a chance to win this contest but he would have to break the milling rules on ducking and weaving.

"Start milling," Sergeant Thorpe shouted.

Ahmed threw his usual powerful right handed punch, but this time Taylor ducked below the powerful blow and threw a straight left jab aimed at Ahmed's throat. The punch connected with Ahmed's Adam's apple and he immediately fell to the floor squealing and gasping like a stricken dog. Taylor's punch had landed exactly where he intended the punch to land and he knew that the contest was now officially over. Doctor Barnes jumped into the ring immediately, shouting furiously at the Captain and Thorpe quickly followed as he knelt down at Ahmed's side.

The Doctor carefully removed his head guard and Thorpe pulled out his gum shield.

"The Doctor shouted over to the Captain, "get me an ambulance now, if this man's trachea is broken he's in mortal danger."

Taylor had taken off his head guard and stood in the centre of the ring. He was covered in his own blood and his face was beginning to swell. Before Sergeant Thorpe could speak, Captain Rogers walked into the centre of the ring to confront Taylor.

"That was an illegal punch," he hollered.

"It was an accident Sir."

Captain Rogers continued to scream at Taylor about breaking the milling rules.

"I'll have you fucking bounced out of the regiment for that."

Taylor said nothing. Captain Rogers soon realised that his shouting and hollering wasn't making the slightest difference to Taylor. He looked hard at Taylor and saw the deadest, maddest eyes staring back at him.

The Captain took a deep breath; "get yourself fucking cleaned up and report to my office in thirty minutes. I swear blind that by the weekend I'll have you back on a fucking train back home to the shit hole that you've come from."

Taylor climbed from the ring, a few of his squad members gathered around, he was clearly unsteady on his feet.

Dave King was the first to speak, "they broke every rule they could mate, as far as we are concerned you just defended yourself."

"Cheers mate," Taylor said, "but I'm in deep shit now, the Captain's out to get me."

King pulled a towel around him and wiped away some of the blood from his face. "No worries mate, I've got an idea, I've a great excuse why you hit the fucker in the throat and there'll be fuck all they can do about it."

As Taylor walked into the office Captain Rogers and Sergeant Thorpe sat behind the big oak desk. Taylor saluted and asked for permission to sit down.

"Denied," Thorpe barked out, "this won't take long, you used an illegal punch which has put a fellow Para in grave danger, he's lying in a hospital bed as we speak, give me one good reason why we shouldn't dismiss you from the Parachute regiment."

"Illegal match Sergeant," Taylor quickly replied, "the man was four inches taller than me, my natural level of impact was throat height not head height."

"It was a fucking deliberate punch," the Captain barked out.

"It was an accident Sir, I threw over one hundred punches and mistimed just one."

Thorpe's mouth fell open as he stared at his Captain in amazement.

Captain Rogers stood, his face beetroot red with anger. "Get out of my office Taylor , you insubordinate bastard, I'll have your travel warrant ready for the weekend."

"Accident Sir, Illegal match," Taylor replied.

"Get out now!"

"Yes Sir."

Taylor saluted the officer, about turned and walked out of the office.

When the door had closed behind him Thorpe turned to his Captain.

"He's right Sir."

"He's fucking what?"

"Better for us to just leave it Sir, we should never have matched Ahmed with Taylor and we have the doc against us now and I'm sure all the other recruits will back up Taylor. They respect him immensely."

"Fucking bollocks, that's what this is. I want him out, think of something for fucks sake."

"Will do sir, have you got a kilo of cocaine hanging around? I can hide it in his locker if you want?"

"Sarcasm won't get you anywhere sergeant? I am warning you that your own conduct will also be under scrutiny."

Sergeant Thorpe kept his mouth shut and listened to the Captain ranting and raving about orders and loose cannons. It all went over the top of Sergeant Thorpe's head as he realised that he now had an unshakable respect for Taylor. He'd gave the lad some shit over the months and not once had he waivered or backed down and he had to admit to himself that his performance against Ahmed in the ring had been nothing short of miraculous, if not a little naughty. He'd already decided that enough was enough and from now on he would treat Taylor like any other recruit.

CHAPTER 11

Bradford City, June 2008

Imam Aasif was deep in thought as he drove into the Manningham area of Bradford. He was listening to some local radio station that was debating the delay in the arrival of the new buses that Bradford City council had promised its citizens.

He drove through the supposedly 'nice' white areas every Friday afternoon on his way back to Manningham. He often watched the young white women with their short skirts and tight T shirts walking up the High Road. *Fucking Infidel bitches*, he thought, *sluts and whores, pathetic non-believers*.

The non-believers would get their just desserts, the grooming gangs would see to that, teach the little white bitches a lesson. It was all so easy. They targeted the girls in care, the vulnerable ones, the press described it as grooming but he much preferred to call it old-fashioned trickery. It started with alcohol, cider and vodka mixed with Red Bull, occasionally soft drugs and always attention and friendship and compliments, something most of these young girls had never before experienced. The gangs didn't want the girls comatose when they were raped, they much preferred a little spirit and a distinct knowledge of what was happening to them. The leaders of the grooming gangs told them they were being punished by God for the error of their ways and that under Sharia Law the brothers were justified in their actions, it was their duty, they took no pleasure in the act. Imam Aasif totally agreed with the actions of the muslim grooming gangs!!

And the infidel adults weren't much better. They were obsessed about making money and then spending it on bigger houses and more expensive cars. What was that saying the English used? Yes, 'keeping up with the Joneses.' If there was ever a saying that summed up the English that was it.

Aasif entered into Manningham, a district he felt comfortable in. He liked the hustle and bustle of his home area. There were virtually no whites and those that remained only did so because they were too poor or too old to move. One day soon they would also be gone, every last one of them.

He pulled up outside a Muslim grocery store in one of the most deprived areas of Manningham. He walked into the small shop and nodded to the owner, then picked up a basket and selected a few bits and pieces from the shelves. He walked up to the fruit counter and picked up several kiwis, checked them over then returned them to the fruit counter. Any casual observer would have seen a customer who was not happy with the fruit on offer.

Imam Aasif, looked around, waited until the last customer left the shop and then approached the counter.

"Good evening, Imam," the shopkeeper said.

"Good evening, have you got any fresh kiwis?"

"I have some fresh kiwis that have just arrived, would you like to choose the best before I put them out in the shop?"

"Yes I would, thank you," he said.

The shopkeeper ushered the Imam through to the back of the shop and then returned to the store. The Imam did not look at any kiwis but instead walked down some stairs into the basement. There he opened up a large wardrobe and pulled aside the back to reveal a hole through the wall of the basement which led into the basement of the adjoining house.

The lights were already on as he walked through to the neighbouring basement and upstairs into the house. The house was boarded from the inside and the only light came from one stark lightbulb located in the kitchen. Imam Aasif made his way to the kitchen where a masked man was sitting at a table.

"Sit down Imam Aasif," the man said.

Aasif hated these meetings. They had been going on for several years now and he still did not know the identity of the man he was talking to.

"How many converts have you now?" The man spoke in English but with a strong Afghani accent.

"We have fourteen converts," said the Imam.

"How many white converts?" asked the man.

"Three whites, two Chinese and five blacks, the rest are Asian."

"I asked for white converts, not niggers," he scowled.

Aasif sighed deeply, "There are three whites," he spluttered, "I cannot magic them out of thin air, the whites are very suspicious of Islam these days, I do my best."

The man waived a hand in the air, "Okay, that's enough for now, perhaps we do not need any more converts, it is becoming too dangerous. Do not underestimate the security services, do you understand?"

"I never do brother."

"And Bakar in Full Sutton, I believe he has found someone interesting for our cause?"

"Yes, he is white, English born and bred. I know him personally and he is devoted, I mean really devoted to Islam" Aasif said.

"How long until he is released?"

"A few years. It depends on his behaviour."

"Well, that fits into our timescale."

They talked for some time and the masked man looked at his watch. Pleasantries and good manners were not his forte.

"You can go now Imam."

Aasif stood, bowed and then started to retrace his steps back to the grocery store as his eyes strained in the darkness. He went back through the secret door and made his way up towards the shop. In the back room he picked up a brown paper bag full of kiwis and then returned to the shop. He picked a few other products from the shop shelves, paid and walked towards the door that led to the street outside.

"Thank you for the kiwis," he said as he opened the door and stepped onto the street.

As he climbed into his car he looked at the boarded up house next to the shop. About fifty per cent of the houses in this road were boarded up and it made for a grim setting but it was perfect for their needs.

He drove up the street heading for home but as he did so he failed to notice two occupants of a battered silver Vauxhall Astra parked on the side of the road. As the Imam took a left turn at the top of the road the silver Astra slowly pulled out, drove to the end of the road and made the same left turn.

Anti-terrorism officer DC Marsh sat in the passenger seat of the silver Astra. He opened up the laptop and a road map of Bradford City came onto the screen. The map showed a blue arrow that moved slowly through the street map. The tracker on Imam Aasif's car gave a clear signal.

"Nothing going on as usual, prison, shop then I bet home," he said.

DC Bennet rubbed his hands together and smiled. "Then we can call it a day eh?"

"Yeah, the tracker will keep a tag on him."

The Imam had been doing the same routine for the past year and many at Mi5 believed that following the prison Imams was becoming a waste of time. Operation

Mensa was a tedious affair. There were now seven Imams under close surveillance and each team had reported nothing out of the ordinary despite the length of the surveillance.

CHAPTER **12**

Mi5 headquarters, Thames House, London.

The phones began to buzz as news of the Edinburgh Airport bombing flashed across the screens. First reports were that two Asian men had tried to ram a car full of propane bottles into the entrance of Edinburgh international airport. One of them had been confirmed dead but up to now there had been no reports of civilian casualties.

Mark Baxter slammed down the phone and grinned. "Sir, we are in luck, we've got a live one, the other mother fucker is a piece of toast though."

His Section Chief, Gordon Fletcher rubbed his hands together gleefully. "Fan fucking tastic Baxter, you'd better get your arse into gear and go up to Scotland. I want you to handle the transit personally and bring him back safe and well. As soon as that lot of fundamentalists know he's alive you can rest assured they will want him eliminated. Take Clarke with you, remember do not give any indication whatsoever to the Police regarding our procedures for questioning."

"Will do," said Baxter as he picked up his car keys and hurried from the room.

Twelve hours later Bidal Abdullah was driven through the underground car park of Thames House. He had been blindfolded throughout the journey and his hearing had been taken away with ear muffs. No one had spoken to him for the duration of the trip. He was dressed in a white police issue jumpsuit and as he was bundled out of the car he was chained to a wheelchair and wheeled into the building, straight to the Enhanced Interrogation Room for interview. It was no ordinary room, this was Mi5's secret interrogation suite and despite the flashy terminology the room was nothing more than a torture chamber.

Officer Clarke wheeled Abdullah into the centre of the room where his wrists were forcibly placed into two padded shackles that hung from chains suspended to a pulley above his head. His ankles were placed in padded shackles tied to short chains and secured to the floor. Clarke took a deep breath and pulled on the end of the chain as he adjusted the pulley so that Abdullah's body weight was suspended by the shackles on his wrists.

Clarke stepped forward with a Stanley Knife and sliced into the police issue jumpsuit and ripped it from his body leaving him totally naked. He remained blindfolded and deafened. As Baxter attached a head clamp to Abdullah he started to sob for the first time.

Five feet above Abdullah's head was a drum of water with a little tap. Baxter climbed up some ladders and opened the tap and a drip off water landed directly onto the top of his head. Baxter adjusted the tap to allow one drip every thirty seconds.

"Please tell me where I am, please tell me what you want?" he whimpered slowly.

Nobody answered him, no one had spoken to Abdullah since he had left the Edinburgh Police Station. He heard footsteps leave the room and he was left in silence. Within minutes he was moaning from the pain as he tried to relieve the pressure on his shackled wrists by pushing up on his feet.

"Help me," he cried, "won't someone help me."

This was Abdullah's first round of torture.

Baxter was Mi5's top enhanced interrogator and his first choice of torture was the Chinese water drip. Baxter's hobby was reading books on ancient methods of torture. The top brass at Mi5 had certain levels of torture that were permitted and the general rule was that no physical marks should be left at the end of the enhanced questioning session, anything else was fair game.

Baxter and Clarke stood by the coffee machine drinking the foul tasting liquid as Baxter explained exactly what was in store for the terrorist in round two.

The prisoner was left in the same position for the next six hours. The room was silent apart from the creaking and clanking of the chains as Abdullah tried to change position to alleviate the pain. Nothing could describe what the constant drip of water was doing to his brain.

It felt like a hammer blow every thirty seconds. To Abdullah those six hours seemed like six days.

The Mi5 officers returned to the enhanced interrogation room. They had slept for a few hours and showered and changed. They were more than ready for the next turn of events.

"Okay," Baxter said, "let him down and turn that tap off, that constant dripping is even beginning to annoy me," he laughed.

Clarke removed the head clamp and lowered Abdullah into a plastic chair. His wrists and ankles were still shackled to the chains. Clarke then removed the ear muffs.

"He looks like he could do with a wash, he's pissed himself," he said.

Baxter slapped him gently on the cheek, "you're a dirty stinking Arab and you need a clean-up."

Baxter walked over to the corner of the room. He picked up a bucket of water, the ice cubes still floated on the surface. He walked back to Abdullah and tipped the bucket of freezing water over him. Abdullah let out a scream as the ice cold water hit his naked body.

Baxter knelt beside him and spoke in a pleasant tone. "Now then, now then Mr Abdullah, tell us what we want to know and this will end before it's even started."

"Fuck off you infidel bastard," he hissed.

"Just what I wanted you to say," Baxter said, "bit of a tough guy are you, well we shall see about that." He turned to Clarke, "get the other bucket mate."

Clarke collected another bucket from the corner and walked over to the prisoner. Before he even reached Abdullah, the prisoner could smell it.

"What's that, tell me what it is?" he pleaded.

Clarke laughed. "Ah well, we know what you fuckas think about pigs, you love them don't you? So, as a little treat I'm going to cover you with this foul smelling mixture of pig shit and intestines and you can thank Allah for his little offering."

The prisoner twisted in his seat screaming for mercy. Clarke grinned as he tipped the contents of the bucket over him.

"Okay my little Muslim friend, you can stay there for another few hours and stew in pigs shit. I don't think they will ever let you into heaven now.

Baxter stepped forward. "Haul him up and put the head clamp back on and set that drip for every fifteen seconds."

Clarke did as he was asked.

"And let's get away from this stinking cunt," he said.

Three hours later Baxter and Clarke returned to the room.

"Get him down and clean him up with the hose," Baxter said.

"My pleasure," he replied.

Clarke hosed down Abdullah with freezing cold water. He lingered on his task until the prisoner shivered uncontrollably. Once all the pig shit and intestines had been washed away Abdullah was lowered back into a plastic chair.

"Okay, how we feeling, Abdullah?" grinned Baxter.

"You will pay for this infidel," Abdullah shot back.

Baxter pulled off Abdullah's blindfold. Bright lights shone directly into his eyes as he tried to see his interrogators.

"Listen dickhead, let me explain your situation. You're gonna get tortured until you tell us everyone who's in your network. I'm here for the duration, I'm not going anywhere, in fact I've only just started."

He was crying again, sobbing quietly and at the same time shivering.

Baxter walked over to another bucket and picked it up as he returned towards the prisoner. He stuck a bare hand into the bucket and pulled out a fist full of multi coloured gore. "Pig shit again, pig shit and pigs arse holes, pigs skin and bones, bladders, hearts and curly little cocks."

He stepped forward and thrust it into his face, found the opening to his mouth and rammed his fingers in, "I thought you might like a little taste you Muslim cunt."

"No," Abdullah wailed, "you animals, you fucking animals."

Baxter noticed a slight waiver in Abdullah's eyes. It was true everyone talked, even the SAS men trained to withstand all torture sessions eventually talked, it was just a case of when not if. These crackpot Muslim fundamentalists were not weak and what was worse was that they actually believed in what they were doing and that an invisible man in the sky looked over them. That suited Baxter, the longer they held out the more fun he had.

"Please no, I beg you, please stop."

Fucking religious freaks he thought, don't they realise that god doesn't exist?

Baxter stuck two fingers up his nose and smeared the slop across his face and into his eyes.

"Okay Abdullah, Allah aint nowhere to be seen, just give me some names, who taught you to make the propane bomb?"

"Please stop, please stop."

Baxter nodded to Clarke and Abdullah was hauled up into the air again, the plastic chair was removed and Abdullah was lowered to the floor. This time Clarke handcuffed Abdullah's arms behind his back and secured his ankles to the chains attached to the pulley above his head.

"Haul him up," he ordered.

This time he was left dangling upside down about two feet off the ground. Clarke placed a bucket of water directly below his head. Baxter nodded for the next stage to commence.

Clarke lowered the chains so that Abdullah's head was lowered into the bucket and left there for thirty seconds. He raised his hand and Abdullah's head was lifted out of the bucket. He gasped for breath as the liquid drained from his face. He could smell the urine. His head had been held under urine.

"Enjoy that did you dickhead, what's it like to taste Christian piss, compliments of Mi5?" Baxter laughed, "you got anything to say to me."

"Fuck off and die, go to Hell."

Baxter reached into the bucket of slop and gore, he reached in and grabbed another handful and added it to the bucket of water and swirled it around with his hands.

He looked up at Abdullah, "that should flavour it a little and when you breathe this water in which you will, you'll have a little bit of pig all to yourself. It will be in your lungs and get absorbed into your blood and oxygen, he laughed hysterically, "you'll be part Abdullah, part fucking pig."

Before Abdullah could answer him Baxter had already signalled to Clarke and Abdullah felt himself lowered towards the bucket. He closed his eyes and held his breath. He knew he would be tortured, that was for sure but he also knew that he had to hold out to protect his fellow jihadists. This time it was longer than the first, maybe thirty, forty seconds. Abdullah's lungs were starting to burn with the pain as he fought the urge to breathe.

And then he was pulled out of the bucket.

"How was that dickhead? We're getting nicely warmed up now!"

"Again," Baxter said.

And so it continued for several more hours. Abdullah appeared to weaken. As soon as he coughed the urine and the foul smelling pig shit out of his lungs and took a clear breath he was again forced into the foul smelling liquid. The enhanced questioning session finally came to an end and Abdullah was placed in his original stress position.

"I'll do the tap," said Baxter.

"No more, please, I beg you in God's name."

Baxter pulled up the stepladder. He avoided the pig shit and urine as best as he could and then turned on the tap. He adjusted the drip so it gave a twenty second gap between each drip.

'Fuck it I need a piss,' he said.

Abdullah, instead of feeling the delayed drip suddenly felt a warm liquid splashing over his face. Abdullah's inner soul was beginning to weaken, his dignity had been taken away and his body was in extreme pain. But he had to hold a little longer. He had to be believed when he finally broke. He looked up, his interrogators were gone and the room was silent apart from the timely splash of water dripping.

An hour or two passed, perhaps three or four. He had lost all sense of time.

Fletcher heard a rap on his door and shouted for whoever it was to enter. Fletcher looked up. It was Baxter and he was smiling.

"He's broken, sir."

"You sure?"

"Yes Sir."

"Okay, good work Baxter, what have we got," he said eagerly as he rose from his desk.

"It looks like it's a University medical network, the research unit has done all the background checks and Abdullah and Khalid met at Imperial College in London. They got their degrees there and both went to work at Edinburgh hospital. Two years later they are trying to blow up the fucking airport, can you believe that?"

"Go on," Fletcher urged.

"There's a Muslim trainee doctors association, it's a support group for Muslim students taking medical degrees. Again both Abdullah and Khalid attended this group."

"And?"

"Research tells us that Jamal, one of the two Piccadilly bomb conspirators also attended this Muslim trainee doctors association before dropping out of his medical degree."

This got Fletcher's attention. He took off his glasses and cleaned them slowly and methodically.

"And the live evidence from our friend downstairs?" said Fletcher.

"He's talking big time, he states that there is a professor who does private lectures at this Muslim trainee doctors association. Apparently he offers private tuition for struggling students. Abdullah says he was recruited by this professor Baqri, who trained both him and Khalid on the wherewithal on how to make a bomb."

Fletcher reached for his cigarette packet. "So we have two confirmed connections on two of the last four Muslim terrorist plots," he said.

"Yes, sir."

He reached inside the packet for a cigarette, placed it between his lips and lit it. "Tell research I want the Full Monty on this Professor Baqri," he blew a long plume of smoke high into the air.

"Will do sir, but there is one other thing regarding Abdullah, the Met anti-terror unit are pressing to take him back for formals."

"Already?" Fletcher frowned, "we've only had the bastard for eighteen hours."

"I know, but apparently his doctor friends in Edinburgh know some Scottish MP who is asking where he is and they want him back to charge him, they probably know we've got him and what he's been going through."

Fletcher walked around to the front of his desk and sat down. "And what do you think Baxter, do you think he's worth holding on to."

Baxter was already shaking his head. "No Sir, I have got as much as I can from him. He has been through the mill, I have no more use for him."

Fletcher nodded thoughtfully, "Okay, clean the bastard up and sign him over."

CHAPTER 13

The British government set up COBRA (Cabinet Office Briefing Room A) to implement a plan of action when the nation was either under threat from a natural disaster or in this case a real terrorist threat. The COBRA meeting was instigated after the terrorist attack at Edinburgh airport. The Prime Minister chaired the meeting and in attendance was Beckett, head of Mi5, Minto, head of the anti-terrorism police unit and Samson, head of the treasury department.

The PM had been reading the police anti-terrorism unit's report on the Edinburgh airport incident. He had also read Mi5's top-secret report on the latest Islamic terror threats. Deep frown lines were permanently etched across his face. Not only was he dealing with the biggest economic recession for decades but he also had to finally accept that the UK was at war with home grown Islamic jihadists and more worryingly, they were getting more and more professional with every new attack.

The PM had spent nearly half an hour reading Operation Serpent. Operation Serpent was a treasury backed report highlighting the fact that the Edinburgh bombers had not been under any surveillance, and so had been allowed to carry out the attack. The Prime minister sighed... *our fucking worst nightmare.*

The main recommendation of the report was that extra should be funding be allocated to the police anti-terrorism unit (PATU) to assist in Mi5's surveillance operations against suspected Muslim terror plots. The PATU could double the number of officers involved in these surveillance operations.

"Your views on this Beckett?" the PM asked.

Beckett cleared her throat, she didn't pull any punches. "My view is that any further funding should be channeled through to Mi5. Our officers are specifically trained to deal with this and extra funding would allow more of our officers on the streets. Rather than spend the money on the PATU, who in my opinion are not capable or trustworthy enough to take over these surveillance operations."

"Not trustworthy, how dare you," Minto bleated.

"Mi5 officers are level five vetted," she replied, "in the real world that means no leaks, no mistakes"

"I think the bombing at Edinburgh airport shows Mi5 are as fallible as the rest of us," Minto said as he glanced in the direction of the Prime Minister.

"I totally disagree," Beckett said, "the two bombers were sleepers who had never come under any suspicion in Mi5 or any other government agency. To a degree they were lone wolf terrorists."

Minto let out a little laugh, "ha, two lone wolfs, that's a new one."

"You know what I mean."

The PM intervened in the little spat, "Minto, did the ATU have any information regarding these two individuals that may have given a hint as to their views or intentions?"

"No sir. They were on the face of it completely clean. We have interviewed their family, friends and work colleagues at the hospital and the general consensus is that they were as westernised as you or me. As far as we're concerned they never went to a mosque or had any fundamental views of any sort."

"Exactly my point Sir, please read this internal Mi5 report," Beckett said handing over a file that was headed top secret. Only Samson, head of the Treasury Department had previously seen the report.

The PM read the first few pages of the internal Mi5 report. There were many pointers as to who could possibly be radicalised, from persons who visited outspoken preachers at mosques to those who had a family member who had visited various Middle Eastern countries. The list was long and exhaustive and one suggestion was to step up the level of surveillance on the Muslims who acted completely western, even going so far as those who publically denounced radical Islam. The report was six months old and had been previously presented to the head of treasury when an Mi5 funding review had taken place. The head of treasury department had refused the extra funding for surveillance of potential so-called sleeper terrorists.

The report referred to the profilers at Mi5 and the CIA who had analysed hundreds of attacks and plots, and there was new evidence that revealed up to thirty per cent of all worldwide plots and attacks were carried out by 'sleepers. A sleeper was the 'in' word for an Islamic terrorist who outwardly lived a completely westernised lifestyle and held westernised views. They occasionally even married non-Muslim women and drank alcohol to mask their real objectives.

The PM compared the Mi5 report to the report provided by the anti-terrorism unit. It made the PM's decision much easier.

"The £40million goes to Mi5," ordered the PM.

"Sir," moaned Minto.

"That's my decision, Samson. Make the arrangements," said the PM.

The report made no mention of the Enhanced Interrogation Team.

CHAPTER **14**

Sangin province, Afghanistan, 2009

Sergeant Taylor pulled out his Sony Walkman and started to play his favourite track. It was Delirium's Silence (Tiesto's In Search of Sunrise Remix) featuring Sarah McLachlan . He put one earphone to his own ear and the other to the man sitting in front of him. The broken man's eyes widened as the crazy noise played into his mind. Taylor and a few of his trusted men were entrenched in a small mud hut. There was one Taliban fighter lying dead in the corner, he was mutilated beyond recognition. Taylor's men had propped him up against a wall facing the second Taliban fighter. The dead man's dick was stuffed in his mouth.

"You won't be fucking no more virgins in heaven without your dick," sang one of the soldiers to the dead Taliban fighter, in tune to the music. One of the other soldiers was moving the dead Taliban's arm in motion to the dance music. The second Taliban had been seriously tortured he was living a nightmare on earth as the crazy music hammered into his mind.

He thought to himself, they have to stop soon, they are British soldiers and they don't act this way.

For the next few minutes the crazy scenario played itself out, then Taylor put the end of the rifle in the man's mouth.

Taylor loved the way this particular track built into a crescendo and he watched as the digital reader recorded the track coming to its pivotal seven minute point. The Taliban fighter had never heard music like it. 7.10, 7.11, 7.12. The digital counter continued with the music becoming ever more powerful. Taylor's eyes were staring madly at the Taliban prisoner's eyes as the music reached its peak at 7.28.

At the exact point of 7.28 on the counter Taylor dropped to his knees with the barrel of the rifle still in the man's mouth. The Taliban's eyes opened wide with terror, he tried to make prayer with Allah but he was too late. Taylor said goodbye and smiled as he pulled the trigger. The Taliban's head exploded like a watermelon as blood and brains and shrapnel of skull splattered onto the wall behind him.

"Boom," Taylor said, "I hope you enjoyed a taste of Tiesto my dead friend?"

He pulled out the earphone from the dead fighters ear and wiped it on his sleeve. "Shit, you dirty little rag head, you've left some of your brain on my earphone."

He grinned. "Still it was worth it, we've had enough of you cowardly little fuckers, just look on this as a little bit of payback."

Sergeant Taylor walked out the door of the small hut. The rest of his platoon were waiting outside. They all looked at Taylor waiting for him to say something!!

He stopped at the entrance and spoke abruptly. "No one's got any problem with that have they, we're bringing the war home to the Taliban, that's what we are paid for innit?"

"We're with you Sarge," one of his men said.

One by one they nodded in agreement.

The 3rd battalion of the Parachute Regiment was based in the centre of Sangin and had been under constant mortar and light artillery attack for the past two months. Tempers were on edge, some of the men were at breaking point. Under orders from the commanding officer, Colonel Phillips, two forward operating bases were built to draw attacks away from the command centre in Sangin. The platoon houses provided a buffer against attacks on headquarters. Apart from the odd mortar shell, Sangin command centre was relatively quiet, it appeared the strategy was working well.

Camp Bastion had ordered a Command Change, Colonel Phillips, the acting commander at Sangin knew that there was something going on when he was given a new command in a different province of Afghanistan, in a region far quieter than where he had been in charge for the last few months. Quite simply he was due a rest, a break from the twenty four hour a day stress that he'd endured for so long.

The helicopter landed in Sangin command centre and the new commanding officer jumped out and surveyed his new command. He was led to his office where he sat down at his desk and removed a file from his briefcase.

Colonel Rogers, who had recently been promoted from Captain, again read the file on 'A' company which was based at Platoon House North. There had been some snippets of information over the past three months, of possible field atrocities committed by British soldiers. The military police had started an investigation after two Taliban corpses were found by a US marine platoon who mistakenly patrolled an area that 'A' company had been involved in a 'search and destroy mission.' The two corpses had been badly mutilated, their genitalia removed from their bodies.

There had been no reports of any close-quarter contact by 'A' company, yet the US marines reported evidence of a firefight between the Taliban and a British unit. The two Taliban bodies were taken back to Camp Bastion where they were examined and it was discovered that the cause of death had been a single bullet wound to each head fired from very close range. Ballistic reports suggested that both bullets had originated from a rifle and a firearm issued by the British army to their Paratrooper Division.

The report also went on to say that it had been 'A' Company who had been requesting artillery support close to where the two Taliban had been found and further investigations found that there had been several patrols taken out by Platoon House North when their commanding officer was back at headquarters in Sangin. The commanding officer had been at Camp Bastion recovering from shrapnel injuries that left Platoon House North under the direct command of Sergeant Taylor at the exact time these alleged war crimes were committed.

Colonel Rogers had been ordered to go to Sangin and sort out this troublesome sergeant. On a personal level it was music to Colonel Rogers' ears when he was given the mission. He had never forgotten his humiliation by Taylor at Para Training when he was a captain. He had no doubt that Taylor was the culprit. Now he would have his revenge. Colonel Rogers closed the report and smiled to himself.

He picked up the phone and punched in a number. He waited for a few seconds.

"Corporal Hales," he said.

"Yes, sir," Hales replied.

"Who's in command at Platoon House North," he asked. He already knew the answer.

"I think its a Sergeant Taylor, sir. Captain Henshaw is still at Camp Bastion with shrapnel injuries."

"Sergeant Taylor?" asked Rogers.

"Yes sir, that's him."

"I want you to radio over to the platoon house and obtain a patrol report for the past seven days."

"Yes sir."

Platoon House North was based on the northern outskirts of Sangin, two miles from the command base.

'A' company had used an old mud and brick built compound on a raised part of the terrain to build the Platoon House. The elevated height of the compound gave a good view of the terrain currently under Taliban occupation.

'A' company had spent a considerable amount of time clearing the land of trees, old mud huts and anything that could give the Taliban cover if they decided to mount an attack on the Platoon House. It didn't stop them. In the previous three weeks before Colonel Rogers arrived at the command centre, the Taliban had prioritised the Platoon House North as their main focus of attack. Every single day the Platoon House was subject to constant RPG and mortar fire, along with periodic firefights where the Taliban risked hundreds of fighters in their attempts to overrun the compound.

Low on ammo and with dwindling supplies and hundreds of Taliban in the immediate vicinity, 'A' company had stopped patrolling outside of the Platoon House. Their original orders dictated that patrols must be employed to win the hearts and minds of the locals and install confidence in the local community, that they were under the protection of the British Army. The reality was that in the final four patrols, five paras had been killed and ten severely wounded, including the commanding officer.

Without any officers in charge, Taylor had been thrown in command. He sat in the role nicely, he was a born leader, the men respected him immensely. He thought back to the two previous patrols where he was in

135

command. The capture of the two Taliban fighters was etched in his memory, he'd been harsh, but this was war. What did the top brass and the politicians really know about the mess they had created in Afghanistan? Any thoughts of compassion were well and truly forgotten when he thought about his family. As far as Taylor was concerned the death of his son and wife was just an extension of the Islamic war against the West.

Taylor knew his men were getting out of control and decided to use the low ammunition as an excuse to halt patrols. Once the orders were passed down to stop patrols the men of 'A' company had mixed feelings. They all knew that the patrols were taking a big risk but there was plenty of appetite to take more revenge on any unlucky captured Taliban fighters. But orders were orders and the men followed Sergeant Taylor's instructions, no matter what.

They had no option but to 'dig in' and started to strengthen the defences for the next round of Taliban attacks.

"Sarge."

"Yes, Brown."

"Got a message from the command centre, they want our last seven days' patrol reports."

"What? Why in the hell do they want that? They know full well we aint been out on patrol for nearly ten days now."

"Dunno, Sarge, what shall I say?" Brown asked.

Taylor grabbed the radio mic and had a short conversation with Private Hales back at the command centre. After a couple of minutes he pressed end.

"You okay, Sarge?" Brown queried, "you look a bit angry."

Hales had told Taylor that there was a new officer in charge and that his name was Colonel Rogers. Hales described his appearance and Taylor quickly realised that the same Captain Rogers of the training school at Catterick was now his immediate commander officer in Afghanistan. He knew one thing for certain... there was going to be nothing but trouble.

"Never mind, just get my daily sheet and send over the info to command centre."

"Yes, Sarge."

Taylor's daily sheet reflected on the necessity to conserve ammo and the fact the men were too exhausted to go out on patrol. In his opinion they were battle weary, they had been on the front line for far too long.

Moments later a mortar bomb landed just outside the compound wall leaving a grim reminder of the platoon house's delicate position.

Taylor ordered his men to prepare for yet another assault. "Take cover lads, take up your positions, those cunts are at it again."

One hour later Sergeant Taylor received orders from Colonel Rogers. 'A' company had to resume patrols immediately.

CHAPTER **15**

Sangin Province, Afghanistan

Hassan was twelve years old when his father first showed him a Russian artillery shell. It was good to learn a trade his father had told Hassan and this particular trade would ensure the local warlords would keep his family well fed during those long winter months. Hassan remembered those words and thought how clever of his father was to hand down this skill.

The Russians had left thousands of artillery shells when they withdrew from Afghanistan in 1989 and this stockpile allowed Hassan to practice his deadly trade. Hassan's nickname was 'the fox' and his fellow Taliban warriors never ceased to be amazed with Hassan's ingenuity in outsmarting the foreign infidels who had dared to come into their lands.

Hassan tapped on the big wooden door of the local council building. A small viewing hatch opened and a man with sharp, brown eyes looked out at him. Hassan was quickly ushered into the building and escorted to the office of the local mayor, tribal leader and Taliban warlord, Husam Al Did.

Al Did had two armed guards outside his office and Hassan waited patiently for his audience. After about ten minutes Hassan was motioned into the office. Al Did sat at his desk. He was smartly dressed in a blue suit, he was clean shaven and looked no different from any mayor in any other province in the country. Hassan knew differently.

"Young Hassan, how are you today?" he asked.

"I am good, Emir."

"And what brings you here today? Have you another plan?"

"I need a couple of water bowsers, a diesel generator, a water pump and fifty metres of garden hose with sprinklers."

Husam Al Did raised an eyebrow. He was always intrigued with Hassan's requests and despite today's being unusual there was likely to be great merit to what Hassan had to say.

"Why would my best bomb maker want a water bowser in the middle of the dry season?"

Hassan went into his well-rehearsed sales pitch and Al Did liked the idea very much, so much so that he was prepared to assemble the equipment that Hassan needed to enact his plan. Al Did knew that there would be a few grumbles from the local farmers as their water bowsers were 'borrowed' but a couple of sheep or goats would placate them.

The Taliban decided to use a village approximately four kilometers from Platoon House North to lay their trap. They secretly moved the Afghani families out from the village and set up a perimeter, in effect cordoning off a large area of land from any prying eyes. Then Hassan set to work.

Hassan had studied the British army's operations and the weakness he spotted was that the British always called in a Chinook helicopter to evacuate their wounded or dead, despite the risk. Hassan had studied all the Taliban commanders' reports and noticed a pattern developed when the British retreated after a firefight, they always targeted the Taliban positions with artillery shelling, attack helicopters and occasionally single bombs from fighter planes. These tactics generally allowed the Chinooks to land safely and evacuate the dead or wounded. Hassan's plan was to exploit this weakness and bring down a Chinook helicopter. It would be brutal and spectacular, something that would be talked about for decades to come if he managed to pull it off.

The lay of the land was a small village with no more than fifty houses, surrounded by various fruit tree orchards. To the north of the village and in the likely planned direction that the Brits would retreat was a patch of land that had enough space to land a Chinook. There were no obstacles, no trees, nothing. It was the logical place to land. If Hassan's plan worked the coordinated attack from the Taliban would force the British into his carefully laid trap.

He dug a hole to a depth of half a metre deep and two metres wide. He then dug a small trench ten centimetres deep that ran for twenty metres into the orange orchard and stopped at a particularly leafy orange tree. The dirt was carefully laid onto a tarpaulin. Hassan then delicately laid the five Russian artillery shells in a pentagon shape in the hole in the ground. He then unscrewed the blast caps of each of the five artillery shells and placed a small charge of plastic explosives into the vacated space. The plastic explosive would take over the job of igniting the main charge in the artillery shell as the old blast caps were prone to failure. Hassan then pressed a small electronic detonator into the plastic explosives and meticulously wired up the five detonators to the control wire.

All the earth that had been collected on the tarpaulin was carefully replaced around the artillery shells and then flattened to an even level. The remaining excess earth was placed in a large bucket.

Hassan looked at the ground where the bombs had been hidden and he knew that the Brits would easily see the disturbed ground and steer well clear of the area. But Hassan's work was not quite finished. This was his master plan. He fired up the diesel generator which pumped water from the bowser to the sprinklers. Quickly the earth around the hidden bombs and control wire trench was soaked by the sprinklers and then left to dry.

Hassan inspected the land and noticed the earth above the bomb site had sunk a few inches. He knew this was likely to happen and so topped up this area with some of the remaining earth stored in the bucket. Hassan then levelled off the ground and fired up the diesel generator once again. The sprinklers soaked a wide area and then the area was left to dry in the hot sun. The last of the earth was dumped far away from the bomb site. Taliban guards were posted to keep their fellow soldiers away from the site. Hassan didn't want any tell-tale footprints left in the drying earth.

The next morning Hassan surveyed the entire area. The ground above the hidden bombs and the trench for the control wire blended in perfectly with the surrounding undisturbed ground. He was pleased with his work and thought that the Brits, although very clever at the best of times, would surely fall for the trap. The hardest part of the plan was forcing the Brits to evacuate to this point. That was the one thing that he had no control of but if the attack by the Taliban went to plan then an escape through the orange orchard and to the hidden cache of bombs was a distinct possibility.

Hassan set about concealing the control wire. He'd watched how the British soldiers rarely looked up when searching for IEDs. So Hassan set about hiding the control wire in the canopy of the orange orchard. He then cut through some of the bark on the trunk of the orange tree and prised a thin layer a few centimetres away from the tree. He ran the control wire behind the bark and up, until the leaves of the tree hid the thin wires. He then glued back the bark into position and held it there while the glue dried. It took him no more than twenty minutes and he took a step back to admire his work. Surely the British soldiers wouldn't possibly notice the thin line where the bark had been cut. He wasn't quite finished, he lent a couple of old branches against the trunk of the tree and then ran the remaining control wire through the orange orchard from the top of one tree to the top of another. The control wire was about ten feet in the air and difficult to spot in broad daylight. The Brits wouldn't exactly be going for a nice stroll through an orange orchard, they would be in the middle of a firefight and this increased the odds that they wouldn't look up searching for any signs of a trap.

Hassan ran the control wire to the northern edge of the orange orchard, down the final tree and through a grassy field for about fifty metres to a small ridge. The ridge was about ten metres high above the land and gave Hassan a good view of the village, the orange orchard and the clearing where the bombs had been set. Hassan made a tiny camouflage canopy at exactly the point where the end of the wire stopped. The trap was set and only time would tell if the Infidel soldiers would fall for it. He grinned as he viewed his work, God was good, Allah would be watching over him.

Although Hassan had overall command for this mission he still had to convince the Taliban fighters that it was a good idea and worth the risks. Laying down a consistent mortar barrage often drew a fighter bomber to drop a 500lb bomb on that mortar position. Normally the Taliban fighters would be long gone before the fighter jets actually dropped their deadly load but on this particular mission it required a more permanent mortar barrage to entice the Brits out of their little fort.

The mortar bombardment began early the next morning. There were four teams of Taliban mortar men firing scores of mortar shells every few minutes. There were an additional fifty Taliban foot soldiers positioned approximately three hundred metres to the west of the orange orchard in a motley collection of mud houses. Here they waited and listened as their comrades continued with the mortar barrage.

Although the mortar shells were not particularly accurate and most landed far from the platoon house walls, occasionally one shell would land in the compound to keep everyone stuck behind their sandbag bomb shelters. The soldiers positioned on the northern perimeter of the Platoon House observed the terrain in anticipation of a Taliban ground attack. 'A'company hunkered down in their shelters and waited for the expected ground offensive, but surprisingly no ground offensive materialised.

The shelling continued unabated for some thirty minutes. Sergeant Taylor thought there was only one way to stop it.

"Brown," he shouted, "call into headquarters and ask for logistics to pinpoint the mortar positions, tell them we are requesting air support."

Brown radioed in the request. Another mortar landed in the compound as bits of earth and rock fell around them.

"As quick as they fucking well can," Taylor shouted, "this is getting ridiculous, how many mortars have they bloody got?"

Brown looked across at Taylor, he slowly shook his head.

"What?" Taylor asked, "what is it?"

"Request denied Sarge," Brown said," artillery support only."

Taylor shook his head as he stared at the ground. "I don't fucking believe it," he whispered to nobody in particular.

Here we go again, he thought to himself, *I know what's coming next,* once the Taliban had been softened up with artillery Colonel Rogers would be ordering a seek and destroy patrol.

He looked over the parapet again, trying to gauge where the Taliban mortars were coming from. He estimated that they were shooting their mortars about three kilometres from the platoon house. He was surprised how long they had continued firing as even the Taliban would know that air support was a possibility. It was nearly always a hit and run approach. But today was different. The distant thud of the British artillery regiment's shells made its way back to the platoon house. 'A' Company felt relieved that the Taliban were now getting a bit of their own medicine. The mortar shells soon stopped and all that could be heard were the

145

sounds of the British artillery shells. There were a few insults directed to the Taliban, mainly from the most recent recruits, but 'A' company had long since respected this enemy and many thought that shouting obscenities at them was tempting fate. After five minutes the British artillery stopped firing and almost immediately the Taliban resumed firing their mortar rounds at Platoon House North.

"Brown, repeat the artillery request. This time for ten minutes," Taylor ordered.

This time the British artillery barrage seemed to work as once the rounds stopped the Taliban mortars didn't start up again.

Taylor watched Brown intently and he wasn't too surprised when Brown's radio indicated an incoming call from headquarters. The look on Brown's face said it all. Taylor's stomach churned.

"Seek and destroy patrol ordered," Brown said apprehensively.

"Fucking bollocks. It's that fucking prick Rogers," screamed Taylor, "it's fucking suicide," Taylor took a deep breath, "radio back that we are too low on ammo for any patrols."

"Yes Sarge."

Moments later the radio crackled and Taylor heard Colonel Rogers' voice drift over the airwaves. He had not forgotten the stuck up annoying twang as it burst into his ears.

"Listen Sergeant Taylor, those are orders, I don't want any excuses. If you are refusing this order then you will be immediately relieved of your command. It is your choice."

"That's crazy…"

"No excuses," Rogers shouted.

Before Taylor could argue any more the radio went dead.

"I'll back you up if you want to refuse the order Sarge," Corporal King said.

But Taylor shook his head. "Thanks mate, but what's the point, we'll both get nicked and they'll put some idiot captain in to take over and we might as well say goodbye to our unit, they'll be going back home in body bags. We've got enough dealing with these Taliban fuckers without some untested officers making things that much harder."

"Understood Sarge."

Taylor stood. "We don't have a choice, get the men ready for patrol, we leave in thirty minutes."

Taylor heard the moans and groans coming from some of the men, the murmurs of discontent. They were not cowards but they knew that these patrols were just a waste of time and the most recent patrols had cost 'A' company dearly, and yet some of the men were relishing the chance to go on patrol. Thirty four minutes later 'A' company left the secure compound and was on patrol making its way through the Afghan countryside, heading in the direction of the Taliban mortar position.

CHAPTER 16

The lead soldier was Private Baines. He was an experienced man and was much admired among the men for having a natural ability to spot an IED trap. The patrol was well spread out with each man approximately ten metres between him and the next soldier.

Private Baines led the patrol due north and out of what was called the safety zone that buffered the platoon house. Baines knew the village that had been pinpointed as the source of the Taliban mortar attack and he had to improvise on what route to take to get to that position and make contact with the enemy.

Private Baines zig-zagged slowly across a field and headed towards the small village about 1000 metres due north of their position. Baines headed towards a drainage ditch that ran parallel to the road which led to the village itself. The ditch ran due north east for about 500 metres. The ditch gave his platoon cover from snipers and any RPG attacks that the Taliban were likely to use if contact was made. The ditch also gave Baines an easier job of detecting any signs that an IED may have been planted. Baines was in survival mode, he wasn't taking any chances, just one thought in his mind and that was to get back to his missus and three boys.

He scanned the floor of the ditch with greatest diligence as his life and those of his friends depended upon him. The ditch had not seen any water for weeks and was baked hard by the Afghan sun. Baines liked baked ground because baked ground was easy to detect any disturbance. He scanned it carefully… nothing. He jumped down into the ditch and 'A' company continued northwards towards the small village. Fifty metres from the village the ditch turned into a proper drainage system and was no longer able to provide any cover. Baines scanned the land for his next choice of route to take.

The first house of the village was about fifty metres ahead. The area would provide good cover for a firefight but was also much easier for the Taliban to hide their IEDs. Directly to the right was open scrubland which then turned into an orange orchard. The orchard ran alongside the back of one side of the village. Baines was unsure which route to take. He signaled for Sergeant Taylor to come to the head of the patrol.

Sergeant Taylor was fifth in line on the patrol and saw Baines give a hand signal that halted the patrol. He moved quickly forward and ran towards Private Bains's position, falling to his knees as he got there.

"What is it Bainsey?"

"What do you think, Sarge, which way?"

Taylor gauged the situation. He knew that any seek and destroy mission meant taking a risk but it was his job to minimise that risk to an acceptable level. To the right was the open scrubland and the ditch provided good cover if an attack came from that direction. To reach the houses needed a fifty meter dash.

He pointed towards the houses. "take the point over there, take half the lads and I'll keep the rest here in the ditch to provide cover while you're crossing the open ground. Once you're there, spread out along this side of the houses and then cover our arses. Got that Bainesy?"

"Got it, Sarge."

One by one the first fifteen men made the dash from the ditch to the rear of the Afghan houses. Taylor breathed a sigh of relief as they reached their intended target without a shot being fired. They spread themselves out along the back of the houses and in turn covered the remaining fifteen men as they too made the quick dash to the back of the houses.

The thirty man patrol of 'A' company was now in position, strung along the back of a row of Afghani houses. The small village stretched for about half a kilometre with the orange orchard running alongside the back of the houses.

Taylor watched as a young boy on a motorbike drove slowly through the small village. The boy looked to his right, directly at Taylor and his men and he knew immediately that the rider was a Taliban scout. This was how the war was being fought. It was a classic insurgency where the enemy mingled in with the civilian population and the British soldiers didn't really know who they were fighting until an attack began. Taylor watched as the rider made his way up the main road and disappeared from view.

Taylor listened intently. It seemed very quiet he thought … no one about. It was too quiet. When any British patrol went near a village they were always met by children pestering them for chocolate and sweets. But not today.

Taylor could hear the whine of the motorbike fade as it left the village. His instincts told him that they were about to come under some form of attack, he could sense it. He made the signal to the rest of the company to be on maximum alert.

On the opposite side of the road was a row of houses similar to those that the British soldiers were using for cover. What Taylor and his men didn't know was that these houses held a full complement of Taliban fighters. There were more Taliban entrenched in the various out buildings too, with a good field of fire on the British soldiers as they made their way through the back of the village. The Taliban's plan was to push the Brits back through the orange orchard and into the trap set by Hassan.

The Taliban started their attack. Taylor was using a house as cover when the firefight broke out. He heard the loud crack of automatic fire along with the whip of bullets as they flew through the air. Taylor didn't panic and immediately went to the very edge of the house he was behind and turned his auto rifle round the corner.

He let rip with a full magazine. He quickly reloaded and glanced along the line to see 'A' company returning fire but there was something wrong.

Further down the line there was a body lying prone on the ground. Taylor fired off a dozen more shots for cover and then sprinted towards the body. Private Baines was lying between two houses, he was bleeding profusely from two bullet wounds to the chest.

"Bainsey, Bainsey, you got to move," he shouted, "move soldier, damn it," he screamed.

There was no reply from Baines.

Taylor felt for a pulse still offering words of encouragement, "stay with me Bainsey son, stay with me, we'll get you out of here, that's a promise."

A trickle of blood ran from the corner of the soldiers mouth as his eyes stared blankly into space.

"Where the fuck's the pulse," Taylor muttered to himself as a bullet thumped into the plaster wall behind him.

There was no pulse, no heartbeat, no breathing, no sign of life. Baines was already dead.

Taylor bit down hard on his bottom lip and took a deep breath.

He turned around and screamed at his men. "Smoke."

He reached into his webbing and located a smoke grenade which he threw over the houses into the road separating the Taliban from the soldiers. Other members of 'A' company also began to toss smoke grenades between them and the Taliban. With smoke blocking their direct line of fire the Taliban fighters began to fire wildly in the direction of where 'A' company had been at the start of the firefight. But now the experience and better training of the British army started to come into play and their fifty calibre machine guns started firing on the Taliban positions.

Taylor made his way up and down the line encouraging his men to keep firing. He ran the gauntlet of running between the houses as Taliban bullets whipped through the air. By the time he had completed his recce of 'A' Company he knew that it was turning into a bad day.

"Fucking shit," he muttered to himself, "three dead and two men seriously wounded. They needed immediate medical attention. The Taliban fire began to relent and Taylor ran to radioman Brown's position. Brown was lying on the ground pumping rounds into the Taliban houses.

"Brown, stop firing and get on that radio quick, we've got three dead and two down, call for an immediate med evac."

Brown made the call and just a minute later HQ replied. "At least thirty minutes until the chopper arrives Sarge."

He shook his head, "fucking thirty minutes, that's way too long."

From his vantage point Hassan was keenly watching developments. The British had fallen for the first part of his trap and now he had to force them to use the orange orchard as their escape route. He sent a coded text message to the Taliban commander in the village.

The Taliban fighters began to flank the British soldiers' position in the hope that they would retreat back to the deadly trap set by Hassan.

Taylor squatted down on his haunches. He sensed the fire from the Taliban was coming from three sides now and he didn't want to be surrounded, the situation was getting more perilous by the minute. From the intensity of the Taliban fire he realised that they were not just up against a handful of Taliban fighters, this was well planned, they had plenty men on the ground. He knew he had to get the dead and injured out of there fast. Taylor looked towards the orange orchard. The ground was flat and there was a good field of fire west of the orchard. In open terrain the British always had the advantage with their modern rifles and training. At present they were like sitting ducks.

He looked over towards King. "Corporal, take two men and find a landing zone past that orchard," he ordered.

"Yes, Sarge."

"And check for any IEDs where them choppers are gonna land, I got a bad feeling about today."

"Sarge."

He ordered 'A' Company to intensify their fire giving King and his men the cover they needed to sprint towards the orchard. He gave a brief smile as they all made it beyond the wall without taking any more casualties.

Twenty minutes later Corporal King returned.

"Got a clear area about hundred metres through the orchard. We've checked the ground and there ain't no sign of any IEDs in the area. Looks good for med evac," he said.

"Okay, that's good news."

He turned towards the radio op,' "Brown, get on the radio and ask for some air support. We need to keep these fuckers heads down while we make our way to the extraction zone."

"Okay Sarge."

A few moments later Brown announced that they had air support from a Yankee attack helicopter.

"Good," Taylor said, "that will do the job, teach these mother fuckers a lesson."

He barked out an order. 'A' Company prepare to move positions from the village, we're heading through the orchard to the extraction point, wait for my signal."

'A' Company marked the enemy position with yellow smoke grenades and the US chopper began to lay down its deadly firepower along the Taliban positions and despite taking some return fire the Black Hawk began to inflict casualties on the Taliban. With a reduction in the Taliban's response Taylor ordered the move to the evacuation point.

As they broke cover and sprinted towards the perimeter of the orchard Taylor looked up into the sky.

"C'mon, where the fuck are you?" as he searched the blue Afghan sky for the familiar silhouette of the Chinook helicopters

The Black Hawk chopper hovered above the Taliban positions, every now and then swooping down, peppering the houses with rapid machine gun fire. The Taliban dug in, no intention of trading blows with such a powerful opponent.

Taylor was staring hard at Brown then all of a sudden Brown received the call he was waiting for.

"Sarge, E.T.A four minutes" .

"Thank fuck for that," Taylor whispered to himself and dared to believe that at last, things were going their way. He needed to get everyone to the evacuation point as soon as possible.

"Corporal King, take command of the wounded and get everyone to the evacuation point. I'll bring up the rear and cover. We've got two Chinooks E.T.A. in four minutes."

"On it Sarge."

Hassan watched in great anticipation from his vantage point. He had watched the firefight in the village and how three soldiers did a recce of the exact area where he had hidden the bomb. Hassan knew the Brits were looking for a landing zone and couldn't help feeling rather smug that they were looking at the exact spot where he had prepared his little present for them. He watched patiently. *Not long now*, he thought to himself as the British troops came into view carrying their wounded and dead through the orange orchard.

Hassan had requested that only small arms fire could be used against the Brits as they made their evacuation through the orange orchard. The last thing that Hassan wanted was a stray mortar or RPG round accidentally damaging the control wire.

Private Bennet was one of the soldiers carried from the village through the orange orchard to the evacuation point. He was wide awake and had refused a jab of morphine; he looked at his comrades lined up waiting to get out of there. One of the nearby stretchers had a body bag on it. Poor Bainsey thought Bennet, he was an okay guy and always gave him some of his mother's cakes which she regularly sent over from the UK. No more baking cakes for Mrs Baines.

There was plenty of gallows humour when it came to the dead. It was a fact of life that none of them knew who was next and if you didn't joke about it you would go insane with the paranoia of what could happen. Bennet never thought about death he just somehow sensed that he would be alright, it would never happen to him, it would be others, not him. His spirits lifted even further when he saw the two Chinooks coming into land.

Taylor took charge of the rear-guard, he had every confidence that King would competently deal with getting the wounded on the Chinooks. They still had the Black Hawk laying fire into the Taliban positions and 'A' Company was only receiving sporadic and poorly aimed fire from the village. He ordered his men to leave their positions and take up a defensive semi-circle position in the orange orchard, approximately fifty metres around the landing zone. It would give cover if the Taliban made any attempts to come into the orchard.

Three minutes later Taylor's men had set up their perimeter and were waiting for the Taliban to come through the orchard. He spotted the Chinooks high up in the sky to the west. They were no more than a minute from landing on the ground.

Apart from the thump, thump of the Chinooks' rotor blades it had all gone very quiet. He studied the entrance to the orchard. He expected to see the Taliban burst through at any minute but there were none. It was even stranger that they had not targeted the orchard with RPGs or mortars. What was going on? Taylor started to get an uneasy feeling. Something wasn't right. They were escaping much too easily. Had they booby trapped the orchard? He studied the ground and he knew all his men would be doing the same. Everybody's lives depended on it. Any sign of an IED and they would abort the evacuation. The Chinooks were preparing to land, no more than two hundred metres from the ground.

Taylor watched as the first Chinook landed and his comrades were stretchered into the helicopter. He couldn't help noticing that the Chinook had lurched slightly to the left as it landed, it had settled at an unnatural angle as if it had sunk into the ground.

As Bennet was being loaded onto the Chinook he was aware that the heavy helicopter had sunk a few inches into the ground. It looked damp, as if there had been a heavy rainfall. *Strange*. He could not remember the last time it had rained. Well what did he care, he was off to the military hospital where those pretty nurses would spoil him rotten. Yes, that was all he should be thinking about, those pretty nurses. All of a sudden it hit him. There was something wrong, something seriously wrong and he knew exactly what it was and he began to scream at the top of his voice as he waved his arms frantically. No one could hear anything above the noise of the spinning helicopters rotor blades.

Taylor watched as one of the injured soldiers began to wave his arms frantically as he was loaded onto the helicopter.

"What the fuck" said Taylor to himself as he sensed a bad feeling deep in his gut.

Hassan watched intently as the last of the soldiers boarded the Chinook. Calmly and methodically his thumb found the small red button that was attached to the control wire and he pressed it.

"Allah Akbar."

Taylor watched as the Chinook began to move into the air, and in a split second, as if in slow motion the Chinook was engulfed in a massive ball of flame. Taylor watched on in shock as spinning rotor blades, fuselage and body parts flew in all directions that brought memories of a train journey many years before. The five Russian artillery shells had been planted to send their blast upwards otherwise Taylor and his covering squad of men would have been killed too. The

Chinook was literally torn apart and then there was a secondary explosion as the large fuel tanks on the helicopter erupted into another huge ball of flames. Taylor watched in horror and felt even more disgust as the wind carried the sound of cheering from the Taliban who had obviously planned this delay trap.

And then it was all eerily silent as the dust settled and the flames seemed to die down. He listened for the screams and moans and groans of the survivors but there was nothing. There appeared to be no survivors but as Taylor ran down to the bomb site he saw a hand raised and heard a cry for help. Taylor found corporal King badly injured but alive.

"Its ok Kingy mate. Your gonna be ok" said Taylor as he comforted his long time friend.

A loss of a Chinook with seventeen men on board was a big event. Camp Bastion ordered all available fighter jets to the position to provide cover for the evacuation of the remaining men along with the recovery of the dead. The Taliban were experienced enough to know that the ISAF forces would converge on their positions and so they quickly melted into the civilian population of the surrounding countryside.

ISAF forces secured the Chinook bomb site and the dead were flown back to Camp Bastion in preparation for repatriation to the UK.

The remaining men in Taylor's company were flown back to Platoon House North. Taylor did not get off the Chinook but flew on to headquarters at Sangin. He was looking for one man and one man only.

CHAPTER **17**

Taylor had plenty of time to reflect during his flight back to headquarters. The inside of the helicopter contained more body bags than living individuals. In the centre of the helicopter were several smaller bags zipped up so that the contents were hidden from view. They were the same colour as the larger body bags with a small 'UBP' that someone had written on in an official capacity or perhaps a warped soldiers joke. No one needed to tell him that the bags contained unidentified body parts, he had helped to fill them. By the time he landed and jumped from the helicopter he was seething with anger. He blamed the loss of his men squarely on the shoulders of Colonel Rogers.

Taylor was oblivious to the consolation of his fellow soldiers as he stormed to the building that housed the command centre. He knew he would find Colonel Rogers there. He entered the hallway and saw an Afghani man putting a new nameplate badge on the door. The name plate said Colonel Rogers.

Without knocking on the door he burst into the room. Colonel Rogers was not alone. He was sitting at his desk dictating the report of the Chinook tragedy to his secretary.

"How dare you come in here without permission," he scowled.

"How dare you, is that all you can say you fucking piece of shit," Taylor screamed.

With that Taylor slowly raised his gun and pointed it directly at Colonel Rogers. You could have heard a pin drop as no one in the room dared speak.

Taylor then broke the ice.

"Ever been under fire, sir," he said sarcastically, "I mean really under fire in a hopeless situation"

Colonel Rogers stared at the machine gun like a rabbit caught in the headlights of a truck. He broke the trance and looked into Taylor's face. Taylor looked mad, fucking mad. The scar on his face seemed to glow bright red and his eyes had an intensity that was shitting the life out of Colonel Rogers.

"Well answer me," he seethed.

"No, I …"

"Of course you haven't and do you know what it's like to see your pals burnt alive, what it's like to zip them up in a body bag or what it's like to pick one of your mates arms up from the ground and you haven't a fucking clue where his body is."

The Colonel opened his mouth. He couldn't utter one word.

Taylor turned the gun slightly to the left of Colonel Rogers head and fired a short burst from the machine gun. He knew exactly what he was doing and the bullets embedded harmlessly into the plaster wall behind him. The sound of an automatic assault rifle soon had the base's alarms ringing. Taylor knew that he would not have much time alone with Colonel Rogers.

"Don't kill him, he's not worth it," the secretary said in a calm voice.

"Really, is that so, it may well be worth it," he grunted.

Colonel Rogers sat bolt upright with a blank expression across his face which had drained of all colour. Taylor pointed his gun back at Colonel Rogers's head then cocked the magazine. Rogers began to beg for his life.

"Please don't kill me, please, please, I don't want to die," he pleaded.

"Stand up like a man" ordered Taylor.

As Colonel Rogers stood up from behind his desk a vile stench filled the room.

"You dirty cowardly bastard, you have shit yourself haven't you? That just about sums you right up you miserable cunt."

He looked down at the dark stain spreading slowly on the colonel's trousers.

"Fuck me, you've pissed yourself too."

At that point the door burst open and two military police officers rushed in and pointed their handguns directly at Taylor's head.

"One more move Sergeant Taylor and we will shoot, you have three seconds," one of the military police officers bellowed.

Taylor contemplated his situation. He knew he could kill Colonel Rogers but he also knew that he would be shot dead. Taylor wasn't ready to give up his life just yet. There was unfinished business to attend to.

He dropped his weapon to the floor and while one of the MP's held guard, the other handcuffed Taylor and led him away towards the door.

"You haven't seen the last of me you cunt" he shouted as he left the room, "I'm telling them all they need to know and you'll be serving time just like me."

The Colonel stood in stunned silence.

Taylor still screamed out abuse as he was led forcibly down the corridor.

"Sir, I think you need to get cleaned up" said the Colonel's secretary.

CHAPTER 18

Manningham, Bradford.

Osama Bin Laden had sent a three man terror cell into England. Their orders were very clear, they had to integrate into British society and recruit home grown affiliates to join the war against the western infidels. The order was to bring carnage to the country and seek revenge for the invasion in Afghanistan and all other manner of injustices against the Islamic world.

Their orders were not to give their own lives away in any suicide bombings but to use home grown terrorists to prolong the campaign.

It was the first time the cell had met in two years.

"Abdullah made a great sacrifice; he has sent word from Belmarsh prison. The Brits have taken the bait. We have made our sweeps on the Imams and all the trackers have been removed from their cars. All listening devices have now been removed from their homes," Johiya said.

"That will teach Professor Baqri to sleep with prostitutes... he has shamed Islam," Khalil replied.

"Yes," Johiya said with a satisfied smirk, "but let us focus on the matter at hand, the Imams now have nine converts that are ready to be utilised. We have identified our targets, the vehicles are now ready. The date is set."

"Othmane, let us run through the plan one more time," Johiya said.

"All three converts have mobile phones, they all live in the target area, so they'll not get lost. All three vehicles have trackers that are fitted and working. We can be sure that the vehicles will be parked in the exact target area," stated Othmane.

"And our convert brothers?" Johiya asked.

"As far as they're concerned they're just doing the jobs that the Imams arranged for them on their release. We have no reason for them to suspect anything else. They are bright enough but not intelligent enough to figure it all out."

Dembe Akoli was one of the group of prisoners who had been soft radicalised in prison by the Al Qaeda network of Imams. He was a black male, born in East London of Ugandan descent. He had now been out of prison for nearly one year. He had served ten years for heroin smuggling and converted to Islam halfway through his sentence. Since being released the Imam had given him money for a flat, in Plashet Grove, London, found him a job and given him extra money so he enjoyed a good standard of living. Life was pretty good and not so difficult. Akoli had even got himself a girlfriend.

Upon his release the Imam got Akoli a delivery job dropping off letters and packages to various houses in the East London area. Akoli would get a phone call from the Imam saying that he had left some letters in his car for him to post. It was easy work and usually only took him a couple of hours a day. The Imam even supplied Akoli with a car for his deliveries. However, he couldn't work today as someone had stolen his car. Akoli got straight on the phone and told the Imam about the theft. The Imam smiled, he knew the car had been stolen because he had arranged it. He confirmed that he would be able to supply Akoli with a replacement vehicle in double quick time which was just as well as the Imam had already told him that he would be working this Saturday afternoon on some very urgent and important business.

Akoli went back to bed and put the alarm on. He woke up with the alarm bleeping in his ears and went to his front door and found a set of keys had been posted through his letterbox. The key ring had the registration of a vehicle written on it. His phone rang and the Imam told him his replacement car was parked on the street. It was a ford transit van. The Imam told him it was a temporary replacement and that he would receive a new car on Monday. He also stated that the heater in the van did not work and had kindly supplied a hat and scarf to keep Akoli warm. He went on to say that one of the letters had to be signed for and could not be posted. The Imam made Akoli promise that the letter would be signed for in person. Akoli made that promise and assured the Man he would not let him down. As per his instructions Akoli left his house at 4:15 p.m, found the van outside his flat and saw the small pile of letters on the passenger seat. He walked around to the back and found that the rear doors were padlocked. *Strange*, he thought, *but none of my business*. He didn't bother to check in the back of the van, there was no need to.

There was a typed note that said one of the letters had to be delivered to Green St, Upton Park, at exactly 4:45 p.m. The note said that the letter had to be signed for.

It was bitterly cold. The Imam sat in a small Pakistani cafe drinking coffee, near to Green Street market. He looked at his watch, and walked out of the market onto Green Street. He was carrying a shopping bag and blended in well with all the other asians going about their daily business. The Imam continued walking down Green Street towards West Ham United football stadium. As he got closer to the ground he could hear the chants coming from the supporters inside the stadium.

Green Street on match day was eerily quiet. Most of the businesses close to the ground were closed. They had been smashed up by football hooligans in previous years and took no chances. There were barely any cars on the road either as nobody wanted to get caught up in the match day traffic when the game finished just before 5pm.

The Imam stopped at a bus stop. There was a light drizzle in the air and it was beginning to get dark, a cold wind whipped through the bus shelter creating an ice cold vortex. From the bus stop the Imam saw the white transit van drive up Green Street and park just in front of the main gates at West Ham United, on the opposite side of the road. The Imam saw the driver get out of the van and quickly walk to one of the houses. It was 4:40 by his watch. The bus stop was about 200 metres away from the van.

The Imam shivered and zipped his coat up to the neck. He looked down the street. There were a few police officers milling around chatting to some burger bar owners. They were all waiting for the throng of supporters that would soon embark en masse from the stadium. Akoli parked the van directly outside the address and quickly walked to the front door to deliver the letter. He rang the doorbell and waited. There was no answer. He knocked and banged on the door and waited again. He cursed to himself. Still there was no answer.

Akoli knocked and waited again, he couldn't understand why there was nobody at home, the Imam had definitely said the letter had to be signed for. He looked up towards Upton Park and heard the shrill of the final whistle that had been blown inside the stadium.

"Fucking shit," he mumbled to himself, "that's all I fucking need."

Within minutes a mass of people exited from the football stadium onto Green Street and headed towards him.

"Shit, shit, shit, I'm going to get well and truly stuck in this lot."

His mobile phone rang in his pocket and he answered it and placed the handset to his ear.

It was the Imam. "Hello Dembe, just checking that the Green Street letter has been signed for."

"Sorry Imam but there's no one here."

There was a slight pause. "Hang on and I will find out what's going on and call you right back," the Imam said calmly.

"No problem, I'll wait."

The line went dead.

A few minutes later Akoli's mobile rang again.

"Dembe, I have been told the recipient of the letter is just a few minutes away. He won't be long."

"Okay, no problem."

He wasn't happy as he could see that he was going to get stuck in the traffic and it was bitterly cold so he made his way back to the van and climbed in.

About 200 metres away the Imam stood and watched. This pleased him as it was better that Akoli was inside the van because in would ensure maximum destruction of the body and make the police investigation almost impossible.

The Imam's orders were to wait until Green Street was packed with football supporters. He didn't have to wait long and watched as thousands upon thousands of

West Ham and Liverpool supporters converged onto Green Street and walked ever closer to the white van. Akoli knew he was well and truly stuck now as the fans thronged around his van and he would have to wait at least half an hour for the supporters to clear before he could drive away. He sat back and watched the front door of the house, waiting for someone to arrive so he could get the letter delivered and get out of there.

The van was completely surrounded now, so much so that the Imam couldn't even see it. He smiled to himself and made the coded call to Johiya before calmly joining in with the throng of supporters who had reached the bus stop and continued making his way towards Upton Park tube station. The Imam continued past the tube station then disappeared down one of the many side streets of Green Street.

Johiya had taken the call but just listened. He had said nothing to the Imam. Johiya looked at the smart phone screen and double checked that the tracking device hidden in the van confirmed its position outside West Ham United's main gates.

Johiya glanced across at Othmane and Khalil, "Make the call," he ordered, his brow glistening with perspiration from the surge of adrenaline coursing through his body.

Othmane duly dialed a number. "Allah Akbar," he said as a smile crept across his face.

In the back of the transit van was a large fertilizer bomb. In the centre of the fertilizer bomb was a two kilogram detonator of Semtex. Attached to the Semtex bomb was a detonator that was wired up to a battery pack. The battery pack was connected to a simple mobile phone. The mobile phone was set to vibrate.

The mobile phone attached to the battery pack received the call from Othmane. The phone vibrated and made connection with the battery pack. The battery pack sent an electric current to the detonator. The blast from the Semtex ignited the two ton bomb in a millisecond.

Dembe Akoli was vaporized instantly along with his phone, the letters, the tracking device and everything that could have compromised the terrorists. The gigantic bomb in the middle of Green Street had horrendous consequences to those in close proximity as three quarters of a ton of six inch nails, vehicle shrapnel, engine pieces together with twenty gallons of fuel exploded into a gigantic lethal fireball.

Within seconds of the first explosion Othmane made two further calls to vehicles parked outside football grounds. One in Leicester and one in Blackburn. Both teams were playing a home fixture.

Later that evening Johiya, Othmane and Talpur watched the UK's Prime Minister make an emergency statement to the media outside number 10 Downing Street.

"As a nation we must now accept that we are at a state of war. It is a war that we must win at all costs. These terrorists and their sympathisers can be assured that they will have no place to hide. On Monday an emergency session of Parliament will take place."

The PM spoke for nine minutes, he spoke about morals and decency and the right for every man, woman and child to live a peaceful life and worship whichever god they believed in. He pleaded for all good Muslims to root out the extremists and the radicals.

The Prime Minister went on to call for a day of mourning and gave his condolences to the bereaved families. He asked the British people to remain calm, not to take the law into their own hands, there were not to be any reprisals against the UK Muslim population.

Johiya grinned. "Very predictable from these English infidels, their stupid Prime Minister is telling the entire world when the UK government is meeting and exactly where that will be."

"When do we start phase two?" Othmane asked.

"Why Othmane, the Prime Minister has just told us."

"Of course," he said.

"But we must be very, very vigilant till then, I don't know how long it will take Mi5 to piece all this together, but we cannot underestimate them."

CHAPTER 19

Military Corrective Training Centre, Colchester.

It was 6 a.m. and the military prison was still quiet. Unlike civilian prisons there were no TVs, radios or regular access to the telephone. The regime was strict and designed to instill discipline in the men who were held there, many of whom would return to their units after finishing their sentences. One of the permitted items was a battery operated MP3 player that allowed Taylor the one luxury of listening to music. Taylor was lying on his bunk bed with his headphones on listening to some trance dance music when the Silence by Delirium track came on. Every time Taylor heard the song he thought back to the two Taliban fighters his company had captured in Afghanistan. Taylor felt no remorse or regrets for what he had done. As far as he was concerned war makes good men rise to a necessary evil… that was a fact.

He remembered some of the men when they first landed in Afghanistan and how green they were; they thought they were fighting a noble cause. Once they had picked up a few body parts from their mates who had been victims of an IED that green naivety soon turned to utter hatred for their enemy. The British Army's rules of engagement were nothing more than a joke. Unless you were actually being shot at or caught the enemy planting a bomb, the Taliban could not be touched. It was like fighting a war with both arms tied behind your back.

The rules said that if you captured any Taliban fighters where you had evidence that they were involved with the manufacture and placement of IEDs, you had to bring them back to Sangin headquarters and hand them over to the Military Police. When they'd captured the two Taliban fighters it was the day after Taylor had scraped Private Joey Mathews' body from a wall after he'd walked into an IED trap. It was just a bit unfortunate for the two Taliban fighters when they had been searched that they had found the exact same explosive detonators found in the previous unexploded IED. Not in a million years was 'A' company going to hand over the fuckers to the military police. On that day, 'A' company had decided to be judge, jury and executioner. Taylor remembered how the actual Taliban fighter caught with the detonators was made to watch as a couple of men made sure his buddy's last twenty minutes on earth would be remembered when he landed in paradise. The final act of cutting off the man's dick was quite memorable.

Taylor had walked up to him waving his own dick in front of his face.

"How are you going to fuck seventy-two virgins with no cock?" he had yelled in his face.

But the Taliban had been beyond caring, barely breathing and had accepted his inevitable death. He had given up on life and prayed that the end was close.

Taylor turned to his accomplice. "Your next you rag headed cunt."

He hoped that by seeing what his mate had gone through the detonator fella might blab about where the Taliban stored the explosives for their IEDs.

Did that mother fucker talk? He said fuck all. Maybe if they'd had longer with him he may have eventually spoken out but his platoon could not let this man live after what they had done to him and his Taliban buddy.

The dance music that Taylor was now listening to brought back the crazy moments leading up to the end of the Taliban's life.

The digital reader clicked round to 7.28 and then boom. Taylor remembered pulling the trigger and blowing the man's brains out.

The military police's investigation came up against a wall of silence when interviewing the platoon. None of the men said a word despite harming their own future careers in the British Army. The forensic evidence proved that someone in Taylor's platoon was guilty but without being able to identify who was actually responsible the case was eventually left on the file.

As far as Taylor and his platoon were concerned the two Taliban fighters got what they deserved.

However, the court martial at Camp Bastion had still found Sergeant Taylor guilty of a rack of charges against Colonel Rogers, but taking everything into account including past dispatches for bravery and the real fact that the British Army could do without bad publicity, he was demoted to private and sentenced to three years corrective training at Colchester's Corrective Training Centre. The Colonel Rogers career was also ruined when he was found guilty of gross misconduct and demoted to an NCO role in an office on Merseyside where he could do no harm. In truth Colonel Rogers career was over after he had shit and pissed himself in his own office. No one would ever give him credibility as a soldier again.

Taylor's mind wandered off to Danny and the train bombing and then the carnage of the Chinook disaster.

Corrective Officer Barnes strolled into the dormitory. "Right lads, listen up. There were a series of bombings at three football grounds yesterday evening. Hundreds are recorded as dead with many, many injured. Get on these phones and make sure your nearest and dearest are safe."

He handed out a bundle of mobile phones so the prisoners could make their calls home. Giving the prisoners mobile phones to make calls home alerted the dormitory as to how serious the incident was.

Taylor watched as the prisoners in his dormitory discussed the bombings. Taylor could see the outpourings of hatred coming from this group of men. Many of them had toured Afghanistan and Iraq. Within a matter of minutes the dorm had the full picture of the magnitude of the football bombings. Many were seasoned veterans and they had all seen their mates die in combat for what was nothing more than war mongering by the Ex Prime Minister Tony Hardy. The general consensus was that things were getting worse; now the Muslim extremists were bombing the British people in their own back yard.

Over the coming days the newspapers ran multiple stories on who might be responsible, but with over four million registered Muslims living in mainland UK, it was like finding needles in haystacks. What was worse though, was that there was over a million Muslims who were living in the UK illegally.

It wasn't too hard for Taylor to work out that these attacks were highly coordinated and not just lone wolf suicide bombers. He was thinking. He had plenty of time to think. Enough was enough. One thing that the prime minster was right about was that these Jihadists had declared war on the UK. But Taylor knew what would happen… it would be a war like that in Afghanistan, which would be fought with one if not two arms tied behind their backs. The weak liberal left would preach the good talk, not all Muslims were bad Muslims, Islam was the religion of peace.

"Fucking bullshit," he whispered under his breath, "I'm going to personally bring the war to these Muslims, a war on an equal footing. If they want blood and guts then that's exactly what I'll fucking give them."

Taylor had lost his son and his wife to these so called Jihadists and now the fuckers had the front to kill hundreds of innocent English people, people like him, working class football fans out for a little entertainment on a Saturday afternoon. If they thought they could get away with it they had another thing coming.

"Cunts," he whispered to himself, "the fucking cunts."

Mick Taylor was a natural born leader. From organising football hooligan ambushes to fighting the Taliban, he had the knack of leadership. His main quality was that he led by example. He never hid behind his men like so many other leaders. He was pro-active and hands on. Taylor knew it was this that brought loyalty.

Dormitory B at Colchester Corrective Training Centre became a recruitment centre for the fight back against the Jihadists. Taylor was spoilt for choice. Whereas a civilian prison had inmates from all walks of life such as plumbers, electricians and labourer's, a military prison's inmates came from various skill sectors of the British Army and they were all trained killers. From explosive experts to snipers, to covert surveillance, the military prison was the perfect recruitment centre for Taylor's private army.

He also had an extensive list of contacts from his days in Afghanistan. His entire platoon stuck by him at the court martial and most of those men were now on Civvy Street. There were a few names that he knew would be itching to get something going. Number one on his recruitment list was at least one explosives expert. There was one person who came to mind who was not easily contactable as he was on A dormitory. Luckily for Taylor he played badminton with the ex SAS inmate at Colchester military prison once a week. The gymnasium was the only time A and B dormitories met up.

Drago hit a perfect drop shot that had Taylor running again in vain to return the shuttlecock over the net.

"Twenty one, eight. Game over," Drago beamed.

"Yeah Drago yet again you've beaten me."

"I'm a born winner mate, I can't bear losing especially to you."

Drago was a bit of an enigma. He had no real friends and his Army job was to do special covert ops for the SAS. Rumour had it that he had been undercover in Baghdad for nearly two months pointing laser beams at Saddam Hussein's government buildings for the laser guided bombs to find their targets. Drago had been captured and tortured by Saddam's secret police for months. It was not until the Americans had invaded Baghdad that Drago was discovered in a special prison. Drago was lucky not to have been executed for being a spy but he was in a bad way and only just survived the ordeal.

A few of the Colchester army prison officers had read Drago's prison file and had put it around that Drago was seriously tortured and as a result had various personality defects. Taylor made up his mind that it was worth approaching Drago. He was very likely to have an axe to grind against Muslims in general and following the football bombings, the whole nation was turning against Muslims in general.

"So Drago, looks like these Muzzies are running ring rounds our secret services. It's been a couple of months now and they haven't nicked anyone for the football bombings."

Drago wiped a bead of sweat from his brow.

"Yep, they're running rings around our boys just like I ran rings round you on the court."

Taylor shrugged his shoulders.

"Today your game was well below par," Drago continued, "and I'd guess that you're having an extremely bad day or you're buttering up my ego for something?"

Taylor was caught on the back foot. Drago had side-stepped the comment on the football bombings and didn't offer any comment which may have indicated whether he would be up for Taylor's private army.

Taylor took a deep breath and jumped in with both feet. He told Drago what he thought of the Muslims and their brotherhood and how he would like to fight back against them with a little bit more than diplomacy and the ballot box.

"It's time to fight back Drago, I mean really fight back with guns and bombs, give them a taste of their own fucking medicine. They are a bunch of cowardly fuckas, remember when they slaughtered one of our own, the bandsman?"

Drago nodded. Barely.

Of course he remembers Taylor thought to himself, who didn't?

"It was two onto one," Taylor continued, "and if that wasn't bad enough poor Rigby wasn't even armed and they attacked him with knives and machetes, hacked the poor bloke to death."

Drago listened. He walked slowly from the court towards the shower rooms.

At last he spoke, "and even that wasn't one sided enough, just to make sure that the poor bastard didn't have a cat in hell's chance against them, they mowed him down with a car."

"Exactly, they drove a car at him and made sure he couldn't even stand up. Run over, barely conscious and then hacked to death in broad daylight!"

Drago shook his head. Taylor waited for more but Drago said nothing.

Taylor was frustrated. Drago hadn't given any indication as to whether he would join Taylor's band of brothers or not and yet he seemed to be on the same wavelength.

Taylor tried to remain patient. Drago wiped at his brow with a towel. At least if Drago said no he could be reasonably sure that he wouldn't go squealing to the authorities.

Eventually Drago stood. Taylor waited.

Drago dropped his clothes to the floor and walked off in the direction of the shower.

One week later and Drago and Taylor played Badminton again. Taylor didn't give an inch but still lost twenty one, seventeen. It was his best ever performance against Drago. After the game they sat on a bench at the side of the gymnasium and chatted.

"In or out Drago?" asked Taylor.

"Now that's a bit more like it Taylor boy, direct and to the point. Not pussy footing around like last week are you? Now the question you've just asked is not quite so simple. I'd like to be in, you know I would, nothing I'd like better than to get into those murdering bastards, but I don't want to be ordered to do this or that; it will be me and you on an equal footing or nothing at all. You understand Taylor?" he said.

Taylor was breathing hard, the game had taken more out of him than he thought.

"Okay Drago, if that's how you want it."

Drago put out his hand and Taylor shook to seal the deal. He felt a lot of strength in the handshake but he had no real idea how this deal with Drago would actually go. The SAS types were in a league of their own and if it meant Taylor showing a bit of humility to the eccentric Drago it would be worth it as this man knew everything there was to know about explosives and counter insurgency.

CHAPTER 20

Mi5 Headquarters, Thames House

The three football bombings claimed a total of four hundred and thirty lives. There were nearly a thousand injured and all Mi5 leave had been cancelled. All Mi6 agents not on active duty abroad had been drafted into the biggest manhunt ever undertaken on mainland Britain.

Fletcher stood up in the packed boardroom. He turned on the video and the men of Mi5 and Mi6 and the Met's anti-terrorism unit all watched the three CCTV videos of three almost identical vans parking up outside the main exits to each of the three football grounds. They sat in stony silence as they watched the vans explode in and amongst thousands of innocent football supporters. Fletcher turned off the video.

"Right, I will deal with Upton Park first. The first trace on the CCTV cameras show this van coming on to the Barking Road, no more than two blocks from Green Street. It travels east along the Barking Road, turns left at Green Street and the van parks up. Someone gets out and walks in the direction of a house opposite the main gates. We then see the person get back into the van. The person then stays in the van until it explodes. We are presuming this person was a suicide bomber, he had a hat and scarf covering the bottom half of his face which makes identification almost impossible."

He took a drink from a glass of water and then continued.

"The number plates are false. They coincide with a builder's van in Stratford. The van owner has been interviewed and his plates have not been stolen so they're likely to be homemade. We need to check every number plate kit sold in the UK. We may even have to go Europe wide on this. The engine block survived the blast and has been examined; the engine number has been ground down and also stamped through with blank stamps. Basically we can't read the shockwaves of the original engine stamp. The chassis number has not been found in the debris… it's likely to have been cut out."

One of the men in the audience raised an arm. "So what do we have Sir?"

Fletcher sighed, but tried to disguise it. "We have a plain white van that we have little hope of getting any forensics from. We need to trace all stolen and unrecovered white vans in the UK. Again we may have to go Europe wide on this. The three vans all arrived and exploded at twilight, within minutes of each game finishing. This has made our job that much harder. The Upton Park bomb was actually exploded in nautical twilight, the second phase of twilight with light drizzle. The cameras have great difficulty showing clear images in this light. On that basis the closest camera on the van at Green Street just shows a male getting out of the van. He walks in the direction of the houses opposite then returns three minutes later.

There were five houses in that block that the bomber could have visited. All five houses have been extensively damaged by the blast. Four were occupied. We have six victims from these houses. One survivor, a woman who just so happened to be in the garden at the time of the blast lost both her children and is now under sedation at Newham general hospital. We've managed to contact the owner of the unoccupied house. It has been empty for a year now.

Whoever planned this has managed to make it extremely difficult for us to investigate this incident. As an example, we're trying to trace phone records of all the people in the Upton Park area, this is a mammoth task at the best of times, but there were an extra 36,000 football supporters in the exact vicinity at the time and a large percentage of them used their mobile phones at the end of the game. We're hoping to trace a mobile number that came into the blast zone at 4:45 p.m."

There was a muted but collective sigh from the audience. The terrorists had planned all three tasks with precision and cunning and they were under no illusion just how difficult it would be to track them down.

Fletcher gave a rundown on the football stadium bombs at Leicester and Blackburn.

"Sir, in regards to phone records, it's possible that the bomber was already located close to the blast point before he travelled there," Samuels said.

"Yes that's possible. That's one line of enquiry that needs to be followed up," replied Fletcher.

"We don't even know if the driver of the van had a mobile phone," Samuels said.

"Again that's possible," said Fletcher, frustration clearly etched on his face. "As I said, whoever planned this went to a lot of trouble not to be discovered; you all have your reports and allocated work sheets. The treasury has okayed unlimited resources on this gentlemen, so leave no stone unturned. These bastards are different to the wacko ISIS inspired attacks, they know how to kill hundreds, not tens and twenties."

Two hours later Fletcher sat in his office with his inner council at Mi5 headquarters. His mobile rang, he looked at the number and left the room. It was the Prime Minister. After five minutes of heated and frank discussion Fletcher turned of the mobile. His face was red with anger. He had just been threatened with dismissal. Fletcher had been chastised because extremists had brought death and destruction to British streets despite the massive budget and resources available to Mi5.

When he returned to the room he meant business.

"okay, listen men. I want each and every radical jihadi on our books arrested and questioned. I want them held for the maximum of twenty eight days. I want results." His voice had raised a decibel or two, he was angry. "Whatever fucking happened to the medical ring and this Professor Baqri?" he yelled at no one in particular.

Baxter spoke. "Nothing boss, each and every student who has ever attended his classes has been under close surveillance since Edinburgh. They all have a perfect alibi. At the time of the football bombs they were under close surveillance and couldn't possibly have been responsible."

Fletcher slammed his fist on the table. "Bastards, bring them in, bring them all in, we are at war, bring the bastards in."

A few of the men stood, some made towards the door, some hesitated unsure of what to do.

"What are you waiting for? get going," he yelled, "for fucks sake get a move on."

As Baxter stood Fletcher stopped him in his tracks. "Baxter, you stay behind."

"Yes Sir."

Fletcher waited for his office to empty before he spoke to Baxter alone. "Baxter, tell what the fuck happened with this Professor Baqri. Surely you got something from him?"

"He knows nothing and I mean nothing, sir," Baxter replied.

"Where is he now?"

"We're holding him in our medical suite."

"Will he live?"

"I hope so sir, you did say get blood out of a stone," Baxter said quietly.

Fletcher squeezed at the temples at the side of his head. "I'm at a loss as to what's going on here, you said that Abdullah had been broken and all the intelligence on Professor Baqri came from him."

"Yes sir, we broke him for sure."

"But Baqri and his mob had the perfect alibi?"

"Yes Sir, I sincerely believe that they could not have been involved in any way."

Fletcher stood and paced the length of the room several times as Baxter looked on.

Eventually he spoke. "Abdullah is a terrorist, he was caught in the act trying to blow up the airport. I think you need to speak to him again, don't you Baxter?"

"Yes Sir."

Baxter left the room and met up with Clarke. Walking down the corridor Baxter and Clarke talked privately. Baxter had been thinking. He was number two at Mi5 and more or less ran the show. He had an IQ way off the charts, coupled with an evil streak that left many of his own Mi5 colleagues in fear of him. It wasn't often that Baxter made a mistake but he had this feeling that he'd been led up the garden path by Abdullah. *The bastard,* he thought to himself.

"I don't get this," he said, "this medical ring has been under the most intense surveillance and yet we haven't had a sniff of anything. I'm beginning to smell a rat."

"What do you mean?" Clarke asked.

"No man could have withstood what Baqri went through unless he knew nothing. When they start making up stories to stop the pain you know they know nothing," he said.

"So?"

"Abdullah," said Baxter.

"What the Edinburgh bomber?"

"Yeah, that scumbag. Tomorrow we're going to go to Belmarsh and get Abdullah."

Clarke noticed a glint in Baxter's eyes and they both knew why.

The next morning, at 8 am sharp Baxter arrived at Belmarsh Prison. He wrote out the police visitors information sheet and handed it to the prison officer at the prison entrance. He wrote Abdullah HS 4583 down in the space for the prisoner's number. The prison officer took the form and punched the details into a computer. Baxter was watching the prison officer and saw that a wry smile had come over the officer's face.

A few moments later the prison officer lifted up the speaker vent and spoke. "Abdullah HS 4583 topped himself last night."

"What the fuck are you talking about?"

"Hung himself on the triple A Unit," the prison officer announced.

He then spun round the computer screen and showed an image of the deceased prisoner.

"That's him, yes?"

"Fucking bollocks, okay let me in anyway. We're gonna need to search his cell and double check any calls he made."

"No problem Sir."

The prison officer buzzed open the security door and motioned Baxter and Clarke to step forward. Baxter was angry, on edge, but he wasn't angry because he had lost a potential witness, he was angry that he had lost a torture session.

CHAPTER **21**

HMP Full Sutton

It wasn't by chance that Bakar was the leader of the Muslim prisoners at HMP Full Sutton. Bakar's family ties extended all the way back to the Waziristan district on the Afghan/Pakistani border. Waziristan was a hot bed of radical Islam and the religious teachers of the madrasas of that region had given orders to its worshippers to invite their extended family members living in the west to visit their homeland in Waziristan and undergo the new radical teachings.

Imran Bakar was one of those young men sent off for religious training. Bakar's father had been concerned that his son would fall into the depravity of western society and had sent Bakar on a two year trip to Waziristan. The Imams at the madrasas quickly identified Bakar as an intellectual with an interest in the new radical interpretation of the Qur'an, so Bakar was moved onto a madrasa that specialised in teaching its students to become teachers themselves and indoctrinate their muslim brothers when they returned to their western countries.

By the time Bakar returned to the UK he was a devout believer in radical Islam and took this belief to such a degree that he took it upon himself to murder his cousin in a so called 'honour killing.'

She had been warned, she'd had various relationships with black men and eventually got pregnant to one of them. Bakar couldn't get to grips with it, the man wasn't a Muslim and it simply wasn't acceptable for her family to have an illegitimate black child and the honour of the entire family was at stake. Bakar met with the family and it was unanimously agreed that the family's honour had to be protected and Bakar volunteered to kill his cousin and the unborn child. It wasn't as easy as a straightforward killing, the girl had to suffer, she had to realise the error of her ways before she was dispatched. It was a major error on Bakar's behalf because a bystander had witnessed the kidnap and reported it to the police. It was broad daylight. (Another mistake.) Bakar had driven up north to Bradford, the girls family had given him details of her daily movements and he found her, two hundred metres from the local Tesco supermarket. He had pulled up beside her, wished her good day and asked her to get in the car and he would run her home. But the girl sensed something out of the ordinary, an inbuilt intuition that her cousin hadn't driven all this way for no reason. She politely declined his offer and Bakar got out of the car. There was a brief struggle, a struggle that the girl was never going to win and within seconds he had bundled her into the back seat, a single, well directed punch rendered her unconscious.

The bystander noted down the registration number of the car and alerted police. They found the car outside a derelict building on Saddleworth Moor four hours later. They were too late. The girl had been tortured, her unborn child cut from her belly and then she had been decapitated. They found Bakar digging her grave five hundred metres from the house.

Bakar was convicted and sentenced to life with a recommendation that he serve thirty years before being considered for release. Once Bakar knew that he would be spending virtually the rest of his life behind bars he devoted himself to teaching his view of Islam, ingrained into his psyche at the madrasa in Waziristan. He preached to anyone who wanted to listen, whether they were practicing Muslims or potential converts. He was a natural orator and a born salesman.

Because of the American led war in Afghanistan, it led to the Al Qaeda network escaping to the tribal lands of Waziristan; there they had a new avenue of recruiting members to the Al Qaeda cause. Many of the Imams at the madrasas in Waziristan joined Al Qaeda, and in turn their networks of religious teachers spread through the world. One of the tentacles reached as far as the new Imam taking Friday prayers at HMP Full Sutton.

Although Bakar was a true believer in radical Islam he was not approached to join Al Qaeda until a new Imam took over the Friday prayer group at HMP Full Sutton.

The Imam was a fully pledged member of Al Qaeda who had personally made his pledge of loyalty to the great Osama Bin Laden many years before the war in Afghanistan.

The Al Qaeda leadership had ordered the Imams to go on a recruitment drive to bolster their numbers after the ranks of Al Qaeda had been decimated by the many deaths at the hands of the Americans. The Al Qaeda leadership had also identified western prisons as a target area to recruit new soldiers. The prisons were full of weak young men with a bitter hatred to the society that had taken away their liberty.

When Bakar first met Dodds, he had nothing. No money, no family and no friends. He also had a heroin habit that Bakar knew he could exploit, and a conviction that could cause Dodds trouble on the main wings in HMP Full Sutton. Bakar knew that Dodds would be ripe for conversion to his version of radical Islam. Bakar decided to start by providing him free heroin. He also had money sent to his personal prison account. Through the prison Imam, Bakar arranged for Dodds to be transferred to the Islamic wing at HMP Full Sutton. Once there Bakar could work on totally radicalising his unwitting new recruit.

Bakar did not choose Dodds without reason. Despite his convictions and drug habit, Dodds did not look like a criminal or a violent person. He didn't stand out from the crowd and these attributes would be very useful in the future. He was, as the CIA would describe, *nondescript*. Bakar had also watched how Dodds completed crosswords and puzzles with ease and deduced that he was also highly intelligent. As the years passed it became apparent to Bakar that Khan was more than your run of the mill Muslim convert. Furthermore he had become a firm believer of Bakar's, some would say, distorted version of Islam.

Dodds or rather, Khan, was coming to the end of his sentence and Bakar knew that he needed to finish off the last part of his plan. The Imam had confirmed that the network had plans for Khan and he was ordered to contrive a situation where Khan would no longer be Khan and that he would convert back to Dodds and leave the Islamic wing.

Bakar had arranged and staged the whole incident. This was going to be achieved by an argument breaking out between Khan and another prisoner on the way to Friday prayers.

Before Friday prayers were called Khan went to Bakars cell for the very last time. "Muhammed, my friend, how you have changed in these past five years. Remember everything I have taught you and you will be contacted by the Imam soon after your release. He will guide you through to the next stage of your affiliation to Islam. We are all so very proud of you brother."

"Thank you for everything," Khan replied.

"Remember as soon as you leave this wing you must go back to being Dodds. Muhammed Khan will only be in your heart."

"Yes brother."

"And remember to keep your arm up. We have to make it look authentic but we don't want you seriously injured. We may never see each other again but you will always be my brother," Bakar said.

Tears welled up in Khan's eyes as he embraced Bakar for the last time.

"Goodbye," Khan said as he hugged his brother tightly.

"Goodbye, soldier of Islam," Bakar replied.

Khan turned his back on Bakar and made his way to muslim prayers.

Although Baker could not be one hundred per cent sure, he fully believed that Dodds was ready to fulfil all the teaching and doctrines that he had invested with him. As far as Bakar was concerned he had professionally and methodically radicalised Dodds over the last five years.

Muslim prayers last call, the Tannoy sounded as most of E wing left their cells to make their way to the makeshift mosque located in an old officers' gym that was separate from the main part of the prison.

Bakar made sure he was the last person to leave E wing, he made sure he was a long way away from the incident where Khan would be attacked.

Khan was nervous and more than a little frightened because he knew he had to take a knife. He only hoped that the attacker knew what he was doing. He made his way cautiously to Friday prayers and as usual entered the makeshift mosque. There was one blind spot just inside the gym, Khan knew that this would be the place where he would be attacked. He saw the flash of the blade, noticed at the last moment it was a homemade shank that his fellow Muslim inmate suddenly thrust towards him and as instructed lifted his arm to protect his face. He winced in pain as a splash of blood flew through the air and suddenly he felt quite feint. He dropped to his knees and cried out in pain.

Several of his brothers came to his aid and helped him up the corridor. He had a four inch wound down his left forearm and despite the fact there was a lot of blood his attacker had used a shank with a taped up blade that meant the cut would not penetrate to deeply into Khan's arm. Bakar did not want his protege permanently injured as the network had important plans for Mohammed Khan. Someone had alerted the prison officers and the alarm bells kicked into action. The tannoy announced that Friday prayers were cancelled yet again.

"Twenty stitches Khan, lucky it wasn't your face," the nurse said, "or worse, he could have stabbed you in the chest or the stomach.

The Full Sutton duty police officer looked on. "You want to make a statement?"

"No thanks," Khan said.

The duty officer sighed a sigh of resignation and then grinned. "Well now Khan, you can't go back to E wing, and you can't go back to the main wings. Looks like you gotta go on the numbers with all the nonces."

"Bollocks to all of that, I'll finish off my time down the block." He pointed to the blood stained robe on the floor. "And you can throw that stupid gown in the bin, fuck those carpet kissers, I want be called Dodds again, fuck Islam and all it stands for."

The prison nurse, prison officer and the duty police officer all looked at each other. It was becoming quite regular for so called white converts to give up Islam and go back to their previous selves, although normally it was just before they were released.

"Okay Dodds or Khan or whatever you want to be called. That mark will teach you a lesson for joining them Muslim fuckers. If I had my way you'd be tossed back onto E wing," he grunted, "you're just as bad as they are, kissing their muslim arses and worshipping a peadophile fucking prophet for the last six years. I've no fucking sympathy for you."

Khan nodded. "Whatever, just don't ever call me Khan again."

Dodds spent the next nine months down the block. Prisoners doing time down the block were segregated from each other but Dodds always made an effort to slag off Islam with any Muslim prisoners who ended up down there. This was all part of Bakar's plan and any prison records would show that Muhammed Khan was long gone and Dodds was Dodds again.

Nine months passed and the door of Khan's cell opened; he was led from the block to reception.

"Name and number," said the reception officer.

"Dodds 4836," he replied.

A few moments later the reception officer returned to the desk with a big blue box. The box contained all

Dodd's possessions when he first entered Full Sutton seven years earlier. Khan stripped down into his underwear and dressed in his old clothes. They were a bit of a tight fit but Dodds had remained relatively slim during his prison term.

"Fuck that Muslim shit," said Khan, just loud enough so that the prison Officer heard the remark. He walked through the gates of Full Sutton and into his first taste of freedom in many years. It felt good, the air tasted sweet. He noticed the peace and tranquility as he made his way to the visitors centre. In prison it was never ever quiet, there was always noise. Even when he prayed there was always someone somewhere making noise and interrupting his prayers to Allah.

He walked just a hundred yards from the visitor centre, where he caught a bus into York. From York bus station he got on a coach to Manchester where his probation officer had arranged his first meeting. As the coach made its way into the outskirts of Manchester it hit a traffic jam.

Dodds looked out of the window, he gazed up the road and saw a series of flashing blue lights.

"Bloody hell, what's this all about?" he said to nobody in particular.

"Another Old Bill road block," an elderly passenger answered.

The coach crept along until it too came to the start of the road block.

Dodd could see a police officer motion the coach driver to pull over into a security area. Moments later the coach doors opened and a police officer with a sniffer dog walked through the aisle. The dog never sat down and he sensed the sniffer dog had found nothing untoward. The officer with the sniffer dog left the coach and another police officer entered the coach.

He pointed to the back seat of the bus. "You, you and you off the coach," he said.

The officer went on to order nine individuals off the coach. They were either Asian or black. Dodds watched as other officers questioned each of the non-white passengers and then searched their belongings. After about half an hour the passengers were allowed back on the bus. For the remaining twenty minutes of their journey Dodds listened to the passengers moaning about the police and what had been going on since the football bombings.

Soon after he arrived in Manchester city centre; he had been in prison for a long time and as he walked through the city to his probation appointment he could see that Manchester had changed. Not so much that the city itself looked different but as he walked through the streets he could hear a multitude of different languages being spoken.   He also noticed that many Muslim women were now wearing the Burka, the men wearing other traditional Islamic clothing too. He remembered Bakar's words that Islam was growing and he would see the changes when he was released. He couldn't help as a smile pulled across his face.

Dodds met with his probation officer and went through all the usual talk about drugs and his behavioral problems. He left his probation appointment at 4 p.m. and started making his way to his probation hostel. He saw a phone box and rang the number he had memorised in his head.

"Hello."

Dodds heard a voice he recognised very well and made arrangements to meet the Imam and start the next stage of his training. The Imam referred to him as brother Khan. It felt good to hear his adopted Muslim name again. The Imam reinforced what Bakar had said during his training. He was instructed to go through probation without any incidents that would cause any recall back to prison.

"Yes Imam."

"I know I can trust you Brother Khan."

"I won't let you down."

"I know that Brother, you are a good Muslim."

After a few months Khan was allowed to leave the probation hostel and find his own home. The Imam gave him money for a deposit on a rented flat and also found him a job in a car wash. Khan didn't like his job but the Imam topped up his wages and helped out with regular injections of cash. The Imam told Khan to keep up the act of being a westerner and to show no sign that he had ever been influenced by Islamic doctrines.

The months went by and Khan found himself a girlfriend who he began to have a serious relationship with and it wasn't long before she announced that she was pregnant. It was all part of the grand plan. He needed a wife, he needed a child. They were expendable, it was as simple as that, they were part of his tool kit, the perfect western family. The script had already been written and Khan was more than happy to fill in the pieces.

A few weeks later the Imam made contact with Khan and arranged a meeting. He was told to take a day off work and to leave his mobile phone at home.

A couple of days later Khan met the Imam in a Manchester car park. Khan was told to get in the back of the van and to be quiet during the journey. The van had no windows so he had no real idea where he was going. Approximately an hour later the van came to halt and the van door opened. He found himself in a warehouse of some sort with all the windows painted over. The only light was provided by a few dimly lit bulbs scattered around the building.

"Over here," said a man in English but with a thick foreign accent.

Khan looked at the Imam for guidance. The Imam waved his hand and ushered Khan in the direction of the voice. Khan walked towards the man and as he came closer he could see that the man was wearing a mask.

"I am the person Bakar spoke about," he said.

Khan was drawn to the man, he felt strength in the man's voice and instinctively he knew that he was meeting someone very senior in the organisation he had pledged allegiance too.

"I will take you through to the final part of your training," he said, and you will become a real soldier of Islam."

"Yes brother."

"That is what you want isn't it?"

"Yes," said Khan nervously, "yes, yes, I want to fight," he repeated, this time with more conviction.

"okay Mohammed Khan, soldier of Islam, let us begin." He lifted a large cloth from the table and his eyes looked downwards.

"And this is an AK47 assault rifle."

CHAPTER 22

Sofian Ahmed had never planned to stay in the army very long, had always promised himself no more than a ten year stretch and he knew that the right time had arrived. He'd served his country well and was more than proud. It was difficult for a Muslim man in the British Army but on the whole most of his colleagues had accepted him and he'd made some lifelong friends. The British Army had been good to him, looked after him and even respected his religion, allowed him to practice it, sometimes in the most extreme of circumstances. He was proud to be British, proud of the country's tolerance and multi culturism and while he didn't always agree with some of the battles he had been pitched into involuntarily, he soon realised that it was about following orders and he couldn't begin to understand the politics behind certain conflicts.

CHAPTER 23

Mi5 Headquarters

"Okay Baxter, what have we got," Fletcher questioned.

"Well sir, we have managed to find minute fragments of what appear to be tracker devices at each of the three football bomb sites. These tracker devices work with mobile network SIM cards, the kind found in a mobile phone. The bad news is that the SIM cards would have been incinerated in the blast."

Fletcher let out a sigh, "have we managed to obtain the identities of any of the suicide bombers?"

Baxter shook his head. "At the moment we have bits of eleven body parts with different DNA which we have not been able to match with any of the missing persons reported by the families of those that attended the football matches. However, it's safe to assume that the three suicide bombers are likely to be amongst these eleven Sir."

Fletcher made a note in his work pad and placed his pen on the desk. Progress was being made but it was painstakingly slow considering the resources that the

Home Office had thrown at the investigation. Fletcher himself had visited all three bomb sites and witnessed first-hand the amount of carnage that the bombs had caused.

"And Abdullah?" he queried.

"We have all his phone calls logged Sir, he only made one call in all his time at Belmarsh. The number is recorded as a Pakistani pay as you go mobile phone. Translation of the call revealed that Abdullah left a message stating how the weather was and then he hung up."

"But someone must have answered the phone to get it cleared to take prisoners' calls. I know that for a fact from the Ismail case a few years back?" Fletcher said as he grew more and more frustrated.

"We have ascertained that when the number was cleared by the prison sensor department the phone was located in Bradford. HMP officers don't actually make the calls to non-English speakers, it's farmed out to a local English Language College. There are over one hundred different languages spoken at Belmarsh prison alone and the prison can't find officers who can speak those different languages."

"Unbelievable, un fucking believable." Fletcher said as he slapped his hand on the desk in frustration.

"Quite Sir. The cell site records and record logs from Vodafone confirm that the mobile was immediately turned off and the battery removed after taking the call from the prison sensor department. The mobile was only turned on again three months later for six minutes.

Six minutes is the time that each mobile takes to send a signal to the closest cell site tower."

"Which is just enough time to receive the voicemail message about the weather?" Fletcher questioned.

"Correct, sir."

"So, we have to trace the DNA of these eleven body parts to somehow trace the identity of these suicide bombers."

Baxter nodded.

Fletcher continued. "Has anyone done a criminal records check with the DNA?"

"Not yet Sir, and we have good reason to believe the suicide bombers weren't even English, more likely to have be foreign."

Fletcher eased himself back into his chair. "We don't know diddly squat at this moment so check out the Criminal Records with the DNA, you never know, we might just get lucky."

"Yes Sir."

Fletcher shook his head, mumbled under his breath, "like trying to find a fucking needle in a haystack."

He stood. He looked weary, his patience was wearing thin. "I'm going to speak to the Americans to see if we can use their 'Quartz' programme to trace any patterns from the blast zones to Bradford."

The Quartz programme was a computer programme designed to find patterns with cell site numbers. The CIA's super computers number-crunched billions of calls in relation to location and persons of interest.

Fletcher picked up the black encrypted phone and dialed a number for Langley CIA headquarters.

The operator gave the standard answer. "Good morning, CIA officer McGinley, how can I be of assistance."

CHAPTER 24

By the time Taylor was released from Colchester military prison he had recruited eight good men. All the men that he had approached needed very little persuasion to join Taylor's cause. They were all either already released or due to be released around the time Taylor was due to be freed. None of the seven knew about the eighth man, the man of mystery called Drago. Back on Civvy Street Taylor soon made contact with Corporal King and Private Brown from 'A' company. Taylor explained exactly what he was attempting to set up and both men agreed to join Taylor's cause. Corporal King had recovered from the horrific burns he received when the Chinook was blown up and was lucky to be alive although he had been left with horrific scarring to the upper body, the face and head. He was still a serving paratrooper though, and could be very handy in sourcing weapons to fight the campaign. He was in charge of the armoury records and responsible for taking older or faulty weapons out of commission and claimed it was a simple matter of accountancy, he was at the top, there were no checks after his paperwork had been signed off.

Taylor also made contact with a few of his old ICF mates and was putting out his feelers to source the various assets needed to fight the private war. He wanted a covered yard or warehouse of some sort that was out of prying eyes but also in a suburban setting. As luck would have it Taylor got chatting to one of his old ICF contacts, a man called Darren Swindon, who told him he had bought an old pub in Romford that was due to be refurbished in about a year's time. Taylor told Swindon that he was looking for a place to help out old veterans from the Iraq and Afghan wars.

Swindon had a lot of respect for Taylor and after listening to his request offered him the use of the pub until the refurbishment work started.

He took Taylor down to the pub to check the place over. It was perfect for what he had in mind.

Swindon handed him the keys. "Just one thing, no growing cannabis in there mate."

"Sure thing," Taylor smiled.

Taylor rang his new recruits from a phone box and the first meeting was arranged on a rainy Tuesday night. All the men were told to leave their mobile phones at home and make their way on public transport. Each man was told to inform their family members that they were going to a war veteran's meeting.

There was a buzz of expectation as one by one, the men drifted into the vast boarded up pub.

Taylor welcomed them warmly. "okay lads, we're all here. Most of you know each other from Colchester but I want to introduce you to two more men from my unit in Afghanistan." He pointed to two men at the front of the room. "Kev Brown and Richy King."

The two men looked around and nodded politely.

"I'm not going to do a big speech as you all know exactly why you're here. The average Englishman has sat around too fucking much, we have all had enough and we need to avenge the deaths of those people who died in the football bombings. We have sat on the fence too long, way too fucking long and we have waited for our government to take charge."

He scanned the room and looked at every individual man. "But they haven't acted have they?"

One or two men shook their heads in agreement, a couple of them said no out loud.

Images of his dead son flashed through his mind as he spoke. He took a deep breath, he could almost smell the carnage of that fateful day, taste the death and destruction, burning flesh, black acrid smoke.

He shook the thoughts away before he spoke again. "It's time to fight back, it's time to nip this in the bud, because I'm telling you these new fuckas haven't even started to get serious and if they get serious we might as well run up the white flag now."

"How do you mean Mick?" one of the lads asked.

Taylor took a deep breath before he spoke. "Whoever did these football ground bombs have upped the ante. In the past these so called Islamic State terror attacks have been a bit shit in my opinion. The bombs have been shit, their planning has been shit and they haven't been able to get their hands on anything of real substance. They've used knives and machetes, even fucking trucks, driving them into crowds taking out just a few dozen at a time." His hand pointed at the assembled men. "Most of you know what sort of damage a real bomb can do, and i'm quite sure that the motherfuckers who did these football bombings had military training."

"So far they've had it all their own way and its time we started our own little campaign. We have no way of finding these cunts so were gonna see how they like it when a few of their people get a taste of war. Make the fuckers think before they blow up our people!"

Richy King raised his hand. "I hear what you're saying Mick, you're telling us that if we give them a bit of their own medicine they may well have second thoughts on killing our innocents."

"That's exactly what I am saying Richy, and we need money and we need fucking weapons to put my plan into action."

Richy nodded his approval, a few of the men whispered among themselves. Taylor sensed a positive vibe.

"Our first job is to take down a security van at the Snaresbrook Group 4 depot," he said, "I've being recceing the depot since I was released."

This caused a few raised eyebrows amongst the men but Taylor went on to explain why their first act in their private war was not an attack on an Islamic target but an armed robbery in London. This could have divided opinion amongst the group but none of the men gave any indication that committing this crime was outside the proposition that Taylor had sold them when they were being recruited.

Taylor had prepared well. He gave them all a file containing photos, maps and every detail he had gathered to take down the security van, and most importantly get away with the job. Corporal King had managed to steal some weapons and a small quantity of plastic explosives from his barracks. Cars had to be stolen, disguises had to be made and all manner of jobs needed to be carried out to make sure the security van was taken down like a military operation.

"I'll give you as much time as you need to digest everything, you can do it now, there's no time like the present," he said.

One by one the men read their files and patiently waited for the slower readers to finish. After an hour or so all the men were ready.

"Any feedback?" said Taylor.

"It's a very good plan, Mick. We don't really want to hurt any civilians unless they're Muzzies, right?" Raymond said.

A few of the men laughed.

"Don't worry about hurting Muzzies, they have no idea what's coming to them," he said seriously.

The conversation drifted on, a few questions were asked. Taylor answered each one with an air of professionalism. He had done his homework, all of the men could see that.

Corporal King made a comment. "Mick, what are we going to call ourselves, I mean we to have a name or something?"

"How about, AJI, the Anti-Jihadi Army," one of the other men said.

"Sounds daft that, how about the Anti-Islamic Army?" another said.

Taylor held up a hand. "Okay lads, simmer down, to be honest I haven't given it much thought but yes, we need a name when we announce what we are doing. How about we'll put a few names in a jar and take a vote on them?"

Taylor handed out some paper and pens and after ten minutes deliberation between the group, collected six names and crumpled them up into balls then put them in a glass.

"Kingy, do the honours," Taylor said, offering him the glass.

King jumped from his chair, put his hand in the glass and pulled out one of the pieces of paper. Taylor read the name on the paper and then read it out.

"Okay lads, it looks like we are going to be called the English National Army. I like the sound of that to be honest."

There was a spontaneous round of applause as the group of men signaled their approval. Taylor said it had been unanimously agreed and they could move on to discuss the van theft in greater detail. They sat together for another two hours before Taylor announced that the meeting was over and that they would begin their surveillance of the vans coming to and from the depot within the next twenty-four hours.

Over the next four weeks each and every Group 4 security van that left the depot at Snaresbrook, South London was followed carefully at a distance. The surveillance on the ground was undertaken by Taylor, he walked the leather off his shoes and during some cold days his old injury played up terrible. It took a lot of skill and discipline to follow the vans without anyone noticing the tails but he was fairly confident with the way the operation had went. They had all their notes, long distance photographs and timings, the information had been gathered and the men met at the pub to discuss all of the options including which van was likely to have the most cash and exactly when they were going to take it down.

Eventually Taylor stood and called the meeting to order. "Okay lads, it looks like the best time to take down a van is the first Saturday after the 25th of each month."

"Why's that?" King asked.

Taylor nodded. "Let me explain why. I've done bit of research and most people now get paid after the 25th of each month and logic dictates that most people will have a spend up on the following Saturday.

"Okay, that makes sense, but which van?" King said.

"I'm coming to that Kingy, I have been looking at all your surveillance reports and I reckon the McDonald's' van is our best bet. It looks like Group 4 has a dedicated McDonald's van, whereas most of the other vans visit multiple different businesses.

I've actually sat in the McDonald's restaurants and watched how many people pay with cash as opposed to credit cards. It's nearly all cash and I sat in there for just over an hour counting the people, there was a constant queue with six cashiers taking money on average every two minutes.

"Fuck me," King said, "I never realised they were that busy."

Taylor nodded. "Yes they are, they make fucking fortunes and this is where it gets interesting. The van goes to eight separate McDonald's restaurants on each and every Wednesday and then not again until the next Saturday. So we will have the takings from late Wednesday afternoon until late Saturday afternoon. That's three days' worth of takings from eight shops."

There was an audible murmur of surprise, one or two of the men whispered to each other.

The general consensus of opinion was that the McDonald's van was the one.

Taylor put a map of the Group 4 security depot and the surrounding roads on the large table.

"These Group 4 idiots have done us a right favour. It looks like it's their policy to process one van at a time. The security vans all queue up at the side of the road while they wait to be summoned into the compound. Have a look at these photos."

Taylor handed an IPad to King.

"Show the lads Kingy."

He waited and watched as the IPad was handed from one man to the next.

"Another mistake they make is that their vans all converge at the depot around 6 p.m. after doing their collections. The McDonald's van is usually one of the last vans to arrive back at the depot. They use side of the road to park up while waiting to be called into the depot. So as our van pulls into the back of the line that's when we'll make our move."

The men muttered their satisfaction as Taylor took them through every detail of the well thought out plan.

"Okay," he said, bringing order back to the room, "now, we don't want any boxes or bags thrown out through the chute. They could have delayed dye timers or be bags with small notes in. We have to get them to open up the van so we can take the money ourselves. Sean and Derrick will be a hundred metres north of the van laying down puncture strips ready for any random police cars. Me and Kingy will be a hundred metres south of the van ready doing the same. Brownie will be monitoring the airwaves to see what the Old Bill are up to. Each man has a specific role."

The rest of the evening was spent clarifying various aspects of the robbery. Taylor was more than satisfied that his men were ready and up for the job.

CHAPTER 25

Snaresbrook, East London

Lester Jackson had been driving the security van all day and he was happy to be near to the end of his shift. He was getting the normal banter from his mates in the back of the van which usually referred to them stuffing fifty pound notes up their arses and then flying off to the Bahamas.

He pulled into the depot road and saw the queue of security vans parked up on the left hand side of the road. He pulled his van into the back of the line and waited for his turn. He looked at the clock on the dashboard and let out a little sigh. It was 6.15 p.m. He had done this hundreds of times and it still pissed him off that they had to wait so long to complete the final part of the shift. Lester watched as a dark blue people carrier pulled up alongside him.

Before he had a second to assess what was happening, three men jumped out of the car. They were wearing full face crash helmets, two of them carrying what looked like automatic rifles.

"Oh fuck," Lester whispered to himself, "oh holy shit." One of the men placed a cardboard sheet directly onto his windscreen. Lester read it.

OPEN BACK OF VAN.

The man took a step back, pointed his rifle into the sky and fired a shot. He then pointed the gun at Lester.

Instinct and training kicked in as Lester located and pressed the security buzzer under the steering wheel, safe in the knowledge an instant message had been sent to the depot and to any armed response vehicles in the immediate vicinity. Lester knew he had to sit tight, the van he was driving was bulletproof. Within just a few seconds the man was showing him something through the barred window. It looked like some sort of plasticine with some wires attached to a battery. The man let Lester have a good look at the device before he walked over to the same people carrier that the robbers had arrived and stuck it on the windscreen.

The three men walked back towards Lester and appeared to take shelter on the kerb side of the security van. Lester looked back towards the people carrier. Seconds later he heard a loud bang and saw the people carrier explode in a massive ball of flame. His mates in the back of the van were shouting at him asking what was going on. But everything was happening so fast Lester couldn't find the words to explain. All he knew was he was in the middle of an armed robbery and a bomb had just exploded blowing a people carrier to bits.

The man who placed the device on the people carrier walked to the front of Lester's windscreen. He held up an identical device and showed it to Lester before sticking it firmly on Lester's windscreen. He held up the same cardboard sheet, 'OPEN BACK OF VAN.'

Lester shit himself. He had never known real fear before and he thought he was going to die.

He turned to his mates in the back and screamed at the top of his voice. "For fuck's sake open the fucking van. They've got a bomb, a fucking bomb."

Desmond Driscoll slid the viewing hatch to see what was going on and saw the vehicle burning fiercely out of control. Lester was pointing furiously at the device attached to his window.

"A bomb Des, it's a fucking bomb, open the bloody doors man."

Desmond froze for a second and Lester saw the same fear that he was feeling reflected in Desmond's pale, wide-eyed face. He was petrified.

"Open the fucking van Desmond its a bomb," he begged.

Desmond's nostrils filled with the stench of shit and it seemed to shake him out of his stupor like the worst smelling salts known to man. He turned round and stumbled towards the back of the van and fumbling with the keys he managed to open the back of the van. He saw two men standing there with machine guns. One of them pointed a gun directly at Desmond and the other guard.

"Open the internal safe or I'll shoot you," one of the masked man said.

Desmond didn't need any more persuasion, his hands were in the air.

"Don't shoot please, I'll do whatever you say, the cunts don't pay me enough to be brave." Desmond was on his knees selecting the right keys and immediately opened up the safe.

"It's done, it's open," he squealed out.

The masked man reached for his collar and dragged him from the back of the van. "Okay, lie on the ground and keep your eyes shut and you might just make it home to your family in one fucking piece."

Desmond and the other guard threw themselves onto the ground. Desmond had no intention of opening his eyes. He heard some banging and then cars doors opening and slamming shut, followed by the sound of a car screeching away. Desmond waited about minute or so before he opened his eyes and sat up. He could smell the stench of the burning vehicle and his own shit.

As Desmond burst into tears he looked at his watch. It was 6.18 p.m. The armed robbery had taken just three minutes.

CHAPTER 26

The Pub, Romford

Taylor had listened to the entire robbery on his mic. He was pleased with the way each member of the team had handled themselves and he allowed himself an imaginary pat on the back. He had chosen his men well. There was a big pile of money stacked up on the table. Taylor and King counted out the money in front of everyone.

As he made the final calculations on a scrap of paper he held it up so that everyone could see the grand total. "One hundred and eighty seven thousand pounds. Well done lads, that's not to be sniffed at," he said.

The men were still buzzing with what they had just done the previous evening. They were all watching the TV as the London news channels relayed the whole robbery. They sat with a couple of celebratory beers as the TV showed the grainy images that were recorded on the various CCTV cameras up and down the road. The gang was described as a well-planned group of professional armed robbers who had made a daring attack on a London Group 4 security depot. The media was also speculating that the police had taken the foot off the pedal on domestic crime since the Islamic terror attacks. They said it was another example of under staffing. There were not enough police on London's streets.

A senior police offer came onto the news channel and reinforced the police's view that it was a gang of professional armed robbers. He said they would definitely be caught, referring to their previous track record of solving these types of robberies. When questioned by a journalist the police officer denied any connection with the Islamic terror attacks and the rise in serious domestic crime.

Taylor turned off the TV and faced the men, "okay lads, well planned and well executed, you heard what they said. It went exactly to plan, the added bonus that the Old Bill believe that it was experienced armed robbers." He grinned, "and to the best of my knowledge not one of you has ever done anything like this before."

The cash had been divided into piles. He handed each of the men a bundle of notes.

"It's two grand each for living expenses. We're not criminals, we're soldiers and any soldier needs to be paid," he said.

It was enough to get by but not too much to encourage lavish behaviour that would bring unwanted attention. The rest of the money was hidden by Taylor in the depths of the pub's huge basement. The men left the pub under strict orders to keep a low profile and most importantly not to say a single word to wives, girlfriends and other family members.

CHAPTER 27

The following day Taylor caught a train down to Southend on Sea. He walked down through the High Street and onto the seafront and bought a ticket for Southend Pier. A dilapidated sign said, *'Welcome to the longest pier in the world.'*

"We shut at four p.m.," the ticket man said in a monotone voice.

Taylor nodded as he walked away.

There were a few other people walking along the pier but they were heading in the opposite direction, making their way back to shore. About three quarters of the way down Taylor saw a man sitting in a shelter with a fishing rod propped up against the pier railing. There was a clear bucket close to him that held some fish that he had obviously caught. Taylor's attention was drawn to the fish as he passed by, so much so that he didn't really take notice of the old man and his fishing gear.

"Mr Taylor," the fisherman said.

Taylor stopped and smiled. He knew that it was Drago, not from his appearance but from the sound of his voice. Drago had a full beard and looked a good fifteen years older. There were wisps of grey hair sticking out from under his hat.

"I thought you said meet me at the end of the Pier, Sherlock fucking Holmes, where did you get that disguise from?"

"Just a further precaution." His hand made a circular motion. "Look, we can see for miles in every direction. There are very few people who will take a walk along Southend pier at this hour. It's the perfect place to meet and to get to the end of the pier you would have had to walk past me." He said.

Taylor looked around. Drago was right; it was nearly impossible for someone to eaves drop on their conversation.

"I see the devices worked well," said Drago.

"Yes, very well."

"Your men must have been impressed with your talents."

Taylor nodded. "Don't worry Drago, no one knows who you are. I handled enough IEDs in Afghanistan for the men to think I made the devices myself."

"Good, let's keep it like that Mick. Let's discuss starting this war with something a bit spectacular."

"Yes, let's get down to business," Taylor said.

Drago stood and leaned against the pier railings. He looked out towards the horizon as he spoke. "A long time ago I had a trial for the Surrey County cricket team. I love all sport but cricket is in my blood."

Taylor was getting used to these around the houses conversations, he knew it was Drago's way and he would eventually get to the point.

"I also hate sportsmen who cheat. Especially when they accept bribes for financial gain."

Where the hell was this going Taylor thought to himself.

"Next month England play Pakistan in a series of 20 20 night matches at the Oval," Drago said calmly.

Taylor looked hard at Drago. Both men knew that what they were about to discuss would be upping the ante big time.

After fifteen minutes Drago stopped talking, he had revealed every aspect of his plan…almost.

Taylor was stunned, never would he have believed the enormity of what Drago was planning, it could start a war between England and Pakistan. Taylor didn't know if his face showed weakness, fear or dread but Drago read something in it.

"Remember we lost over three hundred souls last year… many of them children. Just remember why you approached me." He said sternly.

"I know, I am fully up for it," Taylor said, "I just didn't realise it would be so big."

"Big is what I do, this will be huge. I need demolition grade explosives; at least one hundred kilograms. We cannot risk any more thefts from army barracks and in any event after the Snaresbrook incident I imagine all the armouries have tightened their security. It won't be hard for the forensics to realise it was PE - 4 that was used, with a possible source in the British Army."

They ran through the plan again. Drago said the Muslim casualties were sure to be very high, running into the thousands.

"They run down a few tourists with a stolen transit and call it a terrorist attack," he said, "I'll show the fuckers what real terror is."

Taylor looked out to sea and felt the wind change direction. They had talked and planned and now Drago was starting to pack his fishing gear away.

"This is your share from the Group 4 job," Taylor said as he handed Drago an envelope. "It's what I gave to each of the men."

Drago took the envelope and saw it was stuffed full of cash. He handed the envelope back.

"I am here for revenge, Mick... nothing else."

Taylor said nothing. He put the envelope back in his pocket.

"Do you want to walk back first? keep our distance," Taylor asked.

"I'm not walking anywhere," he said.

He walked to the edge of the pier and started to climb down some old pier ladders. Taylor looked over the edge of the pier and saw him climb into a small boat with an outboard motor. He looked up at Taylor.

"Them fuckers deserve it for cheating at cricket," he shouted.

Before Taylor could reply Drago had started the engine and the boat began to pull away from the pier. Taylor could never really be sure whether Drago was toying with him or not but one thing for sure was that Drago was an evil fucker deep down and not a man to be crossed.

Taylor watched as the small craft gradually disappeared from view and he turned and began the long walk back to shore, a wealth of thoughts going through his head.

The next day he called a team meeting at the pub, Drago had his plan but Taylor also had something he needed to get off his chest.

He spoke to his men with passion, he was looking for volunteers but he would head the mission north, he wouldn't ask any of his men to do anything he wouldn't.

"I want to take a small unit to Newcastle," he said, "no more than three or four men and when I tell you why, and what's happening, particularly in the north of the country you won't fucking believe it."

Taylor spoke of the Muslim grooming gangs, men who specifically targeted vulnerable white schoolgirls with the sole purpose of gang raping them. He spoke about a media blackout but couldn't explain why. He said how it had been going on for nearly twenty years and how over two hundred gangs had been found and prosecuted and yet it hardly made page nine in The Sun newspaper.

"Can you imagine the fallout if a British gang had been caught doing this in a Muslim country?"

"They'd be hung drawn and quartered," Richy said.

"They say white girls are filth," Taylor said, "they sleep around and they deserve to be raped. That's why they do it, they say it's a punishment from Allah for their immoral lifestyle and it's their duty."

"They really believe this shit?" Brown asked.

"You'd better fucking believe it."

Brown raised his hand. "So why are we going to Newcastle?"

Taylor had done his homework. The lap top had been power point prepared and rigged up to the overhead projector. He pressed a button. A police mugshot appeared on the screen.

He pointed to the man in Muslim head gear. "Jabbar Kouri, the undoubted ringleader of a gang deliberately targeting fourteen and fifteen year old girls in care. His gang raped at least thirty underage girls that we know of, the case was proved at Newcastle Crown Court and his accomplices jailed for a combined period of over two hundred years."

Richy grinned, "a result then Mick eh?"

Taylor shook his head, "not the result we wanted. Kouri got off on a fake alibi, his gang all backed him up, they took the wrap and the poor girls were too frightened to testify against him in court."

"The bastard," Richy said.

Taylor nodded. "Not one of them would pick him out on an ID parade. The cunt is still walking the streets like me and you."

"Fuck off," Brown said.

"He is, and that's why we are heading to Newcastle, to hang this fucking rapist from the Tyne Bridge.

While Taylor dealt with the Jabbar Kouri matter he also arranged for the remaining men of the English National Army to raid a demolition company in Reading. The robbery went like clockwork and Taylor's small band of brothers now had one hundred kilograms of demolition grade explosives, otherwise known as dynamite.

This robbery was also on the news but the fact a lone security guard was threatened at gun point did not make much of a headline in the UK newsrooms, they had much more pressing stories to investigate. Taylor never told his men why they needed the explosives nor did any of the men seek to ask why. They were soldiers and used 'need to know basis' rule.

CHAPTER 28

The one thing Mick Taylor wanted was a headline making incident, something that couldn't be hidden or brushed under the carpet. In the end he decided to use two of his most trusted men, Richy King and Kev Brown. It was enough. He'd trust them with his life. Kev Brown had been instructed to go to Newcastle and do all the ground work on this Kouri rapist and after three weeks, Brown sent for Taylor and King to make the long journey up North.

The long drive north was exactly that... long. He'd no great desire to head that far north ever again. He remembered the trips up to Newcastle and Sunderland in the old ICF days, even by train it seemed to take forever. This time the train was off limits, too many cameras. They'd stolen a van from Watford, put false plates on and abandoned it just outside Leeds. They'd taken another vehicle for the last part of their journey and dumped it in a multi storey car park in Gateshead. They'd walked from Gateshead to Newcastle across the Tyne Bridge. The arch of the bridge was over fifty metres high and they'd use every inch of that expanse to get their message across. Once they crossed the bridge they slipped into a small bar and met up with Brown and discussed their plan of attack. It was all so simple, Kouri attended the same Mosque without fail, every Friday, for prayers and afterwards, walked a thousand yards to his home in a modest area of Newcastle called Elswick. He walked through a park, an almost deserted park, not the sort of park you'd feel safe in after dark. Brown had not been idle in the previous three weeks and had compiled a detailed dossier on Kouri and his pattern never changed. Photos, maps and even a short video gave the three man team a complete picture of their target.

They hit Kouri just after nine o'clock in the evening, he had finished his Maghrib prayers and hung around the Mosque for a while, just like Brown had said he would.

Brown had asked him the time and as Kouri had looked at his watch he landed an uppercut that shattered his jawbone and rendered him completely unconscious. Brown hadn't been the Southern region boxing champion for nothing, Taylor picked his men personally. Brown signaled to his two accomplices and they had driven another stolen car, the short distance into the park. They'd killed the lights and bundled Kouri into the boot. He was still unconscious when they arrived at their final destination, a small cottage in the middle of the moors, just outside Hexham in Northumberland. It was bleak, desolate, everything it needed to be and they tortured Kouri for the best part of seven days until his heart eventually gave out. He could take no more, it was nature's way.

The next part of the operation was almost certainly the most risky and there was a real danger of being seen and of course caught in possession of a corpse. But they were all professional British soldiers, Richy King was an expert climber, a mountaineering expert and took on the responsibility of scaling the ninety year old iconic structure. It was 4 am as King walked along the deserted road headed towards the Tyne Bridge. It was ridiculously easy, hand and footholds in abundance and he scaled the structure within four minutes. Taylor and Brown had parked the van up a side road only a few minutes drive from the bridge. Both Newcastle and Gateshead were at their quietest with most of the citizens fast asleep and the only real concern for Taylor and his plan was the chance of a random police patrol car discovering them in the final act.

King sent Taylor a text message stating to go now. After a minute King saw the van drive on to the bridge and slow down just before the point where King was positioned. King looked both ways and there was no traffic coming in either direction. He quickly dropped the nylon rope he had been carrying down to the ground along with a second rope attached to a simple pulley system.

Taylor and Brown drove up to the point and quickly open the back of the van and dragged Kouri's body over to the two ropes. They attached one rope around the dead mans neck and then they both pulled hard on the second rope and the pulley system quickly hoisted Kouri's body into the night sky. It took no more than ten seconds. Once the body was safely secured in the correct position, Kingy cut the slack from the pulley rope and then ran a large banner across the bridge.

As dawn broke and the communities of Newcastle and Gateshead began to make their way across the famous Tyne bridge they were met with a gruesome sight. A banner that read in plain and simple terms.

MUSLIM RAPIST

In the centre of the banner and dangling from a rope around his neck was an asian man.

It was midday before a specialist police mountaineering team eventually cut the body of Jabbar Kouri down from the Tyne Bridge. They had been hampered by those responsible as someone had greased all the foot and handholds making access to the body much more difficult. The authorities had closed the bridge just after 8am, but by that time over thirty thousand commuters had passed underneath him, they had taken photographs and video, every news team in the western world had precise, detailed images and video footage of the body dancing in the wind. By two in the afternoon his name had been given or leaked to the press and the more astute journalists and media men had done a little investigating. On the early evening news the topic of Muslim Grooming Gangs and the name of Jabbar Kouri was on everybody's lips, his name was the most searched name on Google that day. Taylor sat in a hotel room at Scotch Corner with his two associates and they all agreed that the operation couldn't have gone any better. At ten, they slipped down to the residents bar to take a well earned celebratory drink. Taylor allowed them two drinks. No more.

CHAPTER 29

Drago bought a second hand IPad and sat in a local McDonald's restaurant. He logged on using the McDonald's Wi-Fi and searched for Lambeth Council planning applications. He typed in the Vauxhall End at the Oval Cricket Ground and the computer screen revealed a detailed architect's drawing of the new stand at the Vauxhall End of the cricket ground.

Drago clicked on the link for the structural engineer's report. Sure enough, up popped a detailed diagram revealing all of the structural loads of the new stand. He saved the document onto his IPad then returned home to his Fulham apartment. He switched on the kettle and made a cup of mint tea and then printed off the structural engineer's report that he'd saved from earlier. Drago studied the document and made detailed calculations to ascertain the load bearing points of the 16,000 capacity stand. He took his IPad and printer to the garage and smashed them to pieces with a hammer. He separated the IPad's hard drive and again smashed that into pulp. And finally, he rode his bike to a local river and threw the smashed up electronic parts into the rushing water of the Thames.

The Oval Cricket Ground, London.

Drago was a cricket fan. He had watched many England v Pakistan matches and had been to the Oval on various different occasions. There was a week to go until England played Pakistan in a third and final 20 20 international match. They were tied at one, one, and with the final game being the decider and in London, it was of course a sell-out, the entire UK Pakistani community was trying to get a ticket. The match was due to be played on a Saturday night, commencing at 7 p.m. The game would be played under the famous Oval floodlights.

Drago had plans to make it a very, very memorable match, but for all the wrong reasons, or maybe right reasons depending on which side of the fence you were sitting on.

Drago had been an explosives expert in the SAS. He was trained to blow up military targets. One of his skillsets was the demolition of buildings. It could be said that it was his specialty bringing down a building with explosives was not as easy as it looked in the movies. Structural points had to be assessed, discovered and taken out first and foremost. If it were executed correctly the structures own weight normally took down the rest of the building.

Drago had a very simple plan. Surrey were playing a home test match against Durham seven days before the International. The match was a non-entity as Surrey and Durham counties were both mid table in the English cricket league and had nothing really to play for. This meant a low attendance, which in turn meant very little match day security personnel.

It was perfectly normal for cricket fans to bring large ice boxes to matches as a typical day at a test match could be seven to eight hours. Drago had bought his ticket for the new Vauxhall End main stand at a London kiosk. He had a full beard, an Australian style floppy hat and big dark sunglasses, all the things needed for a long day watching a cricket match. It would also ensure that the limited security cameras could not pick out Drago's face as he entered the stadium.

The CCTV security system was basic and old. The pictures were grainy and not very detailed. But then again there was never any trouble at a cricket ground so it didn't really matter. The few elderly ground stewards at the stadium soon settled down to watch the match and didn't notice an inconspicuous gentleman leave his seat at about 4 p.m. He made his way towards the maintenance area of the main stand. Had anyone taken any notice they may have noticed that the gentlemen had not taken any refreshments from the large ice box that he had brought to the ground, not once.

Drago was strong, very strong and it took all his strength to carry the icebox in a way that hid the weight of its contents. Drago had memorised which door would take him into the depths of the stand. The door was locked as he'd envisaged, so he quickly picked the lock and entered into a stairwell. He locked the door behind him and made his way downwards into the basement in the depths of the main stand.

There was a corridor that ran the entire length of the new Vauxhall End stand and here the main steel supports that bore all that weight were located. Working in silence he measured the steel supports to make sure they coincided with the engineer's plans he'd downloaded from the council planning application. Bingo thought Drago, everything was as it was said to be.

He located a storage cupboard, opened it and climbed in. This was the worst bit, he would need to stay there for a good many hours. He was unable to re-emerge into the corridor until the last ball had been bowled and everybody had gone home.

He climbed out of the cupboard just after two in the morning and set to work. He quickly put together the components of the four bombs. Each of the bombs contained twenty four and a half kilograms of the stolen dynamite. The next part was a bit tricky as Drago had to make sure the explosives were not discovered. Drago knew from experience that most people never looked up so he planned to strap the explosives at the point where the steel column touched the concrete ceiling. The only problem was that this point, where the steel column went into the ceiling was three metres high.

Drago searched for some ladders that may have been stored in the basement. He was out of luck. But he always planned ahead and had brought with him some commercial grade Velcro strips which he spray glued onto both sides of the four steel columns. He waited ten minutes for the glue to set and then wrapped rope around his waist and put on some clothes that had Velcro stitched into the inner lower legs and also the forearms. Drago pulled himself up to the top level of the Velcro strips and glued on the next level and then the next until the makeshift Velcro ladder took him to the position where the steel column entered into the concrete floor. Drago completed the same procedure on each of the four steel columns.

Once all the glue had dried he tested the improvised Velcro ladder on each of the four steel columns. He couldn't take the chance of falling to the floor as he carried one of the bombs.

"Perfect" muttered Drago to himself.

He then prepared the explosives and climbed up the Velcro ladders and secured them to the steel column using plastic ties. He wrapped the devices in masking tape and spray painted them as best he could. Drago had even matched the paint with the same colour that was recorded in the architect's building plans.

In normal circumstances when bringing down a building he would have used simple timing devices to detonate the explosives but unfortunately he could not rely on the good old English weather which could well postpone any cricket match. Drago had to use a system of remote control relays that would allow him to choose exactly when to detonate the explosives.

And he knew that the mass of the building would block a normal remote control trigger device so he had to rig a system where the remote control signal was sent to a point just inside the basement and then that signal was passed on to the actual explosive devices.

Drago found an air vent in the basement, unscrewed its cover and placed a remote control signal relay box inside the vent. He switched it on and then screwed back the cover. He carefully turned on the four explosive receivers to a bandwidth of 843mhz. The detonator switch actually attached to the four bombs was tuned to 957mhz so it could not be detonated by mistake. He sent a signal to the relay box which in turn sent a signal to the explosive receivers. Drago's monitoring equipment showed that everything was working correctly but he had rigged up a backup system to double check the system was working. Drago had chosen infrared antennas on the four bombs so that only someone with infrared, night vision glasses could detect the bombs' antennas and therefore the bombs ignition system. Each antenna had a tiny red light that flashed to indicate the receiver was working.

He turned off the lights in the basement, put on some infrared goggles and saw that each of the four explosives' antennas were flashing. He smiled to himself. The receivers were on and working. Drago turned the lights back on and tuned in the relay signal box, the explosives' receivers and crucially the detonators, all to 957mhz. Once he was positive that all the bombs were working correctly he scraped off the Velcro strips from the steel columns and studied his work. At eye level there was the faintest of marks where some of the clear glue had been sprayed onto the steel columns but he was confident no one would notice. He looked upwards to the bombs. Again, all that any observer would have seen was the tiny tip of the antenna sticking out from some uneven metal on the steel columns.

His work in the basement was finished so he headed outside to find the corresponding air vent. Again all the air vents were recorded on the architect's building plans so Drago knew exactly which one corresponded with the air vent where he had placed the relay box in the basement. He placed another relay box in an air vent located on the outer wall of the huge stand and set the frequency to 957mhz.

Afterwards he slipped into one of the cricket ground's toilets and sat in a cubicle. He changed back into his cricket spectator clothes and poured a miniature bottle of whiskey over himself. If he was found before the ground opened he would just say he fell asleep drunk in the toilet. Drago had thought of everything.

At 11 a.m. he heard the first of the days spectators come into the toilet. He waited a few minutes before he calmly left the toilet and went to his seat. Drago watched the final day of the Surrey v Durham test match with one eye on the game and the other on the basement door where the explosives were hidden.

Drago left the ground with the remaining few thousand supporters.

Taylor turned on the Sky Sports channel and sat watching a 20 20 cricket match for the first time ever. The cameras regularly panned to the Vauxhall End stand to show the thousands of Pakistani cricket fans massed at that end of the ground. The stand was a mass of green and the Pakistani national flag was draped over the sidings of the stand, revealing the white crescent against a vivid green background. Taylor remembered the flag from his time in Afghanistan and each and every British soldier knew that some elements of the Pakistan government were the main backers of the Taliban in Afghanistan.

As the camera focused in on the action a Pakistani player took a spectacular catch and the whole of the Vauxhall End jumped up to celebrate the loss of an English wicket. Taylor watched as the cameras panned round to show the gleeful faces of fathers, mothers, sons and daughters of the Pakistan team supporters cheering and hugging each other.

Drago was also watching the game in a cafe behind the Vauxhall End stand having a glass of wine while watching the game on the cafe's outside TV. It was a warm pleasant evening and the cafe was busy with cricket fans who hadn't been able to get a ticket for the match. Drago sighed at the loss of another English wicket.

"The black bastards," he whispered to himself as he calmly slipped his hand into his pocket.

He felt for the switch on the remote control transmitter and pressed the button. He settled back in his seat, calmly picked up his glass of wine and his eyes returned to the TV to watch the forthcoming spectacle.

Deep in the bowels of the Vauxhall End stand the explosives rigged to the main support columns received the signal. The little red light flashed twice and the dynamite exploded, cutting through the steel columns like a hot knife through butter.

It was a sight that Taylor nor anyone else would ever forget. Similar to the 9/11 New York attacks, the Sky TV cameras stayed on the Pakistani supporters as their joy turned to concern. Everyone in the ground heard the four intermittent dull thuds that came from deep within the Vauxhall End stand. The vibrations from the explosives reverberated throughout the ground.

"What the hell was that, did you feel that?" said the Sky TV cricket commentator.

"Look, oh my god," his co-commentator screamed as he rose from his seat.

The Sky TV cameras instinctively panned from the players on the pitch back to the Vauxhall End stand. In those initial seconds the joyous faces of the celebrating Pakistanis turned to concern as they heard and felt the deep thuds coming from deep within the stand. The whole stand began to shake and vibrate as the weight of the entire structure transferred to peripheral support columns straining to hold the load.

The tearing and grinding noise from the stand was deafening as each structure started to crumble but this noise was soon drowned out by something far worse as the screaming of the thousands of Pakistani supporters echoed around the famous sports arena. As they desperately tried to leave, some of the fans in the front ran directly onto the pitch but the rest stood little chance.

Moments later there was an eerie noise as the upper tier, unable to support the weight, leaned forward and crashed down onto the second upper tier. One by one the concertina effect resulted in all three tiers crashing down onto the lower stand. It was a complete carnage, sheer horror as thousands of tons of concrete, steel and masonry collapsed like a pack of paper cards onto the people below. Only a few hundred supporters in the front of the stand appeared to have escaped. They stood looking back at the lifeless, crushed and broken bodies, yards from where they stood. They should have run further away, much further as the steel loop framed roof gave a groan and a series of loud bangs and cracks brought the huge structure crashing down on top of them. There was no escape.

In the proceeding hours the London emergency services battled to save the thousands of Pakistani supporters trapped in the tangled wreckage. The Sky TV cameras continued to film the chaos as the world witnessed the horrific scene being played out on social media. The Pakistani cricket team were seen as heroes as they joined in with the rescue until late into the night, clearing rubble and lifting debris from dead and dying bodies, occasionally managing to pull a survivor from the tangled twisted mess of steel and concrete.

But Drago wasn't finished. Notwithstanding the carnage that he had caused, he was going to use the chaos at the Oval cricket ground as a decoy to implement his true target. Drago would have been a psychiatrist's dream if they could have got inside his head and found out how his mind worked. He could always find a means of justifying the ends, and as a side issue in the fight against Islamic terrorism, Drago had come to the conclusion that the Pakistani cricket team also had to be punished for their cheating ways. Bribes, ball tampering and match fixing, it had been going on for decades. *Part of their culture*, Drago told himself. *Cheating bastards, how dare they meddle with our beautiful British game.* He recalled how it had been the Australian players Shane Warne and Mark Waugh who accused the then captain, Salim Malik, of offering them bribes to perform poorly. The Pakistan's denied it of course but just a few years later they had them bang to rights and Malik and bowler Ata-ur Rehman were found guilty of match-fixing.

While the Pakistani players and backroom staff were helping with the evacuation and rescue mission, their team coach had been left unattended in the Oval cricket club's members' car park. *They've even left the fucking door open* Drago laughed, and of course the driver was nowhere to be seen, most likely trying to help the injured. No one paid the slightest attention as Drago sneaked onto the Pakistani players' coach and planted two, two kilogram, remote controlled bombs under seats at the front and rear of their team coach. Drago had trimmed half a kilo of dynamite from each of the bombs that took down the Vauxhall End stand. He'd kept this part of the plan to himself. Taylor knew nothing!

By midnight the Pakistani cricket board had told the players to leave the Oval and make their way back to the hotel. The world's media were heading to London and the Pakistani cricket players would be the centrepiece of the world's attention. The players and backroom staff boarded the coach, relieved to get away from the scenes they had just witnessed. Most of the players were in shock, distressed and some of them in tears at the sight of the horrific casualties they had witnessed and the thousands of dead and seriously wounded. They were just cricket players after all, they had lived privileged lives, this bloodbath was completely alien to them.

The coach pulled out of the Oval car park and made its way through south London towards the Lambeth Bridge. Drago followed behind on his scooter. The coach then went through Horseferry Road and onto Buckingham Gate. Drago was not sure which exact route the Pakistani cricket team's coach driver would take. However as luck would have it, the coach took a turn onto Spur Road and would now have to pass Buckingham Palace to get to the Marriot Hotel in Park Lane. That's where he would hit the bastards. He had one other car between himself and the coach as it came to a halt at the Victoria Memorial roundabout, directly outside the gates of Buckingham Palace.

Drago pulled up in the queue of traffic behind the coach. He slightly unzipped his leather jacket and put his hand inside his coat. He switched on the receiver and held his hand over the send button. After a few seconds the roundabout was clear and the coach began to move off. As the coach was directly outside the main gates, Drago pressed the remote transmitter send button. The signal was received by the two bombs in the coach. He watched the macabre scene play out in a kind of slow motion. A small explosion at first, hardly a sound and then a deafening crescendo of noise as the bus exploded into a massive ball of flame.

He sat and smiled. "Don't fuck with the Brits you cunts," he whispered to himself, "fucking terror, I'll show you terror."

Drago pushed the scooter into gear and crawled slowly past the burning wreck of twisted molten metal. He drove back down Spur Road and disappeared into the London traffic.

A Birmingham based news team was driving through central London, making its way to the Oval cricket disaster when their smart phones began to buzz. Images of a burning coach outside Buckingham Palace were being posted live on the net by members of the public who were at the scene. The news team were about five minutes away in Trafalgar Square and they became the first news team to arrive.

CHAPTER **30**

The UK Embassy, Islamabad

It was 3 a.m. in Islamabad. The UK ambassador had just gone to bed to try and catch a couple of hours' sleep after the terrible events of the Oval cricket bombing. The ambassador had been informed by the Foreign Office that the cause of the tragedy was almost certainly a bomb, but was asked to keep this secret from the Pakistani government. He had spent the last four hours in lengthy calls with London and several meetings with the Pakistani Minister of Foreign Affairs.

The embassy ambassador's phone rang. He answered it, "yes, what is it?"

It was one of his diplomats. "Sir, please get dressed, there's been another terrible incident in London."

"What something else?" he asked.

"Another attack against Pakistan, you're not going to believe it and you've been summoned to the Pakistan Ministry of the Interior. You'd better turn on the TV," he said anxiously, "it's the cricket team this time.

The ambassador turned on the news and stared, eyes glazed at another horrific scene from the capital. The scene was of a fiercely burning coach directly in front of the Victoria memorial roundabout at Buckingham Palace. An eyewitness was being interviewed by a news team and he was saying that it was the Pakistan cricket team coach as he had being following it. The eyewitness said no one escaped from the coach and that he himself was lucky he had not been killed in the blast.

"You've got to be kidding me," he muttered into the phone as he raised his hand to his mouth, "don't tell me that's the entire Pakistan cricket team"

"Yes sir, we believe so," he said.

As the ambassador left the UK embassy he saw that a small crowd of protesters had already gathered outside the gates of the embassy. There were several placards that read 'Death to the English, one group was setting fire to a Union Jack Flag. The ambassador knew he was in for a very long night.

Taylor couldn't believe his eyes as he sat watching Sky News early the next morning. Drago hadn't mentioned anything about taking out the Pakistani Cricket Team. This was beyond belief, it was in another stratosphere. *And the repercussions,* he thought to himself, Drago had murdered a group of men who were almost God like in their home country.

"Fuck me," he whispered, "the cunt has just started World war three."

He took a large drink from the brandy he had poured himself soon after he had turned on the television, "and I was the one who recruited him."

The Sun newsroom was bedlam, dealing with the Oval cricket disaster and now the Pakistani Cricket Team bombing.

At 6 a.m. Their WhatsApp story hotline phone flashed a message:

'THE ENGLISH NATIONAL ARMY TAKE RESPONSIBILITY FOR YESTERDAYS ATTACKS IN REVENGE FOR THE FOOTBALL BOMBINGS BY ISLAMIC TERRORISTS.
WE ARE WARNING THE ISLAMIC TERRORISTS LOCATED IN OUR COUNTRY THAT FOR EVERY ONE CITIZEN THAT THEY KILL, WE WILL KILL TWO MUSLIMS. TODAY WE HAVE PROVEN OUR CAPABILITIES.'

This news flashed around the world and the UK yet again became the centre of the world's attention.

CHAPTER **31**

Baxter's phone vibrated on the table. He picked it up and read the display. *Annalisa*, his wife.

He pressed the answer button. "Hi darling, how are you?"

"Fine, just calling to remind you we have your brother in law coming over for dinner night."

He smiled, "do I really have to spend the whole evening with your crazy brother?"

"Yes, I am afraid you do," she laughed, "you love him to bits really and anyway it's only for one night."

"Okay, if I must, I'll be home just after six."

"Perfect, see you then, you've a nice sirloin steak to look forward to."

"Great, just what I need, see you later."

Baxter pressed end and slipped the phone in his pocket.

"My fucking crazy brother in law," he mumbled.

He is one crazy fuck, he thought to himself, even the thought of dinner at the same table unnerved him just a little.

They had met in the SAS, Baxter would never forget the first day he had met the mad Greek with the crazy eyes.

Baxter looked at his watch. "Your brother's late," he said.

Annalisa looked at the clock on the kitchen wall but before she could say anything they both heard the familiar, forceful knock on the front door.

"Talk of the devil" joked Baxter.

Baxter eased himself from the table and walked towards the front door, opened it.

"Hello Drago"

"Baxter you old pen pusher, how are you?"

The remark was taken in jest, but Drago left him in no doubt that it was yet another quick dig at his current employment. After they finished their SAS training Baxter had gone into SAS signals while Drago went into the full military units of the SAS. It was only when Baxter was recruited by Mi5 and as he worked his way to the top and gained higher levels of security clearance did he learn that his brother in law was part of a unique team of SAS black operatives.

After dinner they retired to the drawing room, the only room in the house where Annalise allowed anyone to smoke, and only if the windows were wide open, no matter the season.

"Another glass of wine boys?" Annalisa asked.

Drago nodded.

Baxter shook his head, "I've had enough I think."

"Come on Baxter, you've only had half a bottle of wine, let's have a proper drink."

"Go on Mark, let your hair down for once," Annalisa said.

Baxter sighed, stood up. "Okay Drago, okay, I'll get out some brandy I have had stashed away."

"And a couple of cigars."

Baxter nodded.

Annalisa frowned, "well, I am off to bed if you're starting with those things and don't make a noise when you come to bed and wake up Jamie."

"Yes, yes. Good night love."

"Good night Drago, love you forever," Annalisa said as she cuddled her brother.

Baxter felt slightly annoyed as he saw his wife and Jamie's mother warmly embrace her brother and tried hard to recall the last time she had hugged him like that.

As the night wore on the brandy flowed like cheap lemonade. It was like old times, Baxter opened up and Drago probed and probed, gently at first, like a good salesmen.

"So have the pen pushers managed to fathom out who these terrorists are yet?"

Baxter lifted his glass, shrugged his shoulders and took another long mouthful.

"I would have thought with all your computer programmes you would have them hung drawn and quartered before now."

"That's typical of you," Baxter said, "you'd want us to round up every Muslim in the country and send them to the gas chamber."

"Well that's an idea I hadn't thought of," Drago joked.

Baxter shook his head. "Not all Muslims are bad Drago," he slurred, "let me tell you a secret, I have a good Muslim at Mi5."

"Really? In my opinion the only good muslim is a dead one" said Drago as he cut off Baxter. Baxter ignored that off the cuff comment and continued on.

"Yes, really," Baxter said, "remember that armed robbery in South London?"

"Should I, which one?"

"The one where they used stolen military plastic explosives."

"Yeah vaguely"

"Anyway, listen, the Police thought they were just a bunch of criminals with some soldier buddies who had robbed the MOD. But because the criminals used military grade explosives, protocol meant Mi5 had to have one of their officers review the Police investigation. The Police had spent hours reviewing CCTV cameras and presented a detailed report on a potential suspect to our Mi5 man. Anyway to cut a long story short one of the suspects had a limp and by miraculous chance our muslim Mi5 man thinks he knows him."

"So what, thousands of people have limps."

"Listen Drago, our Muslim mate used to be in the Paras and he remembered one of the recruits had the exact same limp."

Drago listened intently. He was stone cold sober, his brother in law was three sheets to the wind.

"And he's named him?" Drago asked.

"Can't say, top secret."

"Top secret my arse, he's probably told everyone in Mi5."

"Not yet," Baxter slurred, concentrating hard on holding onto his glass.

Drago reached for the near empty bottle and filled Baxter's glass.

Baxter nodded, "thanks," he was having difficulty focusing. "He has only just seen the CCTV films two hours ago. He called me immediately, he said that he remembered a man with the exact same limp but wanted to be one hundred percent sure."

"No way."

"I've called a meeting tomorrow and we are going to get the records from the Army and find out exactly who was in the barracks at the same time as Ahmed. Baxter's hand instinctively clamped over his mouth as he realised his slip up.

Drago sat back in his chair and laughed, "not that wet fucka you had at the christening a few years back?"

"Yes, I mean no, look he's one of us now and I shouldn't have told you his name. Forget you ever heard that Drago, okay?"

"Don't worry brother in law, my lips are sealed."

The night lingered on. The lap top was on the table along with a couple of bottles and they were watching nonsense on YouTube and laughing like schoolboys.

Drago changed the address bar at the top of the page to Facebook.

"Fuck off," Baxter said, "why do you want to go on there?"

"Come on mate, show me your birds before you married my sister."

"I didn't have any ugly ones mate."

"Fuck off."

"I'm telling you man."

Drago filled up two glasses with brandy, slid one over to Baxter, "drink up you pussy."

Baxter was having trouble focusing. "don't you be telling my sister I still have some old birds as friends."

"My word is my bond mate."

Baxter reached for the brandy glass and missed it completely, the palm of his hand hit the rim and tipped the contents onto the table.

"Fuck."

"Whoa, steady fella."

Baxter raised himself to his feet. "Fuck you Drago, I'm going for a piss," Baxter said, "and then I'm going to snuggle up with that gorgeous sister of yours. He steadied himself on the table and staggered off in the direction of the toilet.

Once Baxter left the room Drago sprang into action. He quickly found what he was looking for. A picture of Ahmed and Baxter outside a house in Southall taking photos of each other. Drago zoomed in on the picture and saw that the name of the street was in the picture. What luck. Ahmed was posing in his new blue BMW convertible. Drago memorised the number plate.

Fucking idiots. Not very professional at all.

CHAPTER 32

Drago jumped on his scooter just after seven in the morning and rode to a quiet spot where he changed the plates. Satisfied that no one had seen him he made his way over to West London, to Glendale Gardens in Southall and started looking for the same BMW convertible he'd found on Ahmed Masood's Facebook page. He didn't know the exact house number but he soon found the BMW convertible parked outside number 17. As Drago slowly rode past the house he could see there was a downstairs light on

It was five minutes to eight, Drago drove to a neighbouring street, parked up his scooter, picked up his kit and started to walk back to the house.

When he reached the door he pressed the bell.

Ahmed opened the door and immediately recognised Baxter's brother in law.

"Hello Drago, what do I owe this pleasure? It's been a while."

Drago was straight to the point. "Listen Ahmed, Baxter has asked me to speak to you regarding a very serious matter of national security."

Ahmed frowned, "but you, you are -"

"Yes, Mi5 too, sorry, Baxter should have told you."

Ahmed stepped aside. "Okay you had better come in then."

Drago walked into the hallway and closed the door behind him.

"Who's in the house with you Ahmed?"

"Only my brother Bassour."

"No one else?"

"No"

"You sure"

"Yes, Drago"

"Okay, go into the living room and pull the curtains shut"

Drago heard Ahmed speak to his brother in Arabic. Drago was fluent in Arabic and listened as Ahmed told his brother he had some very important work stuff that had to be dealt with. From the hallway Drago heard the sound of curtains being closed. Ahmed came back into the hallway. Drago now had a gun pointing at his chest and motioned Ahmed back into the open plan living room and kitchen.

Bassour jumped up, clearly in shock.

"Sit down, sit back down," Drago said calmly, "sit the fuck down and keep your mouth shut."

Drago's initial plan was to simply put a bullet in Ahmed's head and anyone else in the house and then be gone. But as he walked into the living room he had noticed a chess set on a table in the corner of the living room.

"You two play chess?"

The two brothers nodded.

Drago waived the gun at Ahmed. "Go and get the chess set, put it on the kitchen dining table."

Ahmed appeared on the verge of tears as he spoke. "Drago what are you doing? I'm good friends with your brother in law, I work with him."

Drago nodded, "don't I know it, how did a fucking Muslim cunt like you worm your way into his circle?"

"But I work for Mi5, I am as loyal to the crown as you or anyone."

"Just get the fucking chess set like a good Paki."

"But-"

"Get it now, put it on the dining table, I'm running out of fucking patience."

Ahmed quickly got the chess set and put it on the dining room table.

"Go on set the pieces up" said Drago as he waved the gun in Ahmed's direction.

Drago opened his bag and tossed Ahmed a roll of heavy duty duct tape.

"Tie your brother to that chair good and proper but leave one arm free."

"But please Mr Drago…"

"Just do it you sniveling cunt or I'll put a bullet in both of you right now."

Ahmed nodded and reluctantly wound the duct tape around his brother's body leaving only one of his arms free.

It was Bassour's turn to question Drago. "You are seriously wanting us to play chess?"

Drago grinned. "Why not, it's a great game?"

He turned to Ahmed, waving the gun menacingly. "Your turn, sit down."

Drago took the duct tape and strapped Ahmed to the chair. He found two dish cloths on the bench tops, stuffed them into the brother's mouths and sealed a piece of duct tape from ear to ear.

"There we go, that should keep you two fuckas quiet. Chess should always be played in complete silence" he slapped Ahmed playfully on the cheek, "it's the rules brother."

He rubbed his hands together gleefully. "Speed chess, thirty seconds a move. Understand?"

The two brothers nodded.

Drago walked over to the sink and carried a chopping board to the kitchen table. He searched in a draw and found a large chopping knife. He placed the chopping board and the knife next to the chess set.

He looked at his watch. "Play"

Bizarrely Ahmed moved one of his pawns out and then Bassour followed. Drago counted down the thirty seconds until each move and it wasn't long until Ahmed sacrificed one of his pawns.

"Oh dear," Drago said, "you've lost a pawn."

He opened up his kit bag and pulled out a pair of pliers. Ahmed's face fixed in terror, his eyes were bulging out of his head. He held Ahmed's free hand. "Don't worry," he grinned, it's just a little pawn."

Ahmed's nail was thick and long, well overdue a cut. The pliers fixed on quite easily, had plenty of grip. Drago pulled slowly and the nail began to give. Beads of sweat stood out on Ahmed's brow as he did his best to pull his arm away but Drago was far too strong. Ahmed thrashed in the chair as Drago pulled even more and eventually the whole of the nail broke free and the blood began to pour from the end of his finger. Drago flicked the nail onto the table and did his best to clean up the blood.

"Every time you lose a chess piece your lose something else," he laughed, "rules are rules, by the end of the game you will be greatest speed chess players in the world."

Pawns have the lowest value and that's why you've only lost a finger nail. For god's sake be careful with your rooks and bishops."

The game resumed. Ahmed was sobbing gently, his brother frozen in terror. Drago looked at the fear on their faces, the pain in Ahmed's eyes. But still they played on, he was beginning to enjoy himself.

The two brothers soon became entrenched in a battle of wits against each other. Ahmed lost another pawn and another nail, soon after Bassour lost three in quick succession as any question of brotherly love went out of the window.

Drago studied the play hard. Ahmed swooped and grabbed at Bassour's bishop with a slight exclamation of joy.

"Oh dear brother Muslim, you have just lost a Bishop," Drago said.

Bassour twisted and thrashed around in his chair squealing beneath his gag. Drago stood behind him and bent down to whisper in his ear.

"This might hurt a bit" said Drago quietly.

The knife was well kept, razor sharp in fact and mercifully the pain was bearable as Drago held the top of his ear and sliced down hard with the knife which cut through the flesh like butter. It was Ahmed's turn to let out a silent wail as he looked at the plod pouring down his brothers cheek as Drago symbolically held up the severed body part before laying it on the table.

The chess game continued.

Bassour lost a rook and a finger, Ahmed's loss of a knight cost him his thumb. The kitchen table was awash with blood, the body parts lined up in two neat rows.

Both players were now nearing unconsciousness. Drago threw a dish of cold water over them both to wake them up a bit.

"Now listen up you Muslim fucks," Drago said, as he held a second ear in his hand, "we are reaching the end of the game so it's time to tell you what's at stake."

He explained that they were both going to die because Ahmed was going to squeal on the man with the limp. "He's a good friend of mine and a man on a mission."

He continued. "The winner of this fascinating game will have quick and painless death but the loser will suffer. I promise you that."

Despite the savage attacks on their bodies both chess players somehow began to put some clever moves together and all of a sudden Ahmed was motioning that he had won.

Drago checked the board. Ahmed had symbolically pushed over his brother's king.

"Well blow me down Ahmed, you have check mated your brother."

He stood, patted Ahmed on the head as he walked over to the cooker and switched on one of the gas rings.

He found a barbecue fork and placed it over the flame. Bassour bucked and kicked and thrashed around for some minutes as the steel fork eventually glowed red. Drago removed it from the flame and walked over to Bassour. He held the double prongs just above his nose but seemed to stall for a while. And then he smiled. "Right eye it is Bassour, I believe the right is very significant in Islam, more noble and honoured. Bassour closed his eyes, he knew it was hopeless to fight and he was right. Drago touched his eyelid with the fork and there was a slight hissing noise and the room filled with the pungent smell of burning flesh. He pushed, slowly at first as he buried the fork no more than a centimetre into Bassour's eye socket. Bassour's instinct was to move his head away from the unbearable pain but Drago placed a hand around the back of his head and took a handful of hair. He gripped hard. He pushed again, more forcefully as the fork moved forward and all of a sudden there was pop as the eyeball exploded. After several more inches Drago stopped as the steel found the back of Bassour's skull. The man's head flopped to the side and Drago released his grip on the fork.

He turned to Ahmed, "there are some things so much worse than death don't you think?"

Ahmed said nothing, he was living in a nightmare, the likes of which he would never have imagined.

"Now Ahmed, I am a man of my word so if you want to close your eyes I will give you your prize."

Ahmed nodded. Drago ripped the makeshift gag from Ahmed mouth.

"now open your mouth and suck on the gun. I don't want to make a noise as I have forgotten my silencer. Bit of a rushed job this Ahmed" said Drago

Ahmed closed his mouth around the gun.

"Ok Ahmed, don't close your eyes. Look at me" said Drago

In the next instant Ahmed was dead.

CHAPTER 33

In Bradford, Othmane, Talpur and Johiya were also watching the latest developments on TV. The three battle-hardened Al Qaeda soldiers were not shocked by what they saw on the news, just angry.

"Well, well, well, looks like we have a mirror army," stated Johiya.

"We must avenge our brothers," Othmane shouted with rage in his eyes.

Talpur watched the Sky news reporter as she brought the latest death toll from the emergency services. "They've killed thousands of our brothers, this English Army or whatever they're called. They must be seen to suffer."

"Interesting that they're adopting the same tactic as our enemies in Israel... a two to one ratio," Johiya said thoughtfully. "It is a policy that is readily endorsed, a policy that in a war of attrition the Palestinians cannot win."

"We'll kill ten times more of these infidels to teach them a lesson," Othmane screamed at the TV as another image of a dozen body bags filled the screen.

Johiya paused before he spoke again. He was the epitome of calm. Nothing seemed to faze him or ever make him angry. Neither Othmane nor Talpur had ever seen Johiya lose his cool.

"Remember the words of our father, Osama. It is not to win a war in little England, it is to fan the flames of war in the entire world. Once the Muslims rise as one, we will once again rule our own lands. Let all Muslims return to our holy lands. Let the westerners have their money based lives and their filthy Western debauchery. Osama's dream is for our holy lands to be governed by Muslims without the influence or proxy governance by these western infidels. We are sleeper cell terrorists and we have a strict line to follow, we must stick to the plan. Let us be calm and take notes. Whatever this English Army have set out to do they have achieved it. But when we next strike it will be bigger and more destructive.

Johiya pointed to the TV screen, "We must mourn our brothers but this attack is good news for us for it has fanned more flames than we could ever have dreamed of. Remember it was what Osama predicted."

He stood up and switched off the television. "Othmane, how is Khan's training progressing?"

"He's coming along remarkably well. He's becoming quite a marksman on our target range. His technical capability is also good, he can do the blindfold test now on our AK-47s and the Glock 19. He's physically fit, he's also passed all our drugs tests too."

"Excellent, and the Islamic classes?"

Othmane nodded, "our brothers in prison did a very good job, his belief is unquestionable in my opinion."

"Talpur, what's his personal life like?" Johiya asked.

"I have followed him on many occasions and we have given him one of our spy phones, so we know where he's going at all times. He has no idea that his phone is also a listening device which gives us a real insight into his private life."

"And?"

"As far as I'm concerned he's acting like a perfect westerner when he's with his family. As far as his partner is concerned he's hard working and only has Sundays to spend time with his family. As you know he has recently had a baby," he added.

"And what of tonight?" Johiya asked, what are they saying about the attacks in London?

"Our spy phone works a treat. We listened to his wife bleating on about the state of the world and how it had all gone crazy. Khan just said his family were lucky to live away from London. He gave nothing away, not even to his wife."

Johiya lowered himself into a chair, and tapped one of his teeth with his index finger as he thought. "Do you both think that he's ready to be tested?"

"Yes I do," replied Talpur

"Me too," Othmane said as he nodded in agreement.

"Excellent," Johiya said, "and the fact that he has his child gives us an added insurance at this point." Johiya stood. "Make the arrangements immediately."

Othmane nodded and walked out of the room.

Khan was finishing off a practice session in the basement, firing off the last few rounds in his AK-47.

Othmane looked on, more than a little impressed and jealous at Khan's accuracy. "Okay brother, tonight we have work to do. Your training is now complete and you're ready to become a real soldier of Islam."

"I'm ready brother?" Khan asked.

"Allah knows it is so and now we must pray together"

Both Othmane and Khan prayed together. It was a strange setting. An ex-junkie, house burgling criminal praying to Mecca with a fully-fledged Al Qaeda operative. The prayer session was taking place in the terror cell's firing range in their sound proofed basement.

CHAPTER **34**

Later that same evening Khan and Othmane drove to a Manchester suburb. It was raining as usual and there was very little moonlight. They parked the car and Othmane rang a number on his mobile phone. Talpur answered.

The phone was handed over to Khan. He listened as he heard his girlfriend's voice talk about his friend who had brought round presents for their daughter. His girlfriend handed the phone to her visitor. Khan could hear his baby daughter crying in the background.

"Hello my friend, I'm sorry you're not here but I'll wait for your return. Your girlfriend and beautiful daughter will look after me in the meantime," Talpur said, "I'll let you speak to her."

Khan's girlfriend came back on the phone and rattled on about how nice this gentleman was and that she didn't know that he had any Indian friends. The phone call ended and Khan turned to Othmane.

"What are you doing? I am with you," he said, "what kind of stunt is this?"

"You must prove you are with Islam," Othmane said, "you are not stupid, you know you have to prove yourself to the cause, tonight you will demonstrate how much you love Allah and Islam."

"You know I will not let you down brother."

Othmane pulled out an envelope from the glove compartment. He showed Khan a photo of a man.

He pointed to another piece of paper. "That's his address. It's a three minute walk from here."

Othmane opened up a cloth and revealed a hand gun; it was the same Glock 19 that Khan had regularly trained with. Othmane gave Khan a pizza box and a crash helmet.

"You see that scooter parked over the road"

"Yes"

"It's stolen, your cover is that you will be a pizza delivery man"

Khan grinned, "perfect."

"Its the same scooter you have practised with."

"Ride over there and kill him," he ordered.

"Who is it?" Khan asked.

"He is an enemy of Islam. That's all you need to know," he replied. "Put the helmet on and then use the pizza box to hide the gun. Ring the bell and tell them you have a pizza delivery. The man you need to kill is white, forty three years old with blond short cropped hair and he's slightly overweight. He should be the only man in the house."

Othmane hugged Khan. "For Islam and for Allah, brother, you have done this in your training many times so stay calm, your training will take over and remember, just walk away after the deed is done, don't run."

The stolen scooter had a large box on the back with the name of a fictitious pizza delivery firm and an unobtainable number. Khan made his way to the house knowing full well that his partner and baby were in effect being held to make sure that Khan carried out this attack to the letter. It wasn't necessary; as far as Khan was concerned he was a soldier of Islam and would prove himself to be the equal of Othmane and any of his associates.

Khan saw the house, killed the engine and slipped the keys into his pocket. He walked up to the door and rang the bell. Moments later a little girl opened the door. She was about seven or eight years old.

"Pizza delivery," Khan said softly.

"Pizza, Pizza," she turned around and shouted into the house, "Daddy, daddy we've got a pizza."

Scott Banks was just sitting down to watch the football when he heard his daughter shouting about a pizza delivery. He got up from the sofa and made his way into the hallway.

"Stupid twats," he whispered to himself, "they've got the wrong address again."

He saw a man standing at his front door holding a pizza box. He thought it was rather impolite that he hadn't even bothered to take his helmet off."

"Sorry but I think you've made a mistake," he said as he walked towards the front door," same bloody thing happened last week."

"Dad can't we have the pizza anyway?" the young girl begged. She was pulling at his leg.

"No Lara, we've already eaten," he said, "now get going to bed like I said."

The little girl turned and slowly walked away moaning as she went.

Scott turned back towards the pizza delivery man. "Wrong address mate, what the fuck are you doing still standing there?"

The man opened the lid of the pizza box.

"I've told you, we don't want any pizzas now fuck off."

The man reached inside the box and pulled out a gun. He aimed at Banks head and pulled the trigger. There was a loud crack and then a thud as Banks fell to the floor. The 9 mm bullet entered and exited his head and embedded itself in the wall behind him. Scott Banks, second in command of the British National Party, was dead.

Khan remembered his training and walked away towards the scooter, the screams from the man's daughter getting fainter and fainter. Khan started the engine, kicked it into gear and disappeared into the darkness. He felt no remorse. He only felt honour than he had proven himself a true jihadi. After about half a mile he lifted the visor and as the coolness of the night flooded into his helmet ,a big smile pulled across his face.

He drove the three miles to the rendezvous point. Othmane was waiting for him as arranged. He set light to the motorcycle then both he and Khan calmly walked through an alleyway into a road where a car was parked. They drove for another half hour into the countryside and pulled into a deserted country lane. At the end of the lane was a canal. Othmane took the gun from Khan and tossed it into the canal. He also threw in the mobile phone that he had used to call Talpur.

Later that night Khan returned home to his girlfriend and daughter. His friend had long since gone but had left his daughter a nice array of presents.

"How lovely your friend was," Rebecca said.

"Yes, I have some very good work friends," he answered.

He gave his partner a kiss goodnight and went to bed. That night he slept very well.

The next morning Khan started a new job in Talpur's exhaust fitting company. He worked hard during the day, learning how to remove old exhausts and fit new ones. But once normal working hours were over, Khan and Talpur spent their evenings preparing four more vans for jihadi attacks. It was a complex and lengthy process, uprating the suspension, removing all traces of ownership and making sure they ran perfectly. Khan and Talpur needed to make sure the vans took their cargos to their destinations without any hiccups or undue police attention.

Khan was told never to speak about the murder of Scott Banks, not even with Talpur. Talpur watched Khan closely over the next few days and if anything, he seemed even more fanatical about their jihadi cause.

Khan never missed a prayer session and always prayed in secret so the public's prying eyes were not upon him.

Talpur remembered back to when he was first recruited by Al Qaeda and how he went from being a normal run of the mill youth to a hardened jihadist. Khan seemed no different to him now and it didn't matter that he was once a criminal. Many Al Qaeda fighters were ex criminals and had been recruited in Middle East prisons. In his opinion the difference between an ex-criminal jihadist and a jihadist recruited through a mosque was that the ex-criminals were generally bolder and definitely more cunning.

The vans were prepared and ready after a few weeks. Khan had learned how to make a shaped charge and adapt a sliding roof to one of the vans. The four vans sat secretly in the rear of the exhaust garage, covered in a tarpaulin, waiting to deliver their deadly loads.

Khan had a surprise for the family that night, Talpur had granted him a few days off.

He picked up his daughter and bounced her on his knee. "Hi love, how's my little princess been today?"

Rebecca looked on. "Well she's been teething and crying a bit. Missing you probably, you know how much she loves you."

Khan smiled, "Listen, I've got some good news. I have a week's holiday coming up and I've booked a week on a canal boat… just us three. I think we need a holiday."

"Magic. How exciting, our first holiday together as a family," Rebecca replied, "where, when, what do I need to pack and -"

Whoa, steady on," Khan held up a hand, "all in good time. Now, I'm famished, if you can put some food in front of me I'll tell you all about it.

CHAPTER 35

Kings Langley - Kelly's Narrow Boat and Barge Hire, Grand Union Canal

Khan, Rebecca and Lucy arrived at the narrow boat hire company. Khan went into the boatyard's office and minutes later came out with a boatyard employee who took him onto a large eight berth barge. Rebecca and Lucy watched on the canal bank as he was given basic navigation training on steering a Grand Union Canal barge.

For the girls waiting on the bank side it seemed to take forever as he was given a crash course in navigating the eight berth barge through the locks and canals near to the boatyard. The boatman was impressed as to how quickly the student learnt how to implement the various manoeuvres before the barge could be properly released for hire. The boatman was of course unaware that Othmane had instructed Khan to take various lessons on navigating a barge on the UK canal system.

"Nothing to it," said Khan to the man.

"Yes lad, there's nothing much to it, you're a fast learner, just watch out for the river police who sit outside the canal pubs," he warned as he handed Khan his temporary canal boat licence.

"That's a big old barge for just three people," he said.

Khan shrugged his shoulders, "I suffer from a bit of claustrophobia," he replied, his cover story kicking in without hesitation.

"okay, but there are cruisers with…"

"No, thank you," he said cutting the man off before he could finish his sentence, "you know how it is, why have a little boat when you have the money for a big one."

"Okay, it's your choice pal, have a nice holiday and I'll see you next week."

They waved goodbye to the boat man and set off down the canal. They passed a few other canal boats and everybody waved to each other. It was a great family occasion, Rebecca and Lucy were in their element as Khan took the controls and they moved slowly through the peaceful countryside. It took Khan a couple of days to make his way through the Grand Union Canal and reach the River Thames at Brentford.

He made various notes of any roads or tracks that were connected to the canal. In particular these connections to the canal system had to be away from any prying eyes.

Khan had planned ahead and his barge had been pre-booked to go through the Brentford lock and enter the tidal pool of London. The lock officer came on board the barge and asked Khan if he had been on the Thames before. He lied and said he was knowledgeable with the tidal flow. The lock officer asked Khan to sign the lock gate register and he was manoeuvred through the lock. It was true that Khan was knowledgeable of the Pool of London but only through studying books on the matter.

He went through the lock at high tide on a Saturday afternoon. The reduced strength of the tide and because it was a Sunday meant the large work barges that used the Thames were moored up, which would make the journey on the river as manageable as it could be. Khan had to get to his destination and then return to the Brentford lock late on the Sunday afternoon. He opened up the powerful pair of 300hp diesel engines and made his way down the river to Greenwich.

On his way down river the Houses of Parliament loomed up on the left; he eventually reached Greenwich and moored up for the night. He spent the evening playing with his daughter and relaxing with Rebecca. The next morning they headed back up river. Khan had asked Rebecca to keep the baby inside the barge rather than on the deck as the river had become a bit choppy due to the tidal surge. Rebecca watched the famous landmarks from inside the barge and made a video of anything she thought worth showing her friends and family.

"Can you make sure you film the Houses of Parliament, Rebecca," Khan said.

"Yes John, of course I will," she replied innocently.

The river traffic going up river was designated to be on the right side of the river so this brought the barge close to the Houses of Parliament. Rebecca failed to notice that the barge was steering close to the restricted area located next to the Houses of Parliament. All of a sudden she heard a loud hailer screaming at the boat and she went up on deck with Lucy in her arms.

"This is a restricted area, move your vessel away immediately," a voice shouted from a police launch. The launch pulled up next to the barge and a police officer saw a young couple with baby.

"What's going on John?" Rebecca asked, unnerved by the sight of the police.

"Nothing darling, I think I just went off course a bit, that's all, this thing can sometimes have a mind of its own."

"Sir, this is a restricted area, please move away, we won't tell you again.

Khan was shouting above the noise of the water and the police megaphone. "I'm very sorry mate. I had no idea, my wife and I are on a canal holiday and this is our first trip on this part of the river. The tide took me by surprise."

The police officer looked at the young white couple with the baby and decided that they were nothing more than holidaymakers. The barge had 'Kelly's Narrow Boat and Barge Hire' written on the side. All seemed innocent enough.

Khan watched as the officer talked on his radio and moments later he turned towards Khan.

"Okay, this time there will be no action against you but be aware of the restricted areas here and here. They are marked by the white buoys."

"Thank you officer," he said apologetically.

"Be on your way and have a safe journey."

The Police launch waited until he'd cleared the restricted area and then the boat turned around and sped off.

Khan took note of the menacing 50mm calibre machine gun on deck. Even when the police officer spoke to him a second officer was manning the heavy-duty machine gun.

Khan steered the barge back up the Thames and into the tidal lock at Brentford. He made his way leisurely through the Grand Union Canal and back to Kings Langley.

CHAPTER 36

Bradford Discount Exhaust Centre

Othmane and Khan had had a busy day. Three of the four vans they had prepared for the next phase of their plan had to be driven to secret locations.

"It's very important that when we drive we drive in tandem, Khan. So, do your very best to make sure I can be directly behind you. That means when you pull out of a junction you have room for me to pull out behind you. If we approach any traffic lights make sure I can always be behind you when you stop or when the lights go green. Do you understand brother?" he asked.

"Of course."

"If any police come behind me I will make a mistake and get pulled over. This will allow you to go free. Park up as soon as you can and I'll meet you after. Do not drive to the location without me guarding your backside."

"Yes, I understand all of this. It makes sense," he replied.

Othmane felt assured. The Imam had chosen well when they asked for the recruit with the highest IQ. Khan was smart, he normally only had to be shown something once for him to take it in.

Othmane set the sat nav for an address near Leeds. He took Khan's mobile phone away from him to stop any chance of a random call which might cause Khan to make a mistake and potentially get pulled over by the police.

The first trip went like clockwork with Khan and Othmane delivering the bomb van to the secret meeting point. Khan had no idea who was due to collect it but wasn't too surprised when the Imam from Full Sutton prison arrived.

The fact that Othmane had allowed Khan to meet the Imam further instilled the belief in Khan that he had truly been accepted by his network of brothers. Khan and the Imam embraced affectionately when they met.

"How is Bakar?" Khan asked.

"He is very good, his spirits are high. I have relayed to him your progress and he is very proud of you."

Tears of pride welled up in Khan's eyes. "Tell him I won't let him down."

"I'll pass on the message," the Imam said.

The Imam shook Khan's hand and then excused himself, he spoke for a few minutes privately with Othmane, said his farewells and drove off in the first of the bomb vans.

The day progressed well with Khan and Othmane delivering the remaining two bomb vans to locations north of Newcastle and Cambridge respectively. Both vans were collected by the Imams who took Muslim prayers at HMP Frankland and HMP Whitemoor. The three vans were driven short distances and then parked up.

CHAPTER 37

HMP Full Sutton's Imam attended Friday prayers as normal. He preached to the Muslim inmates and particularly made reference to peace and tolerance of other religions. This was solely for the benefit of the prison guards who sat in the prayer room recording each and every word the Imam said. The prayers ended and there were a few minutes for the Imam to talk personally with some of the inmates. The prayer room became a bit chaotic as the inmates and prison officers prepared to escort the inmates back to their wing. This allowed the Imam to speak quickly with Bakar.

"The new Qur'an I ordered for you will arrive tomorrow."

"Thank you, Imam."

Nothing more needed to be said. Those words were pre-planned and had considerable importance.

Early the next morning three ex-prisoners who had converted to Islam whilst in prison, met with their trusted Imams to assist in a planned escape from the three maximum security prisons where they had previously been imprisoned. The Imams had planned escapes at Full Sutton, Whitemoor and Frankland. The Muslim converts had been told to drive to the outer wall area where five of their Muslim brothers would be coming over the wall and then to drive away as fast as possible. The three drivers had been instructed to position the vans exactly where the Muslim wing exercise yards were designated, at each of the three prisons.

The fact that each of the Muslim converts had been imprisoned on the Muslim wings at each of the three prisons, helped in the positioning of the vans in the escape, however, the Imams had gone a step further in ensuring the correct positioning of the three vans.

They had deployed specialised drones to fly over the prison at night and used infrared cameras to pinpoint exactly where the vans needed to be parked. The Imams then rigged up a laser beam, positioning sensor equipment in the surrounding countryside directly opposite the prison wall.

The laser beam fired an invisible and continuous beam of light at the exact point on the outer prison wall. As soon as the van made contact with that laser beam a small buzzer in the van sounded. They simply needed to drive along the prison outer wall and wait for the laser beam sensor to start buzzing.

On Saturdays, in prison, there was no work or education classes and apart from prison visits and gymnasium, all prisoners normally stayed on the wing.

Officer Beeks called out on the tannoy for gym classes and waited by the gate ready to mark off the prisoners as they left the wing to go to the prison gymnasium.

Beeks waited.

He looked at his watch and stared into the wing of the prison before shouting over to his colleague. "Pikey, never seen that before."

"What's that?" Officer Pike asked.

"No one on E wing gone to the gym."

"What no one?"

"Not one of the goat fuckers."

"That's a strange one, but don't worry about it, it's probably some Muslim fucking holiday or something daft like that."

"Yeah, you're probably right."

Beeks put his pen in his top pocket and tucked the clipboard under his arm.

Half an hour later the call for exercise went out on the E wing tannoy. Beeks stood and watched, clipboard at the ready. He was nearly knocked over in the rush. Every single Muslim prisoner had apparently decided to take some exercise. This caught the attention of the prison officers as it was also raining and from experience very few prisoners would go out on exercise when it was raining.

He looked over towards Pike. "What's going on here? Something's up," said Officer Beeks.

"I've no idea but something's going on. Better get on the radio and tell security," Pike said.

It was 10.30 a.m. and all the prisoners were gathered around Bakar in one corner of the exercise yard. Bakar had in his possession a small mobile phone that had been smuggled into the prison. He hit the send message button.

About a five minute drive away from the prison a white van was parked in a lay-by waiting for the signal to go. The driver's mobile phone beeped and he knew this was the signal to act. The driver of the van sped off towards the prison. He drove past the visitors centre and onto the grass areas that surrounded the prison. The prison's security centre watched the van approach from the CCTV system and the general alarm signal was immediately sounded.

Out on E wing exercise yard a confrontation was developing. The sounding of the general alarm meant every single prisoner had to go immediately back to their cell.

"Right, you all know the drill, that's the general alarm, back to your cells now." Beek looked nervous, he shouted the last command. "Exercise is cancelled, you heard me."

Bakar walked to the front of the group. "We're not going anywhere. We need our exercise."

"Have it your way Bakar, you'll suffer for this, by god you'll fucking suffer," he yelled. He lifted his radio to his mouth. "Code Nine, Code Nine," he stated, trying to remain calm.

Hearing the code nine emergency call, all available prison officers poured into E wing exercise yard within two minutes. They were outnumbered two to one, but some of the prison officers had dogs and all of them had their batons and CS canisters drawn, ready to use force to remove the E wing prisoners from the exercise yard.

The Muslim prisoners were positioned furthest from the outer wall with the prisoner officers located between them and the outer wall. It was all part of the plan. At the exact same time the van driver had pulled up alongside the outer prison wall. He had stopped as soon as the laser beam location buzzer sounded. He jumped out of the van and opened the van's back doors.

Opening the back door triggered a huge bomb which unknown to the driver had been hidden in the van. The blasted ripped the poor man to pieces propelling his body parts in a wave of energy against the prison outer wall which blew a gaping hole through the thick brick work. The blast also ripped apart the steel inner security fence and razor sharp pieces of steel and brick tore into the unfortunate prison officers and some of their dogs who were located near to the blast site. The Muslim prisoners cheered as they looked at the dead and injured lying on the ground. The prison officers still standing looked dazed and shocked, they were in no state to even offer a token fight.

"Let's go brothers, Allah Akbar," Bakar shouted as he raced towards the breach in the prison wall. One hundred fellow Muslim prisoners made the dash for freedom. Some made for the visitors' centre and forced other visitors to hand over their car keys, some made for the road and forced cars to stop with the help of some fake hand guns made out of wood. Some prisoners even went to the prison officers' car park and attacked several officers who just so happened to be parking their cars as they arrived for work.

Within a matter of minutes the one hundred escaped Muslim inmates had managed to commandeer enough cars for all of them to be speeding away from the prison towards to the A166, heading towards the motorway network where they planned to disappear. Bakar, leader of the Full Sutton break out made good his escape.

A second bomb also exploded at HMP Frankland in county Durham, with the resulting escape of a hundred or so Muslim prisoners. However, at Whitemoor prison the escape did not go to plan.

CHAPTER 38

HMP Whitemoor D Wing

There was a staffing issue, not enough officers to patrol the exercise yard. It had thrown Ismail's plans into confusion.

"Come on, come on," he muttered to himself, "we're ten minutes behind schedule, I should have sent the signal ten minutes ago and we're not even on the exercise yard yet."

Abuda and Ismail stood at the locked doorway shouting at the prison officer to open up.

"You can't go on exercise until we have two more officers on duty," the D wing principal officer shouted, "they're on their way so you'll have to wait."

Minutes later two more officers arrived and the D wing exercise yard was finally opened.

It was Prison Officer Henderson who noticed exactly the same thing they had noticed at Full Sutton and Frankland. "That's a strange one, I've never seen an entire wing go on exercise before."

His colleague SO Bradshaw grinned, "they're probably gonna do a mass prayer to their fucking stupid god. Fucking ignore 'em, let the cunts get soaked."

Ismail was the recognised leader of the D wing Muslims. He had managed to spread the word of the intended breakout to his Muslim brothers without any leaks to the prison officers. The fact that the Muslim prisoners kept their mouths shut had more to do with fear of their peers than anything else and so the entire wing was on exercise as instructed. They didn't do much exercise and had all gathered around their leader.

"What's going on Ismail? The men are getting impatient," Abuda said.

Ismail shook his head, "I don't know but something's wrong, I sent the signal as soon as we were all on the yard. That's fifteen minutes ago now."

Julian Toore had parked up in a layby waiting patiently for the signal to drive his Muslim brothers to freedom. The call hadn't come in. It was due at10.30 a.m. He looked at his watch, 10.41. Toore got out of the van, he was bursting for the toilet. Unluckily for him, as he did so a Prison Officer at HMP Whitemoor was driving pass and immediately recognised Toore as a past inmate. Protocol stated that any sightings of ex-prisoners within three miles of the prison had to be immediately reported to security.

Prison officer Delaney stopped his car and rang HMP Whitemoor security.

PO. Lackenby took the call. "What is it Delaney? I hope it's important because all hell is breaking loose elsewhere."

"Probably nothing, but I just want to report an ex-inmate parked up in Church Ave about half a mile from the prison."

Lackenby was on edge. "Look Delaney, there's been two bomb blasts at Full Sutton and Frankland, we haven't got time for this?"

"What's happening?" Delaney asked, clearly concerned.

"Two suicide van bombers have blown through the outer walls at both prisons and caused mass escapes," Lackenby said.

"Did you say vans?" asked Delaney.

"Yeah, two white vans, I've seen the security videos that have just come through the system."

Delaney swallowed hard, suddenly his throat was dry, he found it difficult to form the next sentence. "Listen mate, the ex-prisoner I've just seen is parked up in a big white transit type van."

"You fucking sure?"

"Yes I'm sure. As I was driving along Church Street I saw someone getting out the van and he was having a piss. I recognised him immediately, he's definitely an ex-inmate of the Nick."

"Okay, Delaney, stay on the line."

"What shall I do?" he asked.

He could hear Lackenby shouting out commands to other security officers.

"Okay, listen. We're calling March police and sending our SE squad to the location immediately. Keep the van in sight but don't confront the prisoner, it could well be another fucking bomb."

Delaney turned his car round and pulled up about one hundred yards from the white van. His mobile phone rang and PO Lackenby asked if the target van was still in position. The van had not moved. Delaney watched as minutes later a police armed response vehicle pulled up beside the van. There had obviously been a breakdown in communication as the police had not yet been informed of the fact the van could be a suicide bomber.

Julian Toore cursed his bad luck. But it wasn't his fault, he had carried out his instruction to the letter. The breakout would have to be delayed.

"Driver's license and insurance," the police officer said.

"No problem officer," Toore said as he handed over the documents. Toore was confident he would be on his way as he was completely legal.

The police officer walked back to his car. A prison security car then pulled up keeping its distance from the van. Toore looked in his mirror, he could see the police officer walking towards the prison van, the officers appeared to be shouting at him. As the policeman got closer to the prison van he started to run. Both cars then pulled back about another fifty metres from Toore's van. Other police cars turned up and the road was blocked off quickly.

"Fucking hell," Toore mumbled to himself, "what the fuck is going on here?"

"You, the driver of the van, come out with your hands over your head," said a loud voice over a megaphone.

Toore let out a deep sigh, but decided to do what they said. He thought that he might be questioned for a bit but as far as he was concerned the police had nothing. Toore jumped out of the van and walked into the middle of the road.

"Take all your clothes off," the police officer shouted.

"What the fuck, go fuck yourselves, I'll freeze to death." He shouted back.

Toore heard a loud crack and realised that one of the ARV police officers had fired a warning shot above his head. "What the fuck" exclaimed Toore.

Toore knew that something really serious was going on, something much more than the police getting a whiff of the breakout.

Toore stripped and walked naked to the police road block. As soon as he reached the group he was pounced on, punched and kicked and then dragged to a police van.

"Hold his head up," said the PO of the security wing, "yeah that's Julian Toore. He was on D wing, one of them Muslim convert nuts. He's been released about a year now."

He was thrown violently into the back of the prison van.

"Bye bye, dickhead," another officer shouted as he cuffed him across the back of the head, "you'll be in my block you fucking traitor, I'll make sure of it."

As they locked the doors to the van the Prison officers left to go back to the prison as more and more police turned up. Within five minutes the area was crawling with uniforms and soon after a bomb disposal team in full army fatigues had also joined them.

CHAPTER 39

Mi5 Headquarters

Fletcher answered the phone wearily. He had been organising a response to the HMP Full Sutton and Frankland bombings and was fully expecting more bad news. A wry smile came over his face as he turned towards Baxter.

"They fucked up at Whitemoor, we got the driver and a van. An off duty prison officer saw an ex-con parked up in a layby within the prison security zone. Called it in as a precaution, minutes after the Full Sutton bombings. Initial reports state he was a Muslim convert. Our first big break I think.

"And," said Baxter.

"Cambridge CID are transporting the driver here. E.T.A. two hours," he said.

A big smile beamed across Baxter's face.

HMP Whitemoor D Wing Exercise Yard

Alarms were going of all over HMP Whitemoor, All of a sudden there was lots of shouting coming from B wing, the non-Muslim prisoners were shouting insults out of the windows to the Muslim prisoners on D wing exercise yard.

"Goat fuckers."

"Camel jockeys

"Allah is a peado."

"Muzzie cunts."

The Muslims prisoners reacted and started to hurl back the insults but others were shouting about other things too, they were saying something about bombs.

"Quiet brothers. Let me listen to what they're saying," Ismail shouted.

One of them shouted to Ismail that it had just come on a newsflash that there had been two explosions at Full Sutton and Frankland. Apparently there had been a mass escape by all the Muslim prisoners.

Ismail smiled. "It has begun brothers, our time has come to join our brothers."

The Muslim prisoners gathered around Ismail.

"Our plan is over, there'll be no escape to fight this jihad, but if you believe in the new Islamic order we can start our fight here and now. Are you with me?" he shouted.

The prisoners started to cheer and chant, "Yes Emir, Allah Akbar."

"Let's go," shouted Ismail.

The alarm had sounded, more prison officers started to pour into the exercise yard and the Muslim prisoners started to attack them. Over the coming hours the most serious disturbance ever to have occurred on a British mainland prison took place in HMP Whitemoor. The prisoners quickly overcame the officers and using keys taken from them managed to break out of D wing and take control of C wing which housed the vulnerable prisoners, the prison hospital, the E wing security block, the education block, and the lawnmower workshop.

The Muslim rioters were now everywhere and some of those headed towards A and B wings. Not only were A and B wings short staffed due to it being a weekend shift, but many of the officers on A and B wings had been drafted to quell the ongoing riot that started in D wing. The prison officers had never before experienced such ferocious violence and were unprepared and no match for the Muslims who had armed themselves with knives, scalpels and tools from the lawnmower workshops.

News filtered back to A and B wings that the Muslims were attacking not only the prison officers but also the non-Muslim prisoners too. Reports were coming through that prison officers and non-Muslim prisoners were being murdered by the rioters. As a result, an unprecedented decision was made by the few remaining prison officers on A and B wings to release any locked up prisoners on their wings to help fight alongside the prison officers.

It was a fight to the death, scores of prisoners and prison officers lay dead and injured but after a few hours the Muslim attackers gave in and retreated back to the area of the prison now totally under their control. There were many dead and badly injured prisoners littered along the corridors and reception areas to each of the five wings of Whitemoor. The prison resembled a medieval battle zone from the tenth century. The Muslims had taken about one hundred vulnerable prisoners, the sex offenders and the informers and about fifty prison officers hostage. Any of the main wing prisoners captured were immediately murdered under the orders of Ismail.

As word of the breakouts and riots at Whitemoor spread through the UK jail system, there followed further serious disturbances between Muslim prisoners and non-Muslim prisoners up and down the country. By the end of the day over twenty prisons were under the control of Muslim prisoners. The death toll was mounting by the minute in tit for tat stabbings and beatings. Any captured Muslim prisoners were in turn lynched and sometimes murdered by the non-Muslim prisoners in retaliation.

In total, approximately 250 Muslim prisoners had escaped from the two category A dispersal prisons. In security terms, the 250 Muslim prisoners were classed as the most dangerous in society. As they arrived in Muslim districts some of them in turn created civil unrest and cajoled other Muslims to riot in many cities up and down the country. Some of the UK inner city areas were turned into war zones as the Muslim community attacked western businesses and persons of non-Muslim faiths.

The police and security forces simply couldn't cope, the United Kingdom had not experienced anything on this scale since the Second World War.

Johiya didn't shout about it but he was quietly satisfied. It was all part of his grand plan to create civil unrest and in turn, a massive decoy. Now the real work could commence.

CHAPTER 40

Enhanced Interrogation Room Mi5

Julian Toore was sitting in a chair watching a video of the two bomb blasts at HMP Full Sutton and HMP Frankland. Toore saw both drivers get out of the vans and open the rear doors and then saw how the driver and the van disappeared in a massive ball of flame.

Baxter paced slowly in front of the screen. He was smiling. "You see, you were never going to help a handful of inmates escape, you were just going to be used to blow down the prison walls in a mass escape, you mean nothing to them, you've been conned."

Toore said nothing.

"Now, before we start. I want you to see some photos of other so called jihadists that have entered this room. Here are some before and after photos," Baxter said as he laid half a dozen photographs on the table.

Toore had a good look at the photos. The men looked as if someone had taken an axe to their faces. He really didn't need any further persuading to give information, especially now that he'd seen just how the Imam had tricked him. Only luck would have it that he was not dead right now.

Those videos weren't staged, it was time to talk. "The Imam at Whitemoor gave me the van, he's been good to me, he's looked after me since my release."

"Which Imam Mr Toore?"

"The Whitemoor Imam, the Imam who works at the prison."

"Run that that upstairs to Fletcher," Baxter instructed Clarke.

"Now then Julian, do you know what my hobby is?" Baxter asked.

Toore just stared back at Baxter and saw a big sarcastic grin pull across the face of his interrogator.

"Let me tell you… my hobby is ancient torture methods, the sort used in the Medieval Inquisitions, I just love those old witch hunters don't you?" he took a drink from a glass of water on the table and cleared his throat. "Now my little Muslim convert, I think you've been holding back on me. Come on, what else do you know?"

Manningham, Bradford

As soon as Johiya learnt that the Whitemoor escape had gone belly up he knew it would not be long until Mi5 got hold of the Imams. Johiya immediately summoned the three Imam's to Manningham under the guise that they would be immediately smuggled out of the UK.

The Imams had always been told that an exit strategy had been in place for this eventuality.

One by one they arrived at the Islamic supermarket and made their way down to the basement and through to the abandoned house adjacent. They knelt down on a prayer mat as Johiya joined them in prayer. Johiya gave them dignity and time, just over five minutes to be precise and then as their heads were bowed and they kissed their prayer mat, the executioner stepped out from behind the curtain and calmly put a bullet into their heads and they were carried through to an adjacent room. The owner of the shop heard nothing, the silencer on the gun barely registered a noise. Nevertheless Johiya also decided to murder the shop owner to further distance any links to his cell. He was called down to the basement on the promise of a payment and quietly dispatched the same way.

CHAPTER **41**

10 Downing Street

The PM walked up and down the boardroom impatiently.

"So we now know that these prison escapes were organised by the visiting Imams."

"Yes, sir," Beckett said.

"And their whereabouts?" queried the PM.

"Unknown, sir. We have arrested all their immediate families and they have all stated that they left the house on the afternoon of the incidents and never returned. They have either fled the country or could have even been taken out of the equation."

"You mean they could have been killed to sever all ties with those organising this?"

"Yes sir, it's a pattern. What we now know is that three missing persons were reported in the local areas of the football bombings. All three just so happened to be ex-prisoners who coincidentally happened to be on the Muslim wings at the category A prisons. All three men were living fairly normal lives after their release and had jobs in the same local area as the same three Imams who preach at the prisons."

The PM folded his arms across his body as he listened intently.

"The capture of Julian Toore at HMP Whitemoor has shown us that the Imams were sending the converts on one way missions. They achieved the goal of causing mayhem but by being killed in the bomb blasts removed any chance of a link to the Imams. It's therefore totally logical that the people behind this will silence the Imams too, because they suspect Toore could have talked, they know we will have shown him the CCTV footage."

"So we are in a race against time. We need to find these Imams or their corpses now."

"Yes Sir, we are also arresting every single prisoner who was on the Muslim wings before they were released. Any ex-con who was on the Muslim wings must now be suspected as a potential bomber, either willing or unwilling," Beckett said.

"How many prisoners are we talking about here?" asked the PM.

"It could run to thousands Sir, the truth is we just haven't got the resources to come close to investigating this."

The PM took a drink from a glass on the table as Beckett continued.

"We're in touch with the CIA at Langley and their Quartz programme is currently being used to correlate the three Imams' mobile phones with locations to look for any patterns. If these mother fuckers have made a mistake the Quartz programme will pick it up," she added.

"Very good," the PM responded.

"What's happening in Islamabad sir?"

The PM sighed. "Our embassy is surrounded by the Pakistani Army; it's the only thing that's stopping the locals taking revenge. I just don't know how long that support will last. The entire city is baying for every Englishman's blood, this fucking English National Army is now known all over the world. In fact it's not just Islamabad. Each and every one of our embassies or consulates in Islamic countries are under siege. I don't know how long the governments of these countries can protect them," he added.

Beckett shared her concern. "Whoever this English National Army are, they need to be caught immediately. They could start a war with Pakistan and remember they have nuclear capabilities." The PM massaged his temples. "What are the casualty figures for the Oval?" he asked.

Beckett rubbed a tired hand over her furrowed brow. "We have six thousand dead and over a thousand seriously injured. All live on Sky sports, might I add."

"And not forgetting the entire Pakistani cricket team, you know Beckett, some of our Muslim neighbourhood's have been turned into self-proclaimed caliphates. We have dozens of no go areas in our own cities and we have every fascist or bigot attacking anyone with brown skin regardless of whether they are a Muslim or not. It's total fucking anarchy." He rubbed his temples as he contemplated the situation. "I need to know what you're doing to bring this under control, how the fuck will we win the election with all this shit going on?"

Becket opened a small notebook as she scanned some notes. "The army has been mobilised to take back the Muslim areas in our cities, most of the escaped prisoners will be back in custody and the prisons will soon be back under control. We know it was a network of Imams that were deceiving ex-prisoners to go on bombing missions. We've broken the camel's back Sir."

"Fuck me, some good news," the PM said sarcastically.

"And we are tracing and arresting each and every prisoner who has been released from the category A prisons. They'll be held in custody until we decide they are safe enough to be released and every Mi5 and Mi6 operative is working on tracing this Islamic terror cell and the ENA. These individuals are our priority."

The PM nodded his agreement, gestured towards the door. "Okay Beckett, don't hang around, get on with it, there's the door over there."

"Yes Sir."

As Beckett left he buried his head in his hands. "What a fucking mess," he mumbled to himself, "A real fucking mess."

The next morning Jack Bradshaw serving Prime Minister of the UK resigned.

CHAPTER 42

The new Conservative Prime Minister was quickly appointed by her fellow conservative MP's and despite her being a woman she and her learned colleagues firmly believed she had what it takes to govern the country which was actually on a undeclared war footing. She sat down in her private office and thought back to the open door immigration policy of previous Labour governments and in particular the war criminal Tony Hardy. She knew it was his policy that allowed millions of Muslims into the UK and amongst those millions, god knows how many terrorists. It was Hardy and his war mongering American pal that had started most of the wars in the middle east and in her opinion they had blood on their hands, of that there was no doubt and somehow she would see that Tony Hardy was held to account.

* * *

Fletcher studied the latest report from the Quartz super computer. The computer had been fed the recent information available to both the CIA, Mi5 and Mi6 relevant to the current bombing campaign on the British mainland and forensics had confirmed that the explosives used in the football bombings was of the exact same explosive mixture as used in the prison escapes.

The Whitemoor escape plot had been the real breakthrough as the prisoner had quickly revealed that the Whitemoor Imam had supplied the bomb for the van and it followed on that the Imams at both HMP Frankland and HMP Full Sutton were also involved. Unsurprisingly all three Imams had disappeared, possibly murdered by their own terror cell or secreted out of the country immediately after the prison escapes.

The investigation had also produced another vital piece of evidence. In the areas local to the football bombings three people had been reported missing. It turned out that the three missing people had all been in prison at Whitemoor, Frankland and Full Sutton. Not only were they in the same prisons as the visiting Imams they were also Muslim converts who had been on the Muslim only wings.

The missing ex-prisoners were also recorded by probation officers as being assisted by the same three Imams upon their release from prison and DNA checks on the body parts left at the football bombings had provided positive matches on all three, another three families bereaved and grieving in the name of suicide bombings for Allah and Islam.

It was therefore vital that the computer discovered any pattern in relation to the Imams mobile phones, it was possible that it could point to the discovery of the entire terror cell.

The Imams had to plan the bombings and would have almost certainly met with the explosive experts.

The first round of investigations into the three Imams mobile phones had revealed that they were all turned of at the exact times of the football bombings. It was safe to assume that to avoid detection the Imams' mobile phones had also been switched off at various other phases of the terror operation. Quartz had already produced a print out of 247 UK mobile numbers that were coincidentally turned off whenever the Imams numbers were turned off. These 247 numbers were now being screened to evaluate their potential involvement in the terror plot.

Fletcher held in his hand a document headed *Top Secret* that the CIA had entrusted to him. The report referred to an Al Qaeda suspect who had been recently captured in IRAQ by US Special Forces. The terror suspect had been held under the American rendition programme and Fletcher knew full well that the report could be deemed as 100% accurate.

The latest Al Qaeda interrogation of the suspect suggested that the planner of terror cells did not normally turn off their mobile phone, so as to provide a buffer or a different set of parameters to those in the cell who turned their phones off when meeting and planting bombs.

Armed with this latest information the Quartz super computer searched the three Imams mobile numbers against each and every mobile number used in the United Kingdom. A number belonging to a Mr Michael Cliff was identified as never having made any calls during the exact times the Imams phones were switched off. But what really stood out was that Michael Cliff never sent any text messages, never went online and the phone remained static, in one exact location.

It was enough of a coincidence to prompt Fletcher into action.

Fletcher still had his doubts about the Quartz programme and the reasoning behind the assertion that a number, just because it did not move or make a call was worthy of an Mi5 investigation but it was an experienced operatives hunch that he just couldn't shake off. Still he had procedures to follow so he picked up the phone and called Baxter.

"Baxter, get up to my office pronto."

Baxter read the report intently. The phone number was on but not being used at the exact time of the football bombings and the prison breakouts.

The report also identified each and every number ever linked to the phone and this was where the problem was because all the calls to and from the number had been identified as irrelevant. No suspicious numbers of any other suspects and no calls to the Imams.

"What do you think?" Fletcher asked.

"I don't know Sir, it's a remarkable coincidence but then again it could be nothing. I suggest we put one of the research officers at GCHQ and a surveillance team on this Michael Cliff to see what comes up."

Fletcher shook his head, "Costly, a two man surveillance team as well as a research officer, a bit OTT isn't it?"

"It's your call Sir, but we are getting nowhere on anything else at the moment, I recommend changing the detail to cover surveillance on this Michael Cliff."

Fletcher shook his head, "not just yet, I think GCHQ is enough for the time being and if anything comes up I will review it."

"Yes Sir, as I said it's your call."

There was just an underlying hint of sarcasm in Baxter's voice.

Baxter ordered one of the research team, Sarah Blunt, to monitor the mobile number belonging to a Michael Cliff. She had no idea that the Quartz super computers had identified the number as a number of interest and was only told by Baxter to notify him if the phone remained in the same GPS location without being used. For the next ten hours she sat in front of her computer screen listening to the mundane family and work calls to and from the number.

Blunt learnt that Cliff was going away on a short business trip. By late afternoon the mobile phone was still receiving various calls but they all went to answerphone. No return calls were made which puzzled her. In addition, the phone hadn't logged onto the internet at any time and the GPS revealed that the mobile phone number was stationary at the registered address in Stevenage. More unusual was that GPS positioning of the three other numbers that made the most regular calls, his wife and two daughters were also at the same location of the target phone in Stevenage.

Several times the wife and daughters tried to call 'Dad' and they left several voice mail messages complaining that he wasn't picking up his messages. There was one specific message of interest where his wife berated him, she said that even if he had lost his phone he must surely know by now and at least should have contacted her. Why the wife was leaving messages relating to her husbands 'lost' phone was also irregular, because the phone was switched on but at the same address as the people ringing the number. That could only mean that the mobile phone was on silent.

Sarah Blunt picked up the phone and called Baxter.

Sarah relayed the information to Baxter.

"Good work Sarah," he said as he hung up the phone and as soon as he had replaced the receiver he picked it up again, dialed a number and ordered an emergency surveillance squad to monitor Michael Cliffs home address. He called Fletcher and told him the details.

"You should have run this past me," Fletcher said, "committing to an emergency surveillance squad as a major decision and you're not running the show yet."

"Yes Sir," Baxter said calmly.

Fletcher scratched at the side of his temples. "Where are the team now?"

"Outside Sir, I'm going with them."

"Okay, get your arse into gear and keep me posted."

"Yes Sir."

CHAPTER 43

Bradford Discount Exhaust Centre

A sign stated that the Bradford Exhaust Centre was shut until further notice. Ongoing maintenance work it said. However inside the garage, work of an entirely different nature was being undertaken.

Khan and Talpur had been mixing tons of fertilizer with diesel, in preparation for a huge bomb. The mixture was loaded into forty, thirty gallon steel containers and each steel container had a five kilogram bottle of acetylene added inside the drum. The containers were sealed and loaded into a large delivery truck. Fifty domestic gas cylinder bottles were also loaded into the truck. Khan and Talpur then set about clearing the evidence of their deadly work.

The small side entrance to the garage then opened and Khan saw Othmane and another man enter. He had not met this man before. The door was quickly closed and locked from the inside. Khan studied the second man with a look of surprise. He was small, very slim and with little or no hair and wore old-fashioned spectacles.

He was also white skinned. Johiya's family ties could be traced back to the British Empire's invasion of Afghanistan back in the 1800s. Thousands of Afghan women bore children to the invading British colonial soldiers and Johiya's lineage was the result of this mixing of races.

"This is Johiya, our leader," said Othmane as he introduced Khan to Johiya for the first time.

Johiya was not surprised by Khan's reaction when he met him. Johiya had met hundreds of Jihadi fighters in Afghanistan and each and every one gave him a second look. Johiya just didn't look like a fighter or a Muslim for that matter. If anything, Khan thought that Johiya looked like the type of person who worked in a suburban office doing a mundane nine to five job, probably in accounts or book keeping. And that was exactly what Johiya did. However, one thing that Khan did notice was Johiya had dead eyes. In fact Othmane and Talpur also had the same dead look in their eyes. But Johiya's eyes also portrayed real intelligence.

Johiya shook Khan's hand.

"Pleased to meet you Mohammed Khan," Johiya said.

"Honoured and pleased to meet you."

The simple pleasantries seemed surreal considered that standing next to the men was a truck loaded with enough explosives to blow them into oblivion.

"We are impressed with your work Khan, Othmane and Talpur have spoken highly of you." Johiya said with a polite smile.

"I only wish to serve Allah, I am ready to make my sacrifice."

Johiya looked deep into the eyes of the man before him. He had looked into the eyes of many men who had made the ultimate sacrifice in the fight against the infidels. Khan had the same look of a man who knew and understood his destiny.

"Let us pray," said Johiya.

The four men faced Mecca and prayed. Once they'd finished their prayers they ran through the final phase of their plan. Johiya was a meticulous planner and when he had finished he handed each of them new smart phones and ordered that all communications would now be via these phones.

Johiya paused and stood silent for a few moments. It was not an awkward silence as the group of terrorists knew that the talking and the planning stage was over. Johiya faced the three men.

"So Talpur, my dear friend, if all goes to plan you will soon be in paradise and your martyrdom will be remembered for all eternity."

Talpur stepped forward and embraced Johiya for the last time.

Johiya turned to Khan. "And brother, you too are at the point where your sacrifice will be remembered for all eternity. The long journey you have undertaken has brought you to Islam and you will set an example to all those still suffering in your society that the Muslim way is the true path to freedom and liberty. I applaud you."

"Thank you my emir, I promise I won't let you down. I am honoured that it is me you have chosen to serve Islam."

Othmane and Talpur faced each other.

"Goodbye my dear friend," Othmane said as they embraced.

"Goodbye Talpur, we will meet in a better place," he responded, a place with rivers of wine and beautiful virgins, a place that Allah has chosen for us, a place where we belong."

The battle hardened Al Qaeda soldiers did not need to say anymore. They had reached the point of their existence.

Slowly at first and quietly the four men began to chant in unison. "Allah Akbar, Allah Akbar, Allah Akbar, Allah Akbar."

Talpur walked over and opened up the main shutters to the garage and Othmane drove one of the specially adapted terror vans out into the courtyard. Johiya pulled up right behind the terror van in a silver Ford Mondeo.

Soon after Khan left to collect his family. It was time for another trip along the Grand Union Canal.

CHAPTER 44

Much to Rebecca's surprise, Khan had booked another trip on the canal barge and although Rebecca enjoyed the previous trip she had noticed a slight change in her man's attitude and behaviour in the past few weeks. He had stopped playing with his daughter and had seemed very distant. Rebecca put this down to her working particularly long hours at his new job. She surmised that perhaps that was why Khan needed a relaxing break on a canal boat.

When Khan arrived at the boat yard he was relieved to see the same barge as he had previously hired several weeks before. He had specifically asked for the same boat. He knew how to handle it and wanted no mistakes on their journey south. The perfect little family boarded the boat and waved to the owner of the boatyard as they made their way south down the canal.

Later that evening Khan moored up at a very quiet spot in the Grand Union Canal. He had specifically chosen the location, adjacent to where he had moored up was a track. While Khan waited he chatted to Rebecca and played with his daughter.

"John, are you okay?" Rebecca asked.

"Yeah, all good."

"You seem a little distant that's all, I'm worried about you."

Khan shrugged his shoulders. "Look love, I have a lot on my mind at the moment, with work and things, there's a lot going on."

He was cut short by the noise of a lorry approaching and jumped to his feet. He listened again and then jumped off the barge and onto the bank.

"John, what are you doing?" she shouted after him.

Khan put his fingers to his lips, "Shh…stop shouting."

Rebecca was frightened. John was somehow different, he was cold and distant, he had a blank expression in his eyes and she wondered why they were berthed in such an isolated part of the canal. She spotted headlights and realised that a vehicle was heading towards them.

Minutes later a small truck pulled up next to the barge.

Khan turned to speak to her, "Rebecca, take Lucy below, I have work to do."

"What do you mean you have work to do? We are meant to be on a holiday. What's going on with you John? For Christ's sake it's eleven o' clock at night."

"Shut the fuck up woman. Just do as you're told and take Lucy to the bedroom. Do it now before I take you down there myself."

Khan had never raised his voice at Rebecca before; she felt vulnerable and thought it best to go below and try and get Lucy off to sleep. Minutes later Rebecca heard the door of her cabin being locked.

"John, what the hell"

"It's better that you stay in the cabin for the time being," he interrupted, try and get Lucy off to sleep."

"But John, open this door, talk to me for fucks sake."

Rebecca listened as the sound of his footsteps disappeared along the boat decking and she was left with her own thoughts.

Khan and Talpur transferred the cargo from the truck onto the barge. They loaded sheets of one centimetre thick plating and fixed it strategically around the engine compartment and then into positions that would protect the barrels and gas bottles that they also loaded on. Talpur welded a steel compartment around the helm of the barge and painted the steel compartment with the same paint as the colour of the barge.

They brought on forty drums of explosives and the fifty gas bottles. They arranged them inside the barge in a manner so as to keep the barge balanced in the water.

A couple of Kalashnikov AK-47's and an AK-74 were also hidden on the barge along with one hundred fully loaded magazines.

The next morning Rebecca woke up. She went to the door and found it unlocked. She wandered through to the galley and saw John chatting with another man. She remembered him as the man who had visited her home and given Lucy presents several months earlier. For a few moments Rebecca's fear abated as she remembered the man being ever so friendly and recalled that he was one of John's bosses.

The fear instantly returned when she saw an automatic rifle slung over the man's shoulder. Rebecca looked around the main cabin and could see that the barge was now filled up with steel drums and gas bottles. Rebecca felt sick as she realised that something very sinister was going on, but at the same time she knew that whatever they were up to John wouldn't dream of harming the daughter he idolized. No, whatever it was they were planning, he wouldn't put his family at risk. He had been a devoted father since the birth and now, even in her confused state of muted panic, Rebecca clung to the belief that he could not and would not bring their daughter any harm.

"John, you have to tell me what's going on, what are you doing with this man? What about your daughter, why has he got a gun?"

Khan stared at Rebecca as if she did not exist. It was Talpur who spoke.

"Rebecca, do not worry, everything is going to be okay. You are going to be part of something very special, you will be of great assistance in our fight against the infidels and oppressors," he said.

"Excuse me, what infidels, what oppressors? What fucking fight are you talking about?"

"Islam's fight," Talpur said, almost apologetically.

"Islam, fucking Islam, is this what this is all about, the bloody bombings and the prison riots," she turned to Khan, "how the hell are you mixed up in all this John?"

"It is Allah's will," Talpur said softly.

Rebecca placed her two hands on her head. "Right, that's it, I'm off, I just want to take my child and leave this stupid boat."

Finally Khan broke his silence. "You will stay with me woman, you will be part of this glorious sacrifice."

"What sacrifice, what are you talking about? Have you gone mad John?"

He stepped forward and gripped her tightly by the arm. "Mad, how dare you call me mad. You know nothing."

Rebecca started to struggle, "get the fuck off me, let me go."

Khan was fit and powerful, she was no match for him. He spun her around and started to push her out of the room. He slapped her hard across the face and as she burst into tears he forcefully marched her along the narrow walkway and back into the bedroom where Lucy was still sleeping.

Rebecca threw herself onto the bed beside Lucy. Khan looked at her and his sleeping child and then closed the door. Rebecca heard Khan lock the door behind him. Her first thought was to try the skylight and the port windows to see if she could escape. Her stomach churned as she realised that the skylight and the port windows had been locked from the outside.

A few minutes later Rebecca heard chanting, they were praying.

She was in denial. "No, no," she cried out.

Without warning the boat gave a slight jolt and Rebecca heard the rumble of the diesel engines as the barge lurched forward and started its journey. She buried her face in the pillow and sobbed like a child.

CHAPTER 45

Othmane had driven the white transit van down from Bradford to London. Once he reached the M25 he went clockwise around the motorway until he reached the A127 and then he headed for Southend on Sea. Throughout the journey Johiya followed close behind in a silver Ford Mondeo.

Southend on Sea's new airport had recently opened, it catered for domestic flights and short haul international flights into Europe. Othmane parked his van in a car park just off the seafront, it was 6 p.m. The car park was littered with vans and other commercial vehicles, the drivers and passengers using the seaside hotels to bed down for the night.

Johiya parked alongside the van and joined Othmane as he climbed into the passenger seat. As night descended the two men went through a specially made hatch into the back of the van. One man slept whilst the other man stayed awake, an AK-47 rifle by his side and after a few hours they swapped places.

They didn't get much sleep and by 5.30 a.m. they were both wide awake. Johiya walked over to a small cafe and bought some coffee and then returned to the van.

Southend airport was considered by Johiya to be a soft target. Heathrow and Gatwick airports had serious levels of protection as they were thought to be the most likely target for a terrorist attack, but for some reason the authorities hadn't flagged Southend Airport up as any real importance. Both Heathrow and Gatwick airports had huge airfreight operations and this meant that the surrounding areas had large industrial estates catering for all the businesses associated with the airport and cargo. The areas were extensively protected with numerous security companies patrolling, making both Gatwick and Heathrow airports too risky for the next stage of Johiya's plan.

Apart from the air passenger terminal and a small car park, the area around the airport was residential. Johiya had visited Southend on many occasions as he planned his next outrage.

At 6 a.m. Othmane drove the white transit van into a Lidl car park that was under the flight path of the departing planes from Southend airport. Johiya parked the Mondeo a few blocks away, walked back to Othmane's van and crawled through into the back once again.

Johiya opened up a box and carefully lifted out the surface to air missile. He gently laid it on the floor of the van and both he and Othmane made a special prayer to the missile.

"Let this tool of war bring vengeance for the death of our beloved leader Osama Bin Laden. "Allah Akbar, Allah Akbar," they chanted in unison.

Johiya made a few adjustments and then primed it ready for firing. Othmane removed the specially adapted removable roof which revealed a one metre square hole. And then they waited. At 6.35 the fine drizzle turned into a pitter patter of steady rain on the van roof.

CHAPTER 46

EasyJet Flight 2467 - Southend Airport

They had been at the airport for more than three hours, the little girl was excited but growing impatient by the minute.

The bell from the tannoy sounded and then the operator barked out her command.

Boarding for flight EZY 2467 to Malaga."

Douglas Brown jumped to his feet, he was almost as excited as his daughter. "Okay that's us."

Little Chloe Brown jumped to her feet too. "We're going on holiday, we're going on holiday," she sang as they queued up to board their flight to Malaga.

Chloe Brown sat between her parents. It was her first holiday abroad and she was very excited. She kept on standing on her chair so she could talk to another little boy sat in the row behind.

"Prepare for take-off," said the captain.

"Come on Chloe love, sit down and buckle up. We're taking off now," her mum said.

"Daddy, Daddy, I want you to buckle up my seat belt," she cried.

"Okay, okay," he said as he buckled up the seat belt. Her face was a picture of happiness.

The cabin crew and all the passengers were seated waiting to take off. Moments later the plane's engines roared into full power and the plane began to accelerate down the runway. Within fifteen seconds EasyJet flight 2467 was airborne and climbing fast.

Johiya looked at his watch. It was now 6.37a.m. A distant roar turned into a deafening drone as the first flight of the day left Southend airport bound for Malaga. Ten seconds after take-off the commercial EasyJet flight was directly above the van parked in the Lidl car park.

Johiya was kneeling down in the back of the van waiting to visualise the plane. He could hear it before he could see it but within seconds the EasyJet plane appeared in the sky directly above them.

"They make it easy for us," Johiya said to no one in particular.

He lined up the scope in the rough vicinity of the aircraft and fired the stinger missile. The warhead shot through the van roof and up into the sky.

It seemed to go slow at first, even looked as if it was going to stall but after less than a second or two its infrared radar locked on to the target and started gaining ground on the commercial airliner. A few drivers in the vicinity looked up as they saw the plane climb into the sky, some even noticed a second object hurtling towards the speeding aircraft.

Immediately after the stinger missile was fired, Othmane replaced the removable roof, and Johiya left the van and walked back to the silver Mondeo.

The stinger missile was five hundred metres behind the airliner, the heat seeking radar activated, searching for one of the airliner's engines. Within seconds the missile had locked onto the heat signature of the port side starboard engine.

As Johiya walked back to his car he watched the missile climb quickly behind the airliner. It took eleven seconds before it slammed into the starboard engine.

Douglas Brown was looking out of the small airplane window watching the Southend skyline. He was sitting six rows back from the wing, wondering what to order when the in-flight bar commenced and in a split second he saw an object slam into the plane's left side engine. Time seemed to stand still as there was a blinding flash and the plane shuddered and lurched violently to the left. There was a deafening noise and a rush of vacuumed air as shrapnel from the explosion tore through the fuselage. The oxygen masks fell from the ceiling and the wind howled through the cabin.

"Daddy, Daddy, what is it?"

Douglas looked back at the wing and saw that the engine had torn itself away from the plane and the wing was twisted and tearing apart.

"What's wrong Daddy, what's wrong Daddy."

The plane began to shake and appeared to stall in midair, it lurched to the left then started to dive towards the ground, people were screaming.

Douglas looked at his wife and saw nothing but terror in her eyes as the plane continued to plunge.

"Daddy, stop it, make it stop."

He leaned across and unbuckled his daughters seat belt and lifted her into his lap. He reached over and pulled his wife towards them and they held their daughter close.

"Together," he whispered softly, "together forever."

Above all the screams and noise the plane began to rip apart and plummeted towards the grounds despite the best efforts of the pilot. There was no possible chance of any survivors as it nosedived into the concrete at just over two hundred miles an hour and twenty two tons of aviation fuel exploded on impact.

Johiya sat in his car and waited for Othmane to drive by and pulled up directly behind the van. They pulled onto the A127 and began their drive back to London. As they passed Leigh on Sea they could see a huge plume of smoke coming from the crash site and they smiled at each other. Johiya lifted his right hand towards his friend and Othmane slapped it in a gesture they both recognised.

The timing of the terrorist attack was crucial. The British Government was in session at Parliament. The MP's and House of Lords were all debating various new laws and white papers the ruling conservatives had proposed in parliamentary session. The previous football bombings had also forced an emergency session of Parliament. Johiya had studied this and the recent history of other emergency sessions of parliament and the general rule was that the set timetable of each session was put back until after the 'debate' on the present emergency.

Johiya had to ensure that any terror attack was of enough magnitude to invoke an emergency session of parliament. Killing 253 people on a holiday flight fitted the bill nicely and the fact they had closed United Kingdom airspace for an indefinite period was an added bonus.

Johiya had shot down the airliner on that particular day due to the fact that high tide on the River Thames was at 6.23pm on the next day. Johiya needed a high tide for his plan to achieve maximum results.

CHAPTER 47

Stevenage, Hertfordshire

While Johiya and the rest of the terror cell were making good their plans Baxter was
personally heading up the emergency surveillance squad that had been positioned strategically around the target address for the past twenty four hours. All Mi5 surveillance procedures were fully implemented. Michael Cliff's wife and even the two daughters were now subjected to close personal surveillance. That meant that when Mrs Cliff left for work at the local hospital and the two Cliff daughters attended school, they and their close personal possessions were "tagged" with covert listening devices and where possible, also video recorded. The listening devices allowed Mi5 to monitor every aspect of the Cliff family's lives. When the wife and two children had left the house the Mi5 surveillance team also deployed a special heat seeking drone that had the capability to detect body heat inside a house. The team needed to be sure that the house was empty so they could place listening devices inside the

Cliff home. Once the drone confirmed that there was no evidence of a living person in the house the Mi5 team went in. But they were soon to be disappointed as efforts to bug the family home were soon thwarted by the discovery of a highly sophisticated alarm system.

Baxter shook his head, "Another little pointer I think, why on earth would an accountant and a nurse need such an elaborate alarm system?"

"Dunno Boss, something doesn't seem right with all this." one of the team said.

"Get on to the local plod and see if this house had been burgled or if something untoward happened here recently," Baxter barked out in frustration, "this makes no fucking sense at all or makes the greatest of sense."

Initial background checks had provided Mi5 with copies of UK passport and driving licence and details of Mr Cliff's credit history. The passport and driving licence photos revealed a nondescript Caucasian male. Both the children also took a resemblance to the photo of their father. The Mi5 research team had also hacked all the families Facebook and twitter accounts and frustratingly there was nothing in their personal media that actually pointed to Islamic terrorism. Baxter was getting impatient, this was not a time for pussy footing about. They should just go in arrest the wife and children and then interview them to try a find out where Micheal Clarke was. Interrogation was the way forward. There was only two logical reasons for surveillance equipment like this, someone was having an affair, or he was a terrorist. An affair would also account for Cliff's suspicious behaviour. If that was the case then so be it. If that's what it was least the manpower could be quickly redirected to other Islamic suspects.

Baxter checked his watch, it was 6.45am. He was fed up sitting in a van waiting for something to happen and decided to ring Fletcher. It was a bit early but so be it.

Fletcher answered, "this better be good."

"Sir, we have done all we can do on the surveillance front. This Clarke fella is away and we have no information as to where. The only info is that he is due back soon. In my opinion we need to raid and search the house to put this to bed otherwise we're just wasting time. What have we got to lose, this man could be planning another attack right now?"

He'd barely got the words out when his emergency pager started beeping and Baxter could hear Fletcher's pager also going off at the same time. That normally meant only one thing. He pressed the small black button to reveal the message.

AIRCRAFT SHOT FROM THE SKY AT SOUTHEND AIRPORT. NO SURVIVORS.

"Thats not good," he whispered to himself, "Not good at all."

He heard Fletcher on the other end of the phone with a similar reaction.

Baxter immediately switched to the BBC news channel on the van's monitor and viewed a mobile phone footage of an Easy Jet airliner falling from the sky. The plane disappeared from view for a few seconds then the video showed a huge plume of smoke and a fireball rising from where the plane had crashed to the ground.

The BBC newsreader was speculating that it was terror related, several eye witnesses had reported a possible missile attack.

Baxter had seen enough. "Sir, permission to enter this house now," he implored.

"Okay Baxter, do what you feel is best," Fletcher said.

Within two minutes Mi5 smashed down the door, which activated the alarm. Baxter immediately ordered the arrest of Mrs Cliff at the hospital and also the arrest of the Cliff daughters at their school. He told the arresting Mi5 officers to bring the family back to the house for immediate questioning.

CHAPTER 48

Othmane had driven the van towards London with Johiya following closely behind in the silver Mondeo. As they were nearing Walthamstow one of Johiya's mobile phones vibrated. It was the phone that he carried at all times. The phone did not receive or make calls but had a special SIM card that was linked to the alarm and covert home surveillance system he had rigged up at his home address. Johiya turned on the phone. He had rigged up special cameras hidden in day to day objects around his house. These motion sensor cameras now relayed images of a group of plain clothed men searching his house.

Johiya knew they were not burglars. The special smart phone app not only allowed him to see the images but the cameras also had audio equipment which allowed Johiya to listen to any conversations in his home. Johiya listened intently as the Mi5 officers ransacked his home. Johiya knew his position had been compromised. He felt frustrated as he couldn't think of any mistakes he'd made along the way, he thought he was untouchable, but he knew that the British security forces were the best in the world and somehow they were onto him. It was quite a poignant moment when one of the officers picked up a photo of Johiya and stared hard at his face.

"Where the fuck are you?" he heard, as Baxter studied the photo.

Johiya knew he had to ditch the phone immediately. Mi5 would be able to crack its security codes and trace its location. Johiya flashed his lights and Othmane quickly pulled over in the next available layby. Johiya followed closely behind. Once he was stationary Johiya got out of the Mondeo and had a quick look about to see that no one was close by. He bent down as if to tie up his shoelace and slipped the smart phone that was linked to his house alarm down a drain.

Johiya was annoyed that the security forces were onto him, but it was a minor setback as there were only hours until the final phase of the plan came to fruition. He smiled inwardly, there was no way their security forces had time to stop it.

A few hours later they booked in at a cheap motel in Walthamstow and bedded down for the night. Johiya turned on the 6 p.m. news and watched a bedraggled looking Prime Minister as she said that the downing of the EasyJet plane had been confirmed as a terrorist attack, and that Parliament and the House of Lords would convene tomorrow evening for an emergency session of parliament.

"Looks like they have taken the bait," Othmane said.

Johiya smiled, "Get some rest we have a busy day tomorrow."

The next morning Johiya rose early and got the underground to the Houses of Parliament.

He came out from Westminster tube station and found himself in a queue of people that were being randomly searched. Every single person who came out of the station was spoken to by specially trained police officers looking for potential terrorists. It was bedlam. Johiya waited his turn patiently.

"Sir, your reason for visiting Westminster today?" the police officer said.

"I'm meeting my daughter for lunch," Johiya replied.

Before the policeman had even made the decision to let him pass, Johiya knew exactly what he was thinking. He spoke perfect English, was Caucasian in appearance, he had no bag or rucksack and was smartly dressed. He had to make an instant decision and profile of Johiya didn't raise any cause for concern.

"Will that be all officer?" he asked, "I'm already running a little late."

"Yes Sir, have a nice day."

The policeman waived him through police checkpoint.

"I'm going to have a great day," he whispered under his breath.

Johiya noticed another queue of people all being searched and questioned to the point of aggressiveness. They were either black or of Arab Muslim appearance. He watched as the individuals were even made to lift up their clothes to show that they weren't wearing suicide bomb vests. He smiled to himself as he walked out of the station.

Johiya further surveyed the area around Westminster and the Houses of Parliament. His first thoughts were that the British had been busy. There was a considerable and increased police presence, with numerous patrols dotted around Parliament Square. All the police officers were now armed with machine guns.

The roads surrounding the Houses of Parliament had been closed off with huge concrete slabs. Johiya noticed one thing that the Prime Minister had not announced to the UK population. At each of the main junctions into Parliament Square there was an armoured car and a machine gun nest manned by soldiers. He was amazed by the sheer amount of tourists that chose to visit the Houses of Parliament even though the UK had been put on the highest alert for a possible terrorist attack, severe. Even more bizarre was that so many of the tourists were busy taking pictures of the armoured cars the machine gun nests and the accompanying soldiers.

They were clearly expecting a suicide bomb attack and it would now be impossible to drive a van or truck bomb close to the parliament buildings. Johiya had anticipated this and knew that the heightened security level would not affect his particular plan.

Security was very tight and even the pavement areas around the parliament building had been blocked off. Johiya walked purposely towards George Street and ordered a coffee in Costa Coffee. The view from Costa

Coffee gave him a good view of Parliament Square. He drank his coffee and made his way back to Westminster Tube Station. There was no police stop and search cordon for people leaving Westminster. Johiya took a train to Marylebone and walked to a Q-Park car park in Marylebone.

He bought another ticket for twenty four hours and went to a BMW car that he had parked there the previous week. He removed the old weekly ticket and placed the new twenty four hour ticket in the windscreen. He started the car to make sure it was okay to be moved later that day. Satisfied that everything was okay he looked at his watch. The emergency session of parliament was due to start at 6 p.m. Johiya had six hours to get back to Walthamstow, drive the van with Othmane to the Q-Park car park and then make his own way back to Westminster. Johiya took a brisk walk to Marylebone underground station. As he was walking to the station he made a call.

Talpur took the call and confirmed the barge's position. They were just about to go through the Brentford Lock.

CHAPTER **49**

Khan was waiting in line to go through the lock. He saw the lock keeper motion to him to steer the barge through the gates and waited while the gate behind the barge closed and the lock filled up with water from the River Thames.

Rebecca was still locked up in the barge's bedroom. Lucy was running around playing in the locked room and was oblivious to the situation presenting itself to her mum. Rebecca heard voices.

"Good day sir."

"Hello there."

It was her boyfriend, who was he talking to?

The conversation continued.

"How are you?"

"Fine, I'm here with my wife and daughter, they're down below relaxing."

Moments later Rebecca felt the barge move upwards as the lock began to fill with water. This was her only chance and she started to scream.

"Help, help, please help us."

The lock keeper was chatting to Khan as the water rushed into the lock. It was noisy but the lock keeper noticed something over the rushing water.

"What's that, I thought I heard a woman's voice?"

"I can't hear anything with all this noise," Khan replied.

Rebecca banged on the side of the barge. "Help us."

"Hang on, there it is again, it's coming from your barge."

The barge was near the top of the lock and the noise from the rushing water was reducing.

"It's a woman's voice shouting for help, what the hell is going on?"

"It's nothing," Khan said.

"Tell me what's happening or I'll call the police."

"It's nothing," Khan repeated.

"Nothing my arse, something is wrong, I'm going to phone for some help, you're staying put."

The lock keeper secured the lock and made his way back to the office. He didn't notice another man who had jumped off the back of the barge. As the lock keeper picked up the phone he felt something cold press against the side of his head.

"Put the phone down or I will kill you," Talpur ordered, digging the gun deeper into the lock keeper's temple.

He put the phone down and slowly turned to face Talpur who pointed the gun at his face.

"Open up the lock so we can go through," he demanded.

The lock keeper did as he was told and the lock gate slowly opened allowing the barge into the River Thames. Talpur motioned the lock keeper back into the office. He sat him in his seat. The lock keeper had his hands on his head.

"Please, don't hurt me, I'm an old man, a good Catholic."

"A Catholic eh?" Talpur said, as an interested frown crept across his face.

"Yes sir, don't hurt me, I'm a good man, never done no one no harm ever."

"Put your hands together and pray," Talpur said, "close your eyes and ask your god to spare your life."

The man fell onto his knees and started to pray furiously. "Please god, I …"

Talpur put the barrel of the gun against his forehead and before he could offer any sort of resistance pulled the trigger. The man keeled over backwards and fell to the floor.

Talpur smiled. "I guess your god wasn't listening was he?"

Talpur and Khan dragged his body onto the barge and threw it into the engine room.

"We need to gag your wife." Talpur said, "this incident could have put the whole operation at risk."

"I'll do it now," Khan said without hesitation.

He went down into the barge's bedroom and his daughter ran instinctively towards him trying to cuddle him.

"Daddy, Daddy, Mummy crying," she said.

Khan pushed his daughter aside and turned to his wife, "thanks to you the lock keeper is dead and I can't take a chance on you risking our mission to Allah any more. I need to sort you out."

"Please John, look at our beautiful daughter," she pleaded as her eyes flooded with tears, "this madness has to stop."

Khan stepped forward and punched Rebecca in the face. As she crumpled to the floor he gagged her and chained her to a secure radiator. Lucy began to scream uncontrollably and Talpur came to the cabin door. He looked down and saw Lucy screaming by her mother's side. He picked her up and gave her a cuddle then took her into the main living quarters telling her that mummy and daddy were just playing games. He started to play hide and seek with her. Lucy quickly calmed down as she played amongst the explosive drums and gas bottles.

Khan locked the cabin door and walked back through the main quarters where his child was playing with Talpur. He ignored his daughter and spoke to Talpur.

"We have work to do."

Talpur's mobile rang. He spoke to the person on the other end. It was a one way conversation, Talpur didn't say one word.

Talpur turned to Khan.

"You're right," Talpur said, "and we have just three hours in which to do it."

Khan nodded, turned and left. He went back onto the deck of the barge and steered onto the River Thames.

CHAPTER **50**

Stevenage, Hertfordshire

Baxter had watched as the Cliff's front door was smashed down and then, along with one of Mi5 specialised search teams began to search the premises. They soon found something of interest

"Sir, we've got a private monitor system here," one of the search team members announced.

"Here, got another one," another member of the team called out.

Baxter looked at the array of everyday household items that contained the special cameras and listening devices. He knew that whoever was on the receiving end of this equipment knew that they were onto him. Baxter had encountered these systems before and knew that these cameras were linked to a smartphone. He knew that someone somewhere had probably watched him enter and search the house.

"Richards, get the computer and try and trace the smartphone linked to these cameras," he ordered.

Ten minutes later Fletcher's phone rang.

"Sir, it's me Baxter, we've found a very high tech home surveillance and audio system that's linked to a smartphone by a special app. Whoever was on the end of that phone now knows we are onto him," said Baxter.

"Why is an accountant self-surveilling his own home?" asked Fletcher.

"Exactly. His wife and his children have been interviewed and they claim they know nothing about the surveillance system and the wife is shocked that her husband would put her under surveillance. She claims to never have been unfaithful and loves her husband very much and for what it's worth I believe her."

Baxter glanced out of the lounge window as he spoke. He saw a clearly broken woman being put into the back of an Mi5 car. She would be taken to the local police station for formal questioning .

"These systems are sometimes bought by people who have been burgled but our checks show that this address has never been burgled nor has this Michael Cliff ever reported any crime." Baxter said.

"I see," Fletcher replied.

"Then we have the Quartz programme that has identified this man's mobile phone as relevant, sir. I've got a bad feeling about this. I think we should put a nationwide bulletin on all media platforms to trace this man. I mean we've just had a surface to air missile shoot down an EasyJet flight."

"A coppers hunch eh?"

"Yes sir, call it that if you want and this man was co-incidentally off the grid again at the same time, but more worryingly he remains off the grid."

"Okay Baxter, I see where you're coming from. I'll make a decision but I think we need a bit more. You know what those civil liberty lawyers are like."

"Yeah and half of them are Muslims," Baxter said sarcastically as he hung up.

Fletcher had his resources stretched. He now had one hundred Mi5 officers trawling over hundreds of CCTV cameras in Southend, hoping to find something, a link to identify the persons responsible for shooting down the airliner.

Fletcher looked out over his control room and waited for one of his remaining three analysts still working in the control room to find something more conclusive on Michael Cliff before splashing his photo all over the world. Fletcher lit a cigarette ignoring the no smoking rules.

London, Marylebone

Johiya and Othmane drove in convoy from Walthamstow to Marylebone without any mishaps. Othmane pulled into the Q-park while Johiya found a spot close by to dump the Mondeo. Johiya walked back to the Q-Park and beckoned Othmane to follow him as he made his way to the black BMW previously parked in a very strategic position.

Johiya jumped into the BMW and reversed it out of its parking space; Othmane immediately drove the white van into the vacated space. Johiya parked the BMW in another empty space further along. He walked back to the white van and got into the back.

The Q-Park car park was the only open air car park within a four kilometres of the Houses of Parliament. The car park was specifically chosen because it provided the necessary trajectory to launch the final wave of their attack.

Johiya and Othmane spent the next ten minutes setting up the mortar. The van had been fully prepared back at the workshop in Bradford and all they had to do was bolt the tripod to a pre-drilled and tapped holes, and then attach the mortar tube. This was second nature to both Othmane and Johiya as they had practiced it many times before. Nothing was left to chance.

"OK Tabish, my very, very dear friend, are you ready?"

"Yes."

"This is it now, today we avenge our families and all other Muslim families affected by these infidels. Alaintiqam hu alqarib."

"Yes Jalal, I will see you on the other side. Alaintiqam hu alqarib."

The two Muslim brothers had uttered the words *revenge is nigh* in Arabic.

"Now is the time we will fulfil our pledge to our great leader Osama," Johiya said as he bowed his head, "Allah Akbar."

"Allah Akbar, Othmane repeated as they embraced for the very last time.

"I will call you when I'm in position. Goodbye my friend."

"Goodbye, Jalal."

Johiya left the van and made his way back to Marylebone underground tube station. Johiya knew that it was a bit risky using Westminster tube station so he decided to get off the tube at St. James's Park and make the five minute walk to Parliament Square. Nothing could be left to chance, no risks at this stage of the proceedings.

The Houses of Parliament

Johiya looked at his watch. It was 5 p.m. The emergency session of Parliament was due to commence in an hour. Johiya made his way out of the exit at St James's Park tube station and found himself in another queue of people that were being screened by the police. Johiya was slightly nervous, the police had switched the profiling officers to different stations and he was worried that the same police officer he had met earlier at Westminster tube station might recognise him and his daughter for lunch story would fall apart.

As he reached the police cordon his fears were allayed; he looked around, there were about six police officers, none of which were the same officer as at Westminster. Johiya was asked exactly the same questions as he was previously and to his relief he was waved through.

Johiya walked quickly to George Street and entered the Costa Coffee he had previously visited earlier that day. He bought a coffee and a cookie and hovered around waiting for a window seat to become available. Costa Coffee was packed with tourists and he had to wait nearly ten minutes for a seat with a perfect view.

Johiya made himself comfortable, had a good view of Parliament Square and the Houses of Parliament.

He rang Talpur.

"Your position?" he asked in a whisper.

"Lambeth Bridge."

"Okay, hold up there and wait for my signal," he instructed.

The dry run from Khan's previous trip down the River Thames was crucial in determining the timing of the attack.

Lambeth Bridge

Talpur sat hunched in the cabin trying to keep out of sight. Khan was steering the barge, treading water, waiting to hear the command to go. He was 700 metres from the Houses of Parliament in the downstream lane of the River Thames. Khan watched the river closely. There were two police launches patrolling the Houses of Parliament security zone. The police had clearly doubled their security detail since the recent attacks. The clock was ticking.

Johiya looked at his smartphone, it was 6 p.m. and he watched as Sky news began their live feed on the emergency session of Parliament. He watched as the Prime Minister stood up to address the packed House of Commons and the nation in general.

Johiya made a call to Othmane.

Q-Park Car Park, Marylebone

Othmane removed the false roof on the van. He put on heavy duty ear protectors and a gas mask and picked up a high explosive round and dropped it into the mortar pipe. He turned his face away as the automatic propelling system kicked in and the van shook as the mortar positioning round shot through the roof space and headed in the direction of the Houses of Parliament.

Johiya sat patiently in Costa Coffee. He was expecting the first mortar and was not disappointed when he saw a flash of light followed by a dull thud. The mortar landed in amongst a group of tourists sitting in the grassy area in front of Parliament Square. Johiya could see the panic in the immediate area where the mortar had landed, he could see still bodies and people running around wondering what had happened, but it was as if the thousands of tourists milling around Parliament Square hadn't seen anything.

In Costa Coffee, the atmosphere had stayed as it always had been; people were too busy in their own little worlds to even acknowledge that something untoward might be occurring. The faces of the customers showed little more than slight interest as they tried to understand the strange noise. He typed a text message to Othmane.

ELEVATION 1 DEGREE. 0.5 DEGREE TO LEFT.

Q-Park Car Park

Othmane received the text message and raised the elevation of the mortar by one degree and half a degree to the left. He then fired the second mortar round.

Johiya watched as the second round landed on the pavement about twenty metres directly in front of the entrance to Westminster Hall. Several police officers lay dead or injured on the ground. It drew the predicted response. Johiya watched as thousands of people in the area of the Houses of Parliament scattered in all directions in their panic to escape the mortar attack. He turned to the live Sky News feed. Johiya sometimes couldn't believe how stupid the British could be. The nation was in a state of war where their attackers were within their own borders, yet they were doing a live televised debate on national TV which allowed Johiya to exactly pinpoint the target. He watched the Prime Minister stop mid-sentence in her speech as news of the mortar attack was relayed to her by her cabinet. A few seconds passed as the Prime Minister made enquiries with her front benchers as to the situation. Johiya watched as a dark suited man walked up to the Prime Minister and whispered something in her ear. She appeared to ask a question in response and then the man walked away. The Prime Minister then turned to the packed House of Commons.

"Ladies and gentlemen of the house. It appears we have some sort of security incident going on outside. It does not appear that we are in any immediate danger here so I will continue with the session until we establish the exact circumstances of the incident."

The customers in Costa Coffee had also heard the second mortar round land and then witnessed the mass panic as people began to run past the coffee shop. Some of the customers also started to panic and ran into the street, some stayed where they were. They didn't know whether it was safer to run outside or stay in the coffee shop. Johiya looked at his floor plan of the Houses of Parliament and worked out how to adjust fire so as to reach the House of Commons which was based deep inside the Houses of Parliament complex.

He sent another text message to Othmane.

ELEVATION 1 DEGREE.

Johiya watched the Sky News live feed while the third mortar round was making the short distance through the air from Marylebone to the Houses of Parliament. Johiya watched through the coffee shop window as the third round landed directly on the roof of Westminster Hall. There was a bright flash and the sound of the round exploding.

His eyes switched immediately to the live feed on his smartphone. He watched as the House of Commons shook from the direct hit, the stationary camera trained on the House of Commons vibrating from the impact.

Johiya watched with glee as four dark suited Secret Service men ran onto the floor of the house and quickly ushered the Prime Minister towards the exit. Another dark suited SS man spoke briefly to the Speaker of the House, who in turn stood up and addressed the MPs.

"Ladies and gentlemen the Houses of Parliament are now under attack and I request that you evacuate these chambers. I have been informed that everyone must make their way to the river terrace and wait for further directions. There is no need to panic, everything is under control."

Johiya smiled, "under control? Just you wait and see," he whispered under his breath.

He sent another message to Othmane.

ELEVATION 0.25 DEGREE.

Johiya dialed another number on his phone.

"Go now brother Talpur, may Allah be with you."

Johiya watched as the Prime Minister was led out of the exit followed by the entire entourage of the House of Commons who were evacuating the main chambers in a hasty but orderly fashion.

Johiya knew that the fourth mortar round was in the air and on its way, targeted towards the House of Commons chambers. He anticipated that this would be a direct hit and watched the Sky TV live feed intently. He was not disappointed when the fourth mortar round hot the roof and debris from the explosion began to fall directly onto the members of parliament who had been making their orderly exit. He grinned to himself, this was better than any movie he had ever watched at the cinema, it was so vivid, so real, he could almost smell and taste the death and destruction of the infidels. And he Johiya was the director.

The evacuation came to an abrupt halt as some members of parliament were knocked over by the blast wave and others felled by falling masonry.

Johiya could see that fatalities had occurred, it led to a mass panic in the Commons Hall.

"Now you know what it feels like," Johiya whispered quietly, "you gave the orders to bomb my brothers and sisters in Iraq and Libya and Afghanistan, you murdered their children, you bombed their schools and their hospitals."

The Sky news team abandoned their position but left the stationary camera recording live feeds. In the main, human self-preservation took over and the news feed relayed images to the entire world of the British elected representatives fighting each other and in some cases trampling on their fellow colleagues in their desperation to escape.

Some members of parliament did however show immense bravery and helped those who had fallen to the mortar blast. Johiya heard voices around him commenting on the spectacle as other people in the coffee shop watched the incident on their phones.

Johiya sent Othmane another text message.

SPREAD RANGE 0.5 LEFT AND 0.5 RIGHT DEGREES. ELEVATION 1 ROUND 0.25 BACK NEXT ROUND 0.25 FORWARD. FREE FIRE.

Johiya turned to his phone and watched as the spread of rounds began to land on a wider area to the north of the Houses of Parliament complex.

Clinton Adams was in charge of the Prime Minister's personal secret service guard. He had the PM located in a corridor while he awaited information from his fellow secret service officers as to the best way of escorting her to safety. Adams could feel the building shake from the direct hits of the mortar rounds. His radio buzzed with information as the agents outside reported that the north of the buildings of the Houses of Parliament was now being hit with multiple mortar rounds.

Adams knew that the entire House of Commons and the House of Lords had been told to make their way to the river terrace which was the furthest point away from the mortar attack. Adams spoke to Orca 1 patrol boat and ordered that it should be used for the evacuation of the Prime Minister and the senior cabinet. He ran up the corridor towards the Prime Minister. "Prime Minister we'll make our way to the river terrace and use the police launch to take you to safety. We have space for you and your senior cabinet."

The Prime Minister nodded, she looked dazed and unsure of what to do. Adams escorted her and her entourage through the maze of corridors towards the terrace. As they made their way out of the building and onto the terrace they felt some relief as they realised the blasts were clearly coming from the north of the building. More and more members of parliament made their way onto the terrace and within minutes the entire House of Commons and the House of Lords, along with all the staff of the Houses of Parliament were taking shelter there.

Once Adams, the Prime Minister and the cabinet reached the terrace, Adams ordered Orca 1 to pull up to the embankment.

"Prepare to evacuate the Prime Minister and the cabinet," he barked into his radio.

Within a matter of seconds, a member of the House of Lords pushed his way towards the Prime Minister's group.

Tony Hardy was blowing hard, sweating profusely. "Why should you lot be the first to evacuate?"

"Because she is the Prime Minister and protocol dictates that the Prime Minister and her cabinet are priorities in an incident such as this," Adams responded angrily through clenched teeth.

"Don't you know who I am?" Hardy screamed.

The Prime Minister turned to face Tony Hardy. "Oh we know exactly who you are, you're the one to blame for all this. You and your cronies conspired to bring millions of these people into our country to manipulate the elections and that's the only reason you stayed Prime Minister for so long."

She turned towards the Secret Service man. "Adams"

"Yes Ma'am"

"I want Hardy arrested and taken into custody. Do it right now," she ordered.

Hardy took a step back, panic written across his face, "but we are being bombed I'm not going back into that building."

Adams turned to the nearest Police officer. "Take Mr Hardy to the Guy Fawkes cell, it's well away from the mortar shelling, he will be quite safe there."

"Yes Sir"

The policeman placed his hand under Hardy's arm. "This way Sir."

Hardy pulled back, "unhand me now. how dare you"

The Policeman tightened his grip. "Please don't make it any worse Mr Hardy."

Hardy stepped towards the PM. "What charge am I being arrested on, I've done nothing wrong, tell me the charge this minute or tell this monkey to let me go."

The Prime Minister pondered for a second, she looked as if she was lost for words.

"Well?" Hardy shouted.

The Prime Minister smiled. "I'm not entirely sure Mr Hardy, I'm thinking war crimes at this present moment in time, but that's just for starters."

Hardy lunged at the Prime Minister but the policemen was too quick for him. He forced him into a headlock while another policemen managed to cuff him. He was led away sobbing like a child.

The Sky news helicopter hovered over the River Thames relaying clear live pictures of the terrace filling with the members of Parliament, House of Lords and back room staff. Literally the entire government of the UK was now waiting to be evacuated from the river terrace.

CHAPTER 51

Johiya rang Talpur. "They are in position, it is time."
Talpur went below deck and removed Rebecca's gag.
"Listen, I'm going to take you on the deck with Lucy. If you scream, shout or do anything to bring unwarranted attention to us I will kill you and throw your daughter into the river. If you behave yourself you will come out of this okay."
Rebecca was terrified, "you're lying," she sobbed.
"Do as I say and you'll be fine."
She still had no idea what was going on. In the previous hours her mind had gone into overtime thinking about how this would all end. Would Dodds let them go or was he on a suicide mission which involved taking them with him. Every single scenario had crossed her mind. She still believed that he would never harm his daughter and she clung to that belief as she was led onto the deck of the barge. She glanced out of the corner of her eye, she could see that the barge was full of petrol drums and gas bottles. She also noticed that there was a maze of wires linking the drums together and Talpur was rigging up a dummy in one of the windows. There was

a rifle pointing out of the window attached and bolted to some sort of tripod.

"John please, let us go," she begged, "do what you have to do but let us go."

Khan remained silent, he threw them two coats.

"Put these on, there's a chill wind running down the river and I want you to sit up top." Rebecca held Lucy tight as she was forced to the front of the barge as Talpur joined them.

"Sit down here," ordered Talpur.

Rebecca sat in a chair almost on the bow of the barge and Lucy sat on her lap.

Talpur pulled a length of chain from the deck and wrapped it round them. Rebecca tried to resist but Talpur back handed her across the face. Khan held her hands while Talpur threaded the chain around the back of the seat and locked a padlock in place.

"It's too tight," Rebecca cried, "we can hardly move."

Khan ignored her, knelt down and looked into his daughters eyes. He took her small hand. "Do not be afraid little one."

"Where the fuck are you taking us?" said Rebecca angrily.

"You know where I'm taking you."

"No I don't."

Khan smiled, "you do my love, I'm taking my family to paradise."

He gripped her head tightly as she tried to scream and fixed the gag back in place.

Talpur turned to face Khan. "This is it brother, Johiya's plan has worked and the rest is up to us. Our sacrifices will not be in vain. Make your way under Westminster Bridge and bring us under the second span," he ordered.

Khan opened up the throttle and the powerful diesel engine propelled the barge on its course down river. To travel down river, the designated side of the river was to the right bank, which was the opposite side to the Houses of Parliament. When Johiya had planned the attack he had decided not to attack directly across from the right side of the river as any police patrol boats would have plenty of time to turn their powerful 50 calibre machine guns on the barge.

Those guns had the capability to not only stop the barge but also ignite the huge amount of explosives on board. As Khan steered the barge passed the brightly lit river terrace they could see the entire British government milling about waiting to be rescued. Every now and then Khan could hear the dull thump of mortar rounds carried on the wind.

There was a police patrol boat moored up against the riverbank and Khan could see people boarding it. The second police boat was still patrolling up and down the Houses of Parliament security zone.

Khan passed the Houses of Parliament and went under Westminster Bridge where he made a U turn and then positioned the barge on the upstream side of the river. Khan looked up, he noticed people running across Westminster Bridge away from the direction of the mortar blasts. They waited about 50 metres south of Westminster Bridge. From here they could see through the spans of the bridge. Khan could see the second patrol boat making its sweep up and down the security zone.

Talpur placed a hand on Khan's shoulder. "Remember to wait for the second patrol boat to turn his stern on us before we come out from under the bridge. Do not speed or do anything that will alert the suspicions of the men on that boat, keep it cool. Once we are at the midpoint for the river terrace, go full throttle."

"Don't worry, I know exactly what to do," Khan said.

Talpur smiled, "I have faith in you brother, we are now both soldiers of Islam and we are going to be martyred together for all of eternity. Have no fear Khan, we will be going to paradise."

They hugged for the last time, "Allah Akbar," they called out together.

Talpur went below deck and set up his AK-74 which was specially adapted so that it could fire accurate single shots as well as rapid machine gun bursts. Talpur had also engineered a special silencer which he screwed onto the barrel of the AK-74. The silencer had a special design which reduced the flash when firing the gun. He'd made various holes in the barge's cabin to use as firing positions depending on how the attack developed. Looking through the front firing position, Talpur could see the patrol boat making its downriver sweep facing towards the barge. The 50 mm calibre, front mounted machine gun menacingly pointing in their direction. Those 50mm shells could rip the barge to pieces in seconds, they had to be careful.

It was twilight on the River Thames and the jihadi terrorists planned to use this to their advantage in the last few minutes of the attack. Orca 2 made its sweep and then turned back up river. This was it!

Talpur felt the barge lurch forward as Khan opened up the throttle and steered under the second span of the bridge. The plan was for him to stay in the designated upstream river channel and then at the last possible moment steer directly into the centre of the river terrace.

Khan could see that the second patrol boat in the security zone had now turned on their powerful searchlights and the crew were scanning the river for anything untoward. The patrol boat's crew were clearly on full alert. Khan was about one hundred metres behind the second patrol boat, in the correct river channel and gaining slowly. He had to make the centre of the terrace before the patrol boat made its turn from the northern perimeter.

Orca 1 was busy loading up the Prime Minister and the cabinet. This was taking a bit longer than anticipated as the Prime Minister insisted that the entire cabinet should be evacuated. The panic had caused several members of the Cabinet to be separated from the main group.

Orca 2 had made its sweep down to Westminster Bridge and then turned to go back up to the northern point of the Houses of Parliament. Officer Rodding was on the stern of the patrol boat and saw a canal barge coming out from under Westminster Bridge. The barge was not the only boat on the river and despite the mortar attack, numerous boats were still using the River Thames.

"Sir, got a canal barge coming upstream," he said.

Officer Barnes turned back to look at the boat. It somehow looked familiar and he studied the barge with his powerful binoculars. The barge had its mandatory night lights on and along with the last few minutes of daylight there was just enough light to make out features of the boat. He saw a barge commonly used by holidaymakers visiting the River Thames. The only thing that he noticed different from the other barges was that this particular one seemed lower in the water than normal. This aroused Officer Barnes's suspicions. The light was fading fast and he ordered Rodding to light up the boat with Orca 2's powerful rear searchlight.

Barnes could see a woman sitting in a chair holding a child, on a seat fixed to the bow of the barge. She was wrapped up against the cold, the child cuddled into her. He had a good look at the woman and then thought he recognised her as someone he had spoken to a few weeks earlier. The barge was in the correct part of the river and apart from being low in the water there was nothing really suspicious going on.

"It's okay crew, I know that boat," Barnes said, "holiday makers in a rented boat, just keep an eye on it while it passes the security zone," he added.

Talpur's plan of chaining Rebecca to the front of the boat had given the barge valuable seconds in carrying its deadly cargo to its destination. They were about thirty metres away from the point where they would turn the barge directly towards the centre of the river terrace. He could see that the patrol boat had stopped but had not yet made any attempt to turn and bring to bear the powerful 50mm front cannon on the barge.

Talpur waited. He was ready to fire his AK-74 the moment the patrol boat made any sign of a turn. Moments later the searchlight swung away from the barge and scanned other areas of the river, giving the barge valuable seconds to reach its final destination. Talpur could still see one of the patrol boat's officers looking directly at the barge through binoculars.

Khan reached the centre point directly adjacent to the terrace and opened up the throttle to maximum... he turned the barge and steered towards the centre of the river terrace.

He anticipated it would take about thirty seconds. He hunkered down in the thick, steel, bullet proof box that he and Talpur had built in the hope that it would give him enough protection from the expected hail of bullets. Khan picked up the hand held detonator. Once he squeezed the trigger the bomb would be armed.

This is it thought Khan to himself and he murmured "Allah Akbar" as he squeezed the trigger. Releasing his grip would then activate the detonator and ignite the huge bomb.

As the barge turned to make its final run, Talpur moved his position to face the second patrol boat.

"Sir, sir, Roddings shouted, "the barge, the fucking barge, what the fuck's it doing."

The crew of Orca 2 looked over in the direction Roddings was pointing and saw the barge making its way across the river.

"It's heading for the river terrace."

"Spin us round now," Barnes screamed, "get us over to that barge pronto."

Orca 2's engine screamed out in protest as the skipper turned and full throttled the craft over towards the barge.

The tannoy crackled into life, the voice of the operator menacing and to the point. "You in the canal barge, move away from the security zone. This is a police order."

Talpur watched anxiously as the patrol boat made a tight turn and he heard the demand to leave the security zone.

The politicians waiting to be evacuated also heard the loud hailer coming from the river and many of them moved forward to the river's edge to see what was going on.

Clinton Adams was standing next to the Prime Minister waiting for Orca 1 to take on the last members of the senior cabinet when he too heard the loud hailer. Adams spun round to see a canal barge heading directly for his position. Adams made an immediate assessment and his instincts were that this could well be the second part of a coordinated attack on the Houses of Parliament.

He screamed into his radio. "Code five, I repeat code five, take out that barge now, permission to fire."

Adams pulled out his Glock hand gun and began firing at the barge, his agents on the terrace followed suit as the politicians dived for cover. As the barge drew closer the lights of the river terrace illuminated the barge and to everyone's horror they could see a woman sitting on the front of the barge in a chair, holding what seemed like a small child.

"Hold your fire," somebody cried.

The secret service agents were trained to overcome any feelings of sympathy towards women and children under these circumstances and as the barge crept ever closer they knew there was intent in whoever was at the helm and most continued raining down gunfire onto the barge but many of the police officers hesitated and some even questioned the order on the radio.

All this meant that the barge continued getting closer and closer to its intended target.

Orca 2 also heard the code five order to fire on the barge and watched as multiple flashes of small arms fire opened up from Orca 1 and along the parliamentary river terrace.

Talpur wasn't concerned about the small arms fire; his only concern was the powerful 50 mm cannon that was coming round to bear on the barge as the police patrol boat made its turn. Once the firing from the terrace had started he knew that the order to take out the barge had been given so now he was solely focused on stopping the 50mm cannons from opening up on them.

The patrol boat had its on-board lights on and there was still a touch of light from the sun setting in the west. This allowed the silhouette of the crew to stand out against the blackness of the river.

Talpur fired his AK-74. It was a decent shot considering the uneven ride of the barge on the river and the bullet found its intended target. The first bullet hit Officer Roddings in the chest. It shattered the third and fourth rib of his thoracic cage and splinters of bone and fragments of casing ripped through his heart. There was no noise of a gunshot and he slumped to the floor quietly. In those precious seconds the crew of Orca 2 did not perform well.

Officer Barnes had been standing next to Roddings when the force of the AK-74 bullet killed him. Barnes knelt down to see what was wrong and crucially the boat's gunner leapt down onto the deck to see if he could help.

Barnes felt the blood and then checked for a pulse.

"He's been shot," he said as realisation set in, "the poor cunt's dead."

Orca's 2 crew couldn't believe that one of their team had just been shot dead.

Valuable seconds had passed and the crew didn't even know where the shot had come from. Officer Barnes' training eventually kicked in as he reached for his radio. "Officer down Orca 2, I repeat officer down Orca 2. Officer shot, we are under attack." He turned to his gunner, "Smith, get back onto the 50 mm now. Get back into position he's..."

Officer Barnes' words were cut short as a second AK-74 bullet entered his eye socket and exploded through the back of his skull.

Smith instinctively grabbed the radio, "this is Orca 2, another one down, sniper in the vicinity."

Hearing this situation play out on the airwaves caused each and every armed police officer on the river terrace to open up on the barge looming towards them.

The Sky news helicopter was filming all of it and relaying it live to the entire world. The helicopter had pulled back, high above the river, and the camera panned between mortar strikes on the north of the Houses of Parliament to the hundreds of members of parliament in a blind panic on the river terrace.

The next images picked up by the news team were that of hundreds of muzzle flashes coming from the terrace, aiming for a barge heading directly for them.

The long range cameras of the news team zoomed in on the barge and the pictures of a woman holding a little girl were shown to the world. As the camera panned in, it was clear that the woman and the child were dead. Their heads lolled to one side, they were both riddled with bullet holes, their coats stained crimson with blood. At that point the cameras then picked up the shocking image of the child being released from her dead mothers arms and rolling over the side of the barge into the dark water of the River Thames

In the Q-Park car park in Marylebone, police officers from London SO 19 tactical firearms unit had been called to investigate loud bangs coming from a van parked in the car park. When they arrived it was clear that this van was the launching point for the mortars which continued to rain down on the Houses of Parliament and it only took a few seconds for the orders to come through to take the van out.

Ten SO 19 officers fired hundreds of rounds into the van from their Sig Sauer SIG 516 rifles. Even though Othmane had on his ear protectors he could still hear hundreds of pings as the bullets struck the van. The van had been prepared to withstand small arms fire with welded steel plates attached to the inside of the cargo bay from where Othmane was firing the mortars. Othmane had been ordered to keep firing until the last minute and so he dropped another mortar round into the launcher.

The mortars continued despite hundreds of bullets directly hitting the van. The highly trained and quick thinking SO 19 officers tried another tactic. Under covering fire, one of the SO 19 officers stood on the roof of a car parked next to the van and could see that there was some sort of hole cut out of the roof of the van. The firearms officer pulled a hand grenade from his belt and pulled the pin. The grenade had a five second fuse; the officer counted to three and dropped the grenade into the hole cut out of the roof.

Othmane saw the grenade land at his feet and roll into the corner of the van. He did not make any attempt to throw the grenade out of the van. He smiled to himself and knew that he was going to paradise. Othmane did not wait for the grenade to explode but instead detonated his suicide belt. He knew that he could never be taken alive. The suicide bomb belt and the hand grenade ignited the remaining mortar rounds and the van exploded into a huge fireball. The SO 19 officer who had thrown the grenade was killed instantly.

Johiya knew that Othmane was dead. The mortar rounds had been landing at intervals of fifteen seconds and once those rounds stopped landing it could only have been because Othmane had been killed. Othmane had carried out his duty to perfection and made the ultimate sacrifice for Allah.

Talpur put his AK-74 on full automatic and sprayed Orca 2 with full clips of magazines. He also pressed the remote control for the rifle below deck, and positioned just above the Manikin dummy's arms it released a bullet every five seconds. His number one concern was to keep Orca 2's 50mm gun out of action. Khan had nothing more to do than sit in the steel framed bulletproof box that he had fabricated, holding the spring loaded detonator tight in his hand and counting down the seconds. Khan could hear and feel the hail of bullets as they ricocheted off the barge.

"Wait for it, wait for it," Khan said to himself as the intensity of bullets hitting the boat increased to a crescendo. He could hear Talpur screaming 'Allah Akbar' over and over as he fired his AK-74, right up until the very last moment.

The barge smashed into the embankment of the river terrace and instantaneously Khan released his grip on the bomb's detonator handle. The last thing that Khan thought of was not his child, his parents or Rebecca. He had one thing on his mind and that was fulfilling his pledge to Islam and going on his journey to paradise.

The attack had been timed to perfection and the barge had struck the wall at high tide. This meant that the roof of the barge was above ground level on the river terrace. As the huge bomb was detonated the blast and heat wave traveled out along the river terrace patio. If the bomb had been detonated at low tide much of its destructive power would have been absorbed by the thick wall and bank side. It was well planned and perfectly executed.

The real art of bomb making was to make sure that all the components of the bomb were synchronised to create a blast wave and not a just big fireball. The years of training at Osama Bin Laden Al Qaeda trading camps had not been in vain. At the point of detonation the chemicals ignited to pressurise the surrounding air inside the barge. In a millisecond the super charged pressurised air slammed into the framework of the barge. In the next millisecond the blast wave, along with the entirety of the barge began to spread out in an unstoppable and deadly force.

Racing faster than the speed of sound, the wave of super charged pressurised air, carrying along thousands of fragments of the barge slammed into the living flesh of the victims who had congregated on the River Terrace to make good their escape.

Following milliseconds behind the blast wave was a huge fireball that engulfed the immediate area around the centre of the blast zone. The fireball combusted the bomb blast victims and ignited the Houses of Parliament buildings.

The Prime Minister and his cabinet were sitting in Orca 1. They stood no chance and were amongst the first to die.

By the time the blast wave had dissipated each and every one of the UK members of parliament had been wiped out, the full House of Lords were also dead, along with their back room staff, journalists, and TV crews. At least forty other police and security personnel also lost their lives.

The live sky news reporter had lost it, "fucking hell, fucking hell, fucking hell," he screamed over the airwaves as the catastrophic and unprecedented attack was relayed live to the world.

Johiya watched the huge explosion from his phone and knew that he would soon hear the sound wave as the blast spread out from its epicentre. Everyone around Johiya was screaming, they had just witnessed mass murder live on their screens. Within a second the sound of the blast wave reached the coffee shop. This time a real panic ensued and the people in Costa Coffee felt compelled to get away from Parliament Square as fast as they could.

As everyone left the coffee shop Johiya hung back a bit to view his handy work. Unlike everyone else he knew that was the end of hostilities... at least for the time being. He felt pride surging up within him as a huge mushroom cloud billowed into the London night.

Seeing it with his own eyes gave Johiya a better sense of satisfaction than watching the spectacle on his phone. He felt he had finally avenged the deaths of his family many years ago. In that instant, Johiya thought about the story of Guy Fawkes who had attempted to blow up the Houses of Parliament centuries in the past. He laughed inwardly. The infamy of Guy Fawkes lived on to this day and he had only *attempted* to take out the Houses of Parliament and the British government. Johiya had actually done it.

Johiya had been the planner and instigator of probably the world's greatest terrorist act. Even greater than the twin towers attack in New York and Washington because they had wiped out the entire government of Great Britain. And he'd even had some help from the British government, as they'd broadcast the fact that they would all be in one place at a given time. With a little bit of cunning, the British government had fallen for his simple trap.

It was time for Johiya to make good his escape and he casually joined the throng of people making their way from the Parliament Square area. As he walked away from the scene of his crime he watched as the emergency services sped to the bomb blast. Johiya knew that no one in the vicinity would have survived the bomb that he, Othmane, Talpur and Khan had constructed.

A three man cell, along with the help of a radicalised Englishman and using relatively simple military equipment, and readily available commercial products had destroyed the entire British government and changed the world forever.

CHAPTER 52

Johiya had a spring in his step as he walked along Birdcage Walk with the thousands of other people evacuating the bomb site area. He listened to the general outrage of the public as news filtered through of the carnage and sheer devastation the barge bomb had caused. If only they knew that the chief architect of the outrageous terrorist act that they were so disgusted by, was so close to their company.

The Metropolitan Police, like everyone else, had been watching the attack and had ordered the immediate shut down of the London underground and bus system for fear of further attacks. Getting out of London was going to be difficult. Johiya had pre-planned for this and had parked up a motorbike in one of the numerous motorbike parking zones in Queen Anne's Gate, just off Birdcage Walk. He reached the motorbike, opened up the crash helmet pannier and started the engine. He was relieved to hear it purr straight away.

Johiya headed north west through London and made his way to Denham Aerodrome, where he had pre-booked a helicopter to take him from London to

Manchester on a business trip. Johiya knew that this was potentially a crunch time. Riding the motorbike meant that he had not looked at his phone for about an hour and he prayed to Allah that Mi5 had not splashed his name and photo all over the news networks.

He eventually pulled his phone from his pocket. His news screen was dominated by the reports of the attack on the Houses of Parliament and nothing else. So far so good, he thought. Even with the helicopter flight Johiya had planned ahead. He had flown with the company two previous times that meant that all the checks on his identification had already taken place. This would be his third flight now and as such he was now classed as a regular client.

Johiya entered the reception area and saw that the receptionist was watching the news reports of the bombing in London on a large TV. She had tears in her eyes as she turned to face him.

"Good evening Mr. Cliff," said the receptionist tearfully.

"Good evening," Johiya said.

"Have you seen this, it's shocking isn't it?"

Johiya wanted to tell her that he was there when it happened, the greatest spectacle he had ever seen, but he thought better of it as he suppressed a smile.

"Is the flight still on?" Johiya asked as he also turned to face the TV and tried to fake a look of concern.

"Yes, yes it is, I thought you may have concerns but we have heard nothing from the civil aviation authority regarding cancelling helicopter flight schedules, its only airliners at the moment," she said, trying to regain her composure. "Two of our other clients have not been able to make the flight due to the situation in London. There's only you and a Mr Greyson taking the flight."

Johiya looked over to the waiting area and saw another man dressed in an expensive business suit working on his laptop. The man looked up and nodded at Johiya before burying his head back in his laptop.

"I cannot believe what's happened," Johiya said.

"It's unbelievable so many dead. What's going to happen now?" said the receptionist staring back at the TV screen to see more scenes of devastation.

"This will change our country forever, that's for sure," Johiya responded.

He paused a moment before speaking again, "Well I've also had a bit of a nightmare day myself. I lost my wallet along with all my credit cards this morning but managed to get to the bank and draw out the cash for the flight. Is it okay to pay in cash?" he asked.

"Of course, that's not a problem."

Johiya could not take the chance of paying for anything on his credit card since Mi5 had busted down his door. He knew at the very least that all his cards would be monitored now as a matter of routine. Although he still thought it unlikely that Mi5 could be one hundred per cent sure that he had carried out the attacks.

Johiya counted out one thousand seven hundred pounds in crisp fifty pound notes. The receptionist made a telephone call, a door opened and the pilot walked into the room.

"Hello Mr Cliff, Mr Greyson, we're ready to go, if you can please follow me," he said.

Johiya said goodbye to the receptionist and walked through into the helicopter hangar where he and Mr Greyson were given a set of headphones.

Johiya jumped into the back of the helicopter alongside his fellow passenger. The noise from the engines increased and the helicopter left the ground and climbed steadily into the night.

It was an hour and twenty minute flight to Manchester and after about twenty minutes Johiya reached into his hold-all and pulled out a gun.

He smiled and shot Mr Greyson twice in the chest. The helicopter pilot spun round to see a Glock handgun pointing at his head.

"Okay Mr Pilot, stay cool and do as I say and you won't end up like him. Do you understand me?"

"Yes, I understand"

"Good, now turn off your radio and your radar receiver and drop your altitude to 250 metres above sea level."

Once the helicopter had reached 250 metres above sea level, Johiya ordered the pilot to change direction and head for Belgium.

"Let me know when we're about to leave the UK," Johiya said.

"Yes Sir."

After about twenty minutes the pilot told Johiya that they were approaching the English coastline.

Johiya looked at his phone and saw that his G4 signal was very weak.

"Fly down south until I say so," her ordered.

The helicopter changed direction and continued to fly south until Johiya saw that his G4 signal had reached three bars. He went to his album and uploaded a video.

After a further twenty minutes the helicopter was above the English Channel and Johiya ordered the pilot to reduce the altitude to fifty metres. Flying at night over the English Channel at such a low altitude was risky, but it was only ten minutes of flying before the helicopter reached the Belgium coastline and it was important that they avoided any radar.

"OK, raise your altitude to 250 metres, turn on your auto pilot system and put these GPS co-ordinates into the system."

The pilot typed in the GPS co-ordinates and the helicopter changed direction. After another twenty minutes the auto pilot system buzzed to indicate that the helicopter was five hundred metres from the GPS position.

"OK, take us down and don't put on your landing lights."

The pilot looked anxious as he spoke."This is a very dangerous manoeuvre, how do I know if there are any power lines, trees or anything in this area?" he said nervously.

"I know the area, there are no power lines and just a few scattered bushes. All you need to do is come down vertically on the GPS position and we will not crash. Do you understand?" He was annoyed by the pilot's question and flashed the Glock handgun to remind him who was giving the orders.

The helicopter pilot did as he was ordered and the helicopter landed safely in what turned out to be a public park near to the Belgium town of Gante.

"Okay, turn off the engines and all the navigation and radio systems."

The helicopter's engines soon wound down and the helicopter fell silent.

"Okay," Johiya said, listen to me. I am leaving now. You will wait fifteen minutes before you flick a single switch, is that clear?"

The pilot turned in his seat, "Now just a minute, you -"

Johiya fired a single round into the middle of the pilot's face. His head jerked back and returned to its original position as he slumped into his harness. Johiya pushed the gun into his chest and released another round into his heart.

"You talk too much infidel."

Johiya climbed from the helicopter and he made his way through the park and into a residential area towards a bus stop. Johiya knew that buses ran every half hour to Brussels. After a short wait he boarded a bus to the city centre. Once he arrived in the city he caught a taxi to Molenbeek.

Wherever he went Johiya watched the people on their phones, still glued to the scenes at the Houses of Parliament and he could not help but feel an immense pride.

Johiya walked the final part of his journey and eventually he rang a buzzer on the door of a rundown apartment block. Johiya climbed the stairs to find a man standing at the entrance of an apartment, beckoning him to enter. The man closed the door quietly and at last Johiya began to relax.

The man greeted him with an embrace. "Allah is pleased with your work Johiya, you have done very well. Our new leader has sent you his blessings, but we must not be complacent as your work is not finished. We must get started immediately on your disguise." He handed him a packet of tablets. "Take these Oxsoralen tablets and climb on the sun bed, after a few days we will start to see a difference," he smiled, "we Muslims are normally darker skinned than you my friend."

There was a knock on the door and Johiya tensed up. He was a bit alarmed that so soon after his arrival someone would just so happen to call at such a late hour. He soon relaxed as he heard a voice that he had not heard in a very long time.

The door to his bedroom opened and a beautiful woman walked into the room.

"Hello Jalal," she said Pashtun.

Johiya stepped forward and they embraced. "My dear sister Saadaa, it has been too long."

She kissed him on the cheek and then hugged him again. "Yes brother, and I have been watching your work on our TV screens, I am so very proud of you."

Johiya stepped back and held her at arm's length. "And your uniform, you look so very beautiful."

"Thank you, I've been there nearly six months."
Johiya reached out and traced his finger along the embroidered crest of the nuclear reactor plant of Gravelines, France. "Quality work, real quality."

CHAPTER 53

The Pub, Romford

Taylor had summoned a full meeting of the ENA after the Southend EasyJet outrage and coincidently, as the meeting began the first reports of the attack on the Houses of Parliament filtered in on Sky News. Even the battle hardened ex-soldiers were stunned into silence as they watched the tragic events unfold live on the Sky News channel.

Taylor had to calm the men down as they were all charged up ready to go out and kill as many Muslims as possible. It was not an easy task as emotions were running very high. Taylor ordered all the men to go back home and await further orders. He needed time to think about what would be an appropriate response. Thirty minutes after the men had gone, Taylor received a coded message from Drago requesting an urgent meeting later that night.

Mi6 Headquarters, Thames House London

As soon as the mortar attack had started on the Houses of Parliament, Fletcher had ordered Baxter back to Thames House to organise the man hunt for those responsible. Baxter watched the mortar attack on his phone until he could stand it no more. He summoned a helicopter and headed for central London. The helicopter was about ten minutes away from the Houses of Parliament when the suicide barge exploded. Baxter held his head in his hands.

He composed himself, the devastation was beyond his imagination.

He ordered the pilot to make a short detour to so he could witness the devastation. As they made their way over the north side of the Houses of Parliament, Baxter could see the numerous blasts from the mortar bombs but nothing could prepare anyone for the damage and destruction caused by the suicide barge bombing. From the blast centre point at the river terrace there was a large semi-circle void, approximately two hundred metres wide, where there was nothing but flattened debris. In that blast zone Baxter knew, the entire British political elite had been awaiting rescue. He knew that nobody could have survived that blast. He made his own video on his phone then ordered the pilot to land at St John's Gardens, close to Thames House.

Baxter ran to the Mi5 headquarters and made his way to Fletcher's office. He found a team of medics trying to revive Fletcher.

"What the fuck's happened to him?" he asked.

"Heart attack Sir," one of the medics replied.

Fletcher was stretchered out of Thames House and rushed to hospital.

Baxter took a deep breath as he realised he was now officially head of Mi5 and there would be no government for the foreseeable future to account for his actions. Baxter's mind went into overdrive as he began to think how to track down this terror cell. No one even knew if they'd finished. There could be further attacks waiting to happen.

Baxter went into the main control room and gave his first orders to recall all field officers back to Thames House. He then summoned the editors of all national media outlets to attend Thames House.

He needed a coffee and badly, perhaps something stronger. He was just about to pick up the phone when he was interrupted by one of the analysts working at a computer console.

"Sir, sir you need to come and look at this."

Baxter walked over to the screen and the analyst hit the play button of a video posted on YouTube.

"It was posted just a few minutes ago," the analyst said.

Baxter watched as he saw four men sitting round a table all drinking cups of tea. One of the men he recognised as Michael Cliff. Baxter watched in stony silence as he listened to Michael Cliff talk about the attack at the Houses of Parliament and refer to the mass murder as revenge for the cowardly killing of their leader Osama Bin Laden at the hand of the UK puppet masters the Americans. The video ran on for nearly an hour with each of the four men citing there reasons for giving up their own lives in the name of Allah the almighty.

The video ended with Michael Cliff speaking about his pledge to Osama Bin Laden and urging the fight against the western infidels, encouraging others to rise up against those Islamic countries that accommodate the west for their money. The video finished with all four men praying to Mecca.

Baxter read through all the latest reports since the attack. It had been two hours.

"Okay, listen up everyone. It looks like these fuckers have taken their own lives but until we know for sure this is still a manhunt. We have one attacker who blew himself up at the Marylebone car park. The van he was in exploded, but the police have managed to find some body parts which we can get the DNA from to match against these four mother fuckers," he turned to look at the still images of the men on the screen next to him. "We know that at least three attackers were on the suicide barge. There were three guns or rifles shooting from different positions at any one time.

Baxter drew in a deep breath as he recalled the horrific scene that had unfolded before his eyes as he sat watching the news. "We all know that from explosions such as these there is zero chance of finding any DNA let alone body parts. We have the added complication that the barge was on the river and many fragments will have been washed away down the river. So, until we know otherwise I want a full media search on these four men," he ordered, "the men on the barge could have been anyone, even some of those fucking escapees."

Baxter knew that it was never easy activating nationwide and worldwide manhunts when Islamic suicide bombers were the perceived attackers. Huge resources had been utilised carrying out manhunts only to discover that in most cases the attackers had killed themselves in the process. Some security experts believed that the resources would be better managed in surveillance operations to thwart further attacks when the initial attack clearly pointed to an Islamic suicide attack.

The fact there were martyrdom videos would make it even harder to convince the public that these attackers could be at large. This was not just any old attack... reports were coming in thick and fast that there were no survivors at all on the river terrace. Considering every person located in the Houses of Parliament at the time of the mortar attack had been evacuated to the terrace, it all made for grim reading.

Baxter's phone rang and he was told that two senior military police officers were at reception and that he must speak to them immediately. He went down to reception where he spoke to a colonel of the Royal Military Police. Baxter was summoned to Aldershot barracks, he was told the chiefs of staff of the Army, Air force and Navy would be attending. Baxter made a token protest, said that he was needed at Thames House but the military police officer cited regulations that allowed the army to overrule all civil edicts in time of war.

This was the first time that those words had been used in real terms and Baxter realised that the military were going to play a major hand in the events that were to follow. He was escorted out of Thames House and saw three armoured personnel carriers parked up directly outside the entrance to the building. Baxter was escorted to the second vehicle and ushered into its close confines. The armoured convoy left Thames House with the first and third armoured vehicles providing protection from any potential terrorist attack. The convoy sped through southwest London on its way to Aldershot barracks.

Once the army convoy arrived at its destination, Baxter was escorted by soldiers into a large boardroom. Also present were the head of Mi6 and the commissioner of the Metropolitan police. Sitting at the head of the table was Field Marshal Philip Lawrence, alongside him was the Chief of the Naval Staff and Chief of the Air Force. It had only been four hours since the UK government had been wiped out and the military had decided to play their hand and take control of the country.

The first to speak was Field Marshal Lawrence.

"I am now acting head of the British armed forces. I am sad to announce that by all accounts it looks like Sir Freddie Bradshaw was killed at the Houses of Parliament. I am next in the chain of command. Make no mistake gentlemen, this attack is an act of war," he said bluntly.

Baxter, the police commissioner and the head of Mi6 were not there for any sort of discussions, they were there to be told and to be given the instructions that future orders were to be taken from the Army. Military Rule was now in force, one of the leading democratic countries in the world was being placed under Military Jurisdiction.

CHAPTER 54

It was late on that same evening when Drago and Taylor met up at Canvey Island's own Golden Mile. It was a depressing site, it consisted mostly of tired looking amusement arcades and kiss me quick shops. It was however a good place for a meet as there were very few people out that night. Most people being glued to their television sets watching the tragic events of that day.

But for Drago it wasn't a tragic day, far from it, for him it was a day of opportunity and he explained his thinking as they walked along the sea wall, dimly lit by the line of street lamps.

"The men want to fight back immediately," Taylor said.

"Really, to avenge the British government?" he said sarcastically, "it's those idiots who got us into this position in the first place. Letting every nation of Islam in the world set up camp in your back yard is bad enough but then starting a series of wars against our Muslim enemies when we just so happen to have four million of the fuckers living in the country?"

Drago pointed along the promenade, "keep walking Mick," he said, "the cunts didn't even need to invade us to declare war because they were already here. It's a bit like a Trojan horse in reverse. Instead of being tricked into inviting our enemy into our lands we just invited them in regardless. Listen my friend, this is the biggest opportunity that will ever come our way to change our society once and for all."

"What do you mean?" Taylor asked.

"I mean what do you think the public perception will be after this sinks in?"

"Well, everyone will want to attack the Muslims."

Drago laughed, "yes, some people will probably want to attack Muslims but that will in turn cause Muslims to attack Brits all over the world. Remember, we are seriously outnumbered against the fuckers, there's around 1.6 billion Muslims don't forget, so maybe that's not a great idea."

"Okay, what then?" Taylor said, "what do you suggest?"

"Let's use the shift in the political landscape to really take control. I mean politically."

"What?"

"The electorate will swing to the right, further than it's ever been before and we need to be ready for when that happens."

"But we haven't got a government. They're all dead."

"Exactly. So we have to fill that vacuum with a far right party."

This was not what Taylor had anticipated. He thought Drago would want to plan further attacks. He took a few moments to take in what Drago was suggesting.

"So, what you're saying is that we can start our own far right political party?"

"Yes, we'll be the financial backers behind it."

"We? Who the fuck are we Drago? You're an ex SAS man with a pension of a fifty grand if you're lucky."

Drago was shaking his head...grinning.

"It'll cost millions Drago, we can't rob the Bank of England."

Drago had already lifted his mobile phone from his pocket. He was accessing an app".

"Look at this," he said, it's our network of Offshore Banking."

Taylor was confused, a dozen questions flying around his head. "What do you mean our?"

Drago tapped the screen a few more times. "Our investors," he said without looking up, "ex squaddies mostly, dozens of SAS men and a few right wing businessmen too, even a couple of prominent MPs. I'm in charge of the fund, I've been managing it for nearly two years," he held out the phone. "Look."

Taylor looked down as the numbers came into focus.

Drago pointed at the bottom line. "There's seventy six million pounds all told."

Taylor was stunned, he was speechless as the enormity of everything sank in.

"I'll let you in on a little secret," Drago said, "I did a bit of insider trading and took short options on all

Pakistani airlines before the Oval bombing. Basically Pakistani nationals have stopped flying to Europe and America since the bombing. All Pakistani airline shares have dive-bombed," he laughed, "I doubled the fund within a few short weeks."

"But can't they trace the money?" Taylor questioned.

"They can try, but we bounced the money about electronically all over the world and then we drew out cash to buy gold and diamonds."

"What you mean you've got seventy six million pounds worth of gold and diamonds?"

"Yes my friend, give or take a few million in American dollars and gold prices have shot up since yesterday's attack on our government hence the value of the fund as it stands today."

"Surely they can put two and two together?"

"We're confident that we have our tracks covered and with the loss of the entire British Government, the UK authorities have more pressing matters."

Taylor shook his head in disbelief, "well fuck me."

"I'd rather not Mick thanks."

"You've planned this all along haven't you?"

"Absolutely mate, I was in the SAS for fifteen years and we have connections in every aspect of society."

Taylor thought things through for a few moments.

"Okay, so if we win power we can bring in new laws, Nationality tests that none of these fuckers will have a hope in hell of passing and the law will state they need to go home, back where they came from, along with their families. We'll deport the lot of them, send them

400

back where they belong, and the radicals will be dealt with in a way that will stop any notion of the UK ever being a soft touch on terrorism."

"Exactly Mick, we'll bring back internment and capital punishment, if any of these bastards are found with any sort of arms or bomb making equipment, if any of these Imams preach hatred from the pulpit they'll be sent straight to death fucking row."

"Okay, I'm up for anything as long as we can kick these Muslims out of our country once and for all."

"Good, then we've a lot of work to do mate."

CHAPTER 55

The Aftermath, Downing Street

The United Kingdom woke up the next day to a very different country. Field Marshal Philip Lawrence was promoted to acting Chief of Defence Staff as the previous Chief of the Defence, Sir Frederick Bradshaw was among the victims of the Houses of Parliament terror attack. The world's media was stationed outside Downing Street waiting for the famous black door to open.

Suddenly there was a loud mechanical noise that came from the entrance to Downing Street. The worlds media turned their cameras to record a Challenger 2 battle tank rumble up Downing Street and position itself only a few meters from the media area directly in front of 10 Downing Street. The turret and machine gun then pointed menacingly towards the media scrum. Once the tank was in place the engine was turned off and on cue, the famous black door opened and two men, smartly dressed in military and police uniform, walked purposely towards the lectern. One of the men was the chief of the armed forces, the other the police commissioner for the UK.

Field Marshal Philip Lawrence now head of the British armed forces stood outside Number 10 Downing Street to address the nation and the world. Instead of the usual police officers guarding Downing Street, there were now soldiers in full battle dress. The new chief of the defence staff began to read a pre-prepared statement.

"I regret to inform you that the terrorist attack yesterday evening has decimated our political system. All members of both the House of Commons and the House of Lords have been killed. We the military, in the absence of a functional government have declared the attack on the UK as an act of war on our sovereign state. I am therefore evoking a state of emergency in the country as a whole."

He took a drink of water from a glass placed on the lectern and continued. "In certain designated areas there will be curfews imposed and governance will be by martial law. For the time being I will be governing the UK until further notice. I am not a politician nor will I pretend to be one. The time for political correctness and multiculturalism has come to an end. As for the Muslim community residing in our country, we cannot accept the risk of those seeking to do us harm, using your religion and your community as a vehicle to carry out sustained attacks on our country and people. We accept that many of you are innocent, however at this point in time it is only Muslim people who attack us. I have therefore imposed a curfew and special measures of martial law in each and every Muslim community in the UK. Your mosques will be closed until further notice. My advice to all Muslims is to stay within your communities for your own protection as feelings against you are running very high. As for those so-called Muslim prisoners who have escaped and instigated the riots in Muslim areas, I ask the elders of the Muslim communities to apprehend these men and assist in returning them to prison. You have a responsibility to help us police your own communities. It is 7 a.m. now. If the rioting in these Muslim areas has not stopped by 9 a.m. the army will be drafted in to take back control and rioters and looters will be shot on sight."

He paused to allow his words to be absorbed.

"I am now addressing the Labour, Conservative and other political parties. We have lost our government in its entirety. You must quickly elect new leaders to fill the vacuum that has been created by this act of war. I also wish to say this to the indigenous population of our country. We must not embark on revenge attacks on Muslims or any other races in this country. We must be firm but fair if we are to rebuild from this tragedy and become a stronger nation. We must carry on as normal. Businesses must open, people must go to work, and life will continue as normal, if it doesn't then it means our enemies have won."

Phillip Lawrence took another drink of water and then announced that he was finished. He stepped back from the lectern and the police commissioner took his place.

"I endorse all that the Defence Chief of Staff has said and wish to add the following. To the forty five standing Chief Constables of each of our regional Police forces, I can confirm that you must relinquish all tactical control to the designated army commanders assigned to your area. Thank you, that's all."

Both the Chief of the armed forces and the Police commissioner turned round, saluted each other and walked back to 10 Downing Street. As they did so the media scrum shouted dozens of questions at the two men. All were ignored.

"The speech is over now, make your way out of Downing Street please" a soldier commanded. The tank he was standing on started its engine and moved menacingly towards the media scrum. They got the message and slowly drifted away.

CHAPTER 56

6 Months Later

The recently formed English National Party were at their party headquarters waiting for the final election ballots to be counted. With a lightening political campaign funded by mysterious benefactors, the English National Party had succeeded in fielding candidates in every constituency in the UK. Britain, for the first time in modern history had a real chance of a far right political party winning an election.

The party leader of the English National Party was smartly dressed in a suit, he knew that they had won the general election. However there was one more result to be announced, ironically the last result was Southend East and a victorious result would ensure a landslide victory and complete control of the new government. Everyone in the ENP headquarters watched the TV nervously as the returning officer took to the stage.

He cleared his throat. "The liberal democrats 4578 votes, Labour 9876 votes, the Conservative 16789 votes, and the English National Party 18346 votes."

He tried to announce the name of the new Right Honourable MP for Southend but couldn't be heard above the screams and cheers of the jubilant ENP supporters in the hall.

The ENP headquarters also exploded in a joyous rapture as the news flashed across the TV screens that the ENP had won a landslide victory in the UK general election and the new Prime Minister, Michael Taylor, was duly elected.

The PM sat in a back room with Drago and no more than a dozen close friends, party workers and of course Corporal King.

Taylor turned to Drago. I'm going to have to fucking stop swearing mate, that's going to be the hardest fucking part of this job for me."

Drago smiled and nodded.

King spoke. "Then you have about an hour to get out of the habit because that's when your first press conference will take place."

"Fuck me, that quick?"

Drago stood, slipped a file of papers over the desk. "And then we need to work on this draft."

Taylor picked it up and scanned the first few lines. "Fuck off," he said in amazement, "you want to abolish the fucking House of Lords?"

"One hundred percent," Drago said, "it's a disgrace that an unelected Upper House can influence the major decisions in government, those old bastards delayed and sometimes stopped many a bill and they had no right."

King stepped forward, lowered himself into a seat. "There are twenty six unelected fucking Bishops Mick, and more than half the population of this country are atheist, what right do they have to determine the laws of our land?"

Taylor grinned, "were Dave, I emphasise the word were, there were twenty six bishops, remember they all got blown up."

"Yes I know but if we don't act fast and get rid of the Upper House there will be another twenty six of those bastards sat on their fat arses and another seven hundred hereditary Peers queuing up to sign for their ridiculous expenses package and a nice warm place to sleep the afternoon away."

Taylor was genuinely shocked as King explained how many Lords there were in the United Kingdom

"They cost the country billions a year and all they do is fuck up the plans of an elected government."

Taylor was nodding, "and some of the things we want to get through would be blocked."

"Yes, of course they would."

"One thing for sure is that no one will be blocking the cancellation of the International Development Fund" added Taylor.

"Fucking right' said Drago and King.

"We must be the dumbest country in world, only we could send billions of pounds overseas and yet we can't even care for our own poor"

"Its all back handers in my opinion. I mean we send billions to Pakistan and they are definitely the main backers of the Taliban. Its fucking nuts. Not one of the previous governments ever did a proper audit. Too fucking scared in case they found out what we already know"

"Yeah enough is enough"

The English National Party had drafted up a manifesto prior to the election but some of the proposals for the future had been kept under wraps for the time being.

One of the ENP's manifesto pledges was to try the one surviving Member of the House of Lords for treason. As far as Taylor and the ENP was concerned Tony Hardy was a war criminal and had wilfully caused the deaths of hundreds of soldiers and civilians in stupid self-gratifying and illegal wars.

The newspapers had run continuous stories on how Tony Hardy had been Prime Minister when the Al Qaeda terror cell had been given UK citizenship. It was his policy that had caused the deaths of thousands of innocent people and the ENP had promised the electorate that Tony Hardy would not be able to wriggle his way out of this charge like he had in the Alfred Didcot report on the Iraq war. It seemed like every person with a vote approved of Hardy being tried, and held to account.

The other proposals had the electorate divided. To describe them as extreme was possibly a little harsh, but Drago knew they would not appeal to a vast section of the voting public. He had called it ENP Program 25.

With the House of Lords out the way it was just a case of convincing the likes of Taylor and King and then implementing it all. The ENP Candidates had been carefully selected, the extreme of the extreme placed in the safer seats that they had won convincingly and of course they were now sitting MPs. The ENP controlled the House of Commons and even some of the more right wing Conservatives sang from the same hymn sheets when it came to the Muslim population of the United Kingdom. The death penalty would be reintroduced and any form of treason, sabotage or terrorist activity would mean an automatic execution by firing squad. It had been unanimously agreed between the inner circle of the ENP.

The Muslims would live in specifically designated areas, districts where they already outnumbered the local indigenous population. The locals would be moved out, moved into better areas in significantly superior living accommodation and the additional expenses would be paid for by a five percent increase in taxation for all Muslims in employment and self-employed business owners. If they didn't like it they could return to their homeland. Drago's new proposals to the welfare state were easy enough to implement, there were no grey areas. Muslims would not qualify for any form of benefit including child allowance and in order to qualify for national health service benefits they needed to pay National Insurance. No National Insurance no treatment, even if a husband paid NI and his wife took ill he would need to pay for her treatment. No grey areas.

The state would introduce internment, incarceration without trial. The police knew who the terrorists, the extremists and the radicals were, but proving it was a different matter. Up until now they had walked the streets and been able to spout their radicalism and plan their atrocities if they were clever enough to avoid detection. Not now. The merest suspicion by the state police or the military would warrant arrest and imprisonment for up to twelve months.

Drago, Taylor and King had discussed and drafted the program just a month before the election and it was now time to act.

Taylor dismissed his other friends and colleagues, he told his secretary that the press conference would be delayed by half an hour. He was left alone with Drago and King.

"A mob smashed up all the businesses and Mosques in Bradford last night Mick," King stated as a smile pulled across his face.

Taylor turned to Drago, "did you send the military in?"

Drago nodded, "Yes. As from tomorrow the military pass governance back to the civilians and it was my last chance to have bit of fun."

Taylor picked up the file, opened it and started to read. "We are closing all Mosques?"

Drago nodded.

"Abolishing Trade Unions?"

"Yes."

"No Muslim lawyers?"

"Not a single one."

"No Muzzies in the army"

"None."

"Editors of newspapers."

Drago shook his head again.

King stepped forward as he took a mouthful of champagne and swallowed hard. "We need more money Mick, the more money we make the more chance we have of increasing living standards for the Brits and hanging on to power. We can save billions from the House of Lords, billions from the Welfare System and now that these ragheads have to pay for the health service it will be the pride of the developed world."

Taylor looked at King. He had known him for an eternity, he read him well. "There's a but, isn't there Dave?"

"Yes Mick, we need even more money, the number crunchers say we need to strengthen the military, double the annual budget to 90 billion."

Taylor raised an eyebrow. "Fuck me, how do we raise that kind of money?"

King grinned.

"You have an answer don't you Kingy."

"I certainly do Mad Mick, we seize their assets and properties. Once we implement the Program the Muzzies will be leaving in their tens of thousands but we'll make sure they leave with nothing. Before we let them anywhere near an airport they'll need to sign everything over to the government, property, bank accounts, land and businesses and everyone will be strip searched at the airports in case they try to take their wealth home in hidden gold and diamonds."

Taylor nodded his approval. "Excellent."

And there was more. The three men discussed the proposal to the Halal meat law which meant all Halal abattoirs would be closed immediately. That particular law would be a huge hit with the animal rights activists and meant that no animal would have to suffer in such a way again. All Muslim faith schools would be closed. Muslim teachers teaching in British schools demoted to teaching assistants working under the supervision of a British teacher and one of the most controversial measures, the surrender of precious metals and stones under Muslim ownership.

There was a knock on the door.

"Come in."

It was Taylor's secretary. "The press Mick, you have to get out there, they are at fever pitch."

Taylor stood. He walked over to Drago and King and placed his arm around both of their shoulders.

He pulled them into him hard. "Right gentlemen," he said, "let's get this fucking show on the road."

The End.
To be continued.

Printed in Poland
by Amazon Fulfillment
Poland Sp. z o.o., Wrocław

54587530R00249